Dreaming of Verona

T.A. WILLIAMS

Dreaming
of
Verona

CANELO

First published in the United Kingdom in 2020 by Canelo

This edition published in the United Kingdom in 2020 by

Canelo Digital Publishing Limited
Third Floor, 20 Mortimer Street
London W1T 3JW
United Kingdom

Print ISBN 978 1 78863 832 6
Ebook ISBN 978 1 78863 763 3

Look for more great books at www.canelo.co

Printed and bound in Great Britain by Clays Ltd, Elcograf S.p.A.

With love, as always, to Mariangela and Christina

True, I talk of dreams,
Which are the children of an idle brain,
Begot of nothing but vain fantasy,
Which is as thin of substance as the air.

William Shakespeare

Prologue

Suzie just sat there, stunned. She could feel the wine running down her cheeks and dripping off the end of her nose, but she was too shocked to move. She was vaguely aware of the restaurant door slamming as Alexandra made her dramatic exit, but by now all her efforts were concentrated on struggling to dominate the crushing sense of embarrassment that had turned her cheeks the colour of the tomatoes on the plate in front of her.

She risked a glance up from the table and this immediately confirmed her worst fears. All around the magnificent dining room, faces were turned in her direction, some in disbelief, some amazed and some distinctly amused. A few people were whispering among themselves and there was no mistaking the fact that she was now the object of almost universal attention. As she felt the weight of the eyes upon her, her embarrassment grew even more acute and she came close to getting up and rushing out of the room in her turn. Only the very real fear of looking even more pathetic prevented her from moving from her seat. Dropping her head, she returned her attention to the table and did her unsuccessful best to make herself invisible. She was digging in her bag for a tissue when a shadow fell across her.

'Excuse me, signorina. Perhaps this might help.'

She raised her eyes from the steady drips of Prosecco falling onto the tomato, mozzarella and basil salad in front of her and looked up. It was the immaculate waiter who had welcomed them to the elegant restaurant only a few minutes previously. The expression on his face was studiously neutral as he held out a pristine white napkin towards her. Maybe this wasn't the first time one of his clients had been on the receiving end of a glass of wine in the face.

'Do please take it. I fear there's a real risk of you spoiling your salad if any more Prosecco ends up on your plate.' The hint of a smile appeared on his face.

Automatically she reached out and took the napkin, using it to dry her glasses before wiping it across her face. It came away remarkably wet in spite of the amount of wine that had ended up down her front. Alexandra's glass must have been full before she had thrown the contents across the table at her.

'Are you going to be all right, signorina?' His tone was formal, but sympathetic.

Suzie nodded, dabbing at the wet trail that ran all the way down to the open neck of her blouse. The sensation of wine running down her body beneath the light cotton was disconcerting and she blushed all the harder. Mustering as much resolve as she could, she made an attempt at a smile in return.

'I'm fine, thanks. Just a bit shocked, to be honest. I must have touched a nerve.' And she knew full well which of Alexandra's all too exposed nerves she had touched, but, she told herself yet again, she had had no choice. She did her best to sound positive. 'Thank you for the napkin. You're very kind.'

The waiter gave her a little bow of the head and left her to her salad – and her mopping up. As she did her best to dry herself off, she reflected on the scene which had just taken place. Tonight's outburst signified a marked deterioration in relations between her and Alexandra and she sighed. It looked as though her visit to Italy might be about to come to an abrupt and untimely end.

Chapter 1

'His Lordship will see you now, Miss Cartwright.'

Suzie stood up, straightened her skirt, walked over to the finely carved old door and hesitated, glancing across at the forbidding-looking lady in the twinset and pearls sitting at the desk to one side.

'Should I knock?'

'That won't be necessary. His Lordship knows you're coming.'

Even so, Suzie gave a gentle tap on the door before turning the handle and pushing it open. Taking a deep breath, she stepped over the threshold and blinked in the unexpectedly bright light. Lord Tedburn's study was massive. Tall leaded windows flooded sunlight into the room, illuminating an array of austere moustachioed faces in oil paintings hanging around the oak-panelled walls. The highly polished wood floors glistened in the late August sun and his huge and doubtless antique desk was positioned directly facing the door, with the sun at his back. She hesitated, turning to close the door behind her. As she did so, she heard his voice.

'Good morning, Miss Cartwright. It's good of you to come. Do come and sit down.'

He sounded a bit less intimidating than she had feared and she did as instructed, perching primly on a velvet-upholstered chair in front of his desk, trying not to let the sun dazzle her. His face was in shadow, but she could see the outline of his body, his shoulders more hunched than she remembered, but of course the last time she had seen him had probably been close to fifteen years earlier, and a lot could happen in fifteen years. She had never spoken to him before, although she recognised him, as did all the residents of this part of rural Devon. She clasped her hands together on her lap and waited for him to finish whatever it was he was writing.

'So tell me, if you would – how old are you?' He set down his fountain pen and his eyes subjected her to a searching stare.

She felt the colour rushing to her cheeks as she answered. 'Twenty-eight. I'll be twenty-nine next February.' She wondered vaguely if she should have added a 'sir' at the end, but it was too late now. She had no previous experience of speaking to members of the aristocracy.

'Your father tells me you're an English scholar.'

'I have a PhD in English, yes... sir.'

'Do you have a particular field of interest?'

'My thesis was on Shakespeare. I've always been interested in his plays and poetry.'

To her surprise, there was unexpected warmth in his reply. 'Well, well, a shared interest. I have a fine collection of his works in my personal library. I'll have to show you sometime.'

'I would like that, sir.' Somehow, Suzie had imagined Lord Tedburn as more of a huntin', shootin' and fishin' man. Presumably there was more to him than met the eye.

He returned to the matter in hand. 'I gather you're currently between jobs.'

'Yes, sir. I was working for a charity in London until last month, but the funding was withdrawn and it had to close down.'

'You speak Italian, I believe.'

'Yes, reasonably well. I did A-level Italian at school and then spent my vacations looking after ten- to fourteen-year-olds at a holiday camp on the Tuscan coast for three summers while I was doing my first degree.' She felt she had better explain. 'It helped to pay my way through college.'

'Good, good.' His chair creaked as he stood up and walked slowly round to the side of his desk. Directing his gaze not at her, but out of the windows into the deer park, he laid out his proposal. 'Miss Cartwright, it's my daughter, Alexandra, you see.'

Suzie wasn't sure if a response was required so she said nothing. It didn't seem to matter. A few moments later he turned back to her.

'She wants to go to Italy for a month and I would like somebody to accompany her.'

Suzie began to understand why she had been summoned here to the manor. Presumably all her experience of dealing with children was going to be put to use. His next remark confirmed her suspicions.

'I don't like the idea of her going off on her own, so I'd be grateful if you felt like accompanying her, if you have no other commitments.'

'When would this be, sir?'

'I believe she wants to set off around the middle of September. Would that suit you?'

'Yes, probably, I think so. I suppose it all depends on job interviews and that sort of thing. I've been applying for a number of positions.'

He nodded slowly before responding. 'I wouldn't want you to lose out, so I'm prepared to pay you well for your time. Can I ask how much you were being paid in your last position?'

She told him and waited as he did a bit of mental arithmetic, before coming back to her with a figure that almost took her breath away. He was offering her as much for one month of her time as she had earned in two months in her old job and, along with it, full board and lodging as well as unspecified 'expenses'. Her spirits rose. Four thousand pounds in the bank and a month in Italy were not to be sniffed at, even if she would be looking after a possibly troublesome teenager. She was just about to leap at the offer when he added some extra information and she found herself having to stop and reconsider.

'You need to know a few things about Alexandra, my daughter.' He returned his attention to the deer park as he spoke and she began to realise that he wasn't finding this conversation easy. 'Although she's almost twenty-six, she can still behave in a very immature manner. She appears to be quite incapable of applying herself to anything for any length of time before getting bored with it. She's disobedient, can be rude and sometimes, I'm afraid, she's little more than a fly-by-night.'

'A fly-by-night?' Suzie hadn't heard that archaic expression for years. She lapsed into silence as she took in the full import of his words. She had assumed she was being employed to babysit a minor, not an adult. How on earth could she be expected to look after a woman barely

7

two or three years younger than herself? She would have spoken up, but her natural reticence kept her silent – for now. As it was, Lord Tedburn had more to say on the subject of his daughter.

'She's far too interested in her friends, her clothes and in having a good time.' He looked back over his shoulder briefly. 'And I'm afraid her track record with men is no better. Her tastes leave a lot to be desired, and she always seems to gravitate towards the unsavoury and the unsuitable. Above all, I'll be counting on you to keep your eye on her as and when any Italian men start popping out of the woodwork.' He shook his head ruefully. 'And they will.'

The more she heard, the less Suzie liked the sound of this. Although it was right for Lord Tedburn to make her aware of the true state of things, she was amazed that he should speak so disparagingly about his daughter to a complete stranger and she felt a twinge of sympathy for Alexandra. What, she wondered, did her mother think about this? But then, no sooner did the thought occur to her than she remembered hearing that Lady Tedburn had died quite some time ago. Clearing her throat, she did her best to object, but Lord Tedburn was adamant, waving away her reservations.

'Do you know Italy well, Miss Cartwright?'

'Um, only a limited area, really. I took the train in to Florence a few times when I was working at the coast, and of course I visited Pisa and Lucca, but I didn't see much else, I'm afraid. It was a residential position, you see, and I had very little free time.'

'So you don't know Venice and the area around there – Padua, Verona and the lakes?'

In spite of her doubts, Suzie's heart skipped a beat. The idea of visiting the magical city of Venice was very appealing but, above all, the name that had leapt out at her was Verona. She looked up at Lord Tedburn and explained.

'I don't know the northeast of Italy at all, but I've been dreaming of Verona for years now. Ever since I first started studying Shakespeare.'

A smile appeared on His Lordship's face. 'Of course, the city of Romeo and Juliet. Well, you should have ample time to study it at your leisure.' He returned to his seat and picked up the phone. 'Alice? Please would you ask Alexandra to come and join us? Thank you.'

As he put the receiver down, he returned his attention to Suzie. 'I'm going to spell it out quite clearly to Alexandra. You will have my full support, I assure you. All I ask of you is to keep me informed whenever you have any worries about my daughter's behaviour. It's for her own good.'

By now, Suzie felt herself seriously torn. On the one hand, the idea of visiting the place she had been dreaming about for years was enticing, but she was having ever more serious reservations. Was her presence really for the girl's own good? To her it sounded as if this interfering father was far too controlling and, much as she would have enjoyed an all-expenses-paid month over there, she was already beginning to think of polite ways of refusing when the door opened and a slim, auburn-haired girl slouched in. Her body language screamed at them both. Without a word being spoken, it was plain to see that Alexandra didn't want to be here and certainly didn't want anything to do with Suzie. Apparently unaware of anything unto-ward, her father looked up.

'Ah, good, Alexandra, come and meet Suzanne Cartwright… you know, the vicar's daughter.'

The girl came over and shook Suzie's hand with about as much enthusiasm as if she were picking a rotten apple out of a basket.

'Good morning.' Nothing more.

Doing her best to sound unfazed, Suzie gave her a smile. 'Good morning, Alexandra. It's good to meet you.'

'Suzanne is going to accompany you to Italy, Alexandra. I'm sure the two of you will get on like a house on fire.'

From the expression on Alexandra's face, it was pretty clear she would have preferred it if Suzie had been inside the aforementioned burning house with the fire engine stuck in a ditch somewhere else. For a moment, it looked as if she were about to retort, but instead, she dropped her eyes and nodded, but not before Suzie had noticed another expression flitting momentarily across her face. Suzie had been expecting anger, resentment and resis-tance, but she felt sure the expression she had briefly glimpsed was more one of sadness. In spite of her reserva-tions, she began to reconsider. Unaware of – or ignoring – his daughter's unhappiness, Lord Tedburn carried on.

'Now, Alexandra, I want you to hear what my instruc-tions are to your new companion, so there can be no misunderstanding.' Without waiting for acknowledge-ment from his daughter or for Suzie to protest that she hadn't accepted the job yet, he turned back to Suzie. 'Suzanne, while in Italy I want you to consider yourself effectively in loco parentis. It will be your responsibility to keep me informed at all times if you consider Alexandra's conduct in any way unsuitable. In particular, I need to know if she takes up with any undesirable people – especially men. I need to know I can rely on you. I trust this is crystal clear to you both.'

Suzie felt Alexandra's eyes on her and she decided to prevaricate. Confrontation wasn't her strong suit, but she took a deep breath and made a stab at it. 'I wonder if it might be possible for me to spend a little time with Alexandra so we can get to know each other a bit better, before accepting the job? I wouldn't want her to feel she was being forced to spend her holiday with somebody she doesn't like.' As she finished speaking, she looked across and, for a second, she caught the other girl's eye and read what might have been surprise.

'Yes, of course, Suzanne.' Lord Tedburn also sounded surprised, but he hid it better. 'Why don't you two girls go and sit over there and chat while I get on with my correspondence?' He waved vaguely across to a fine leather-upholstered sofa a few feet away.

This didn't strike Suzie as a good idea at all. What sort of conversation would they be able to have with Alexandra's father listening in? Taking a deep breath, she crossed her fingers and made a counterproposal.

'As it's such a glorious day, I wonder if you'd mind if we maybe went for a little walk in the gardens? It seems too good a morning for staying indoors.' For a moment, she wondered if she had gone too far. From the expression on Lord Tedburn's face, it was clear he was unused to people refusing his orders, but he controlled himself and gave a brusque nod.

'Very well, why not? And after you've had a chance to talk, will you come back and see me again, please, Suzanne, so we can sort out all the paperwork?'

Suzie followed Alexandra out of the study, back along the main corridor and through the magnificent entrance hall to the front door. It was only once they were outside and some distance from the splendid old manor house that Alexandra slowed and turned to her. She was a good-looking girl, but the expression on her face this morning was far from attractive.

'So, what do you want to talk about?' She sounded resigned, rather than belligerent, but definitely not friendly.

Suzie decided to be as open and frank as possible. 'Listen, Alexandra, I feel uncomfortable being asked to play the role of sneak. I've no idea why your father feels it necessary to send somebody along to keep an eye on a grown woman like you and, frankly, it doesn't appeal to me at all. Yes, the idea of going to Italy – my favourite country in all the world – is very attractive, but not if you and I are going to be at daggers drawn all the time. I think it might be better if you find yourself another companion, maybe one of your friends for instance.'

'My friends?' Alexandra's voice was low, her tone morose rather than annoyed. 'My father wouldn't dream of it.'

'I'm sorry to hear that. Then maybe somebody from your father's staff? Surely there must be somebody he trusts and you like.'

Alexandra shook her head. 'Nope, nobody.'

With considerable regret, Suzie decided she had no choice. 'Well, I'm sorry, Alexandra, but I think I'd prefer not to be involved, if you don't mind. I think the best thing would be if I just say no to your father.'

To her surprise, Alexandra reached out and caught her by the arm. 'Don't do that. Please say you'll come.' There was an unexpectedly pleading note in her voice.

'You *want* me to come with you?' Suzie could hear the disbelief in her own voice.

'Yes, please.' Alexandra's hand dropped from Suzie's arm. 'If you say no, my father won't let me go to Italy at all. It's as simple as that. He's already said as much. He trusts you because your father's the local vicar and there's nobody else he approves of. Please say yes. You'll be doing me an immense favour.'

Suzie paused for a few moments of reflection. 'And you won't resent my presence? You heard your father; he wants me to be his spy. That's pretty distasteful.' She held Alexandra's eye for a moment longer. 'And if I take the job, I'll have to do as he says. He's the one paying my wages, after all. You realise what that means.'

Alexandra nodded. 'I understand and I won't hold it against you, I promise. I know my father all too well and I know this is the only way for me to get away. I give you my word I'll be on my best behaviour.'

For a moment, Suzie could hear the voice of a little girl coming from the woman opposite her and she felt a wave of sympathy, maybe even pity for her. After a few moments' deliberation, she came to a decision.

'All right then, I'll say yes. And please try to remember that I'll just be doing what your father wants me to do. I don't like the idea of it, but I'll have to do as he asks.'

Chapter 2

Barely three weeks later Suzie and Alexandra set off for Italy – or, more precisely, for central London first. A luxury saloon with a chauffeur collected them from Devon and deposited them at the Ritz Hotel on the corner of Piccadilly. Suzie had often walked past this world-famous luxury hotel, but had never dreamt of setting foot over the threshold. As the limousine pulled up behind a spotless black Bentley, a pair of liveried porters came out and set about unloading their luggage onto a trolley. As Suzie was still thanking the driver, Alexandra turned and disappeared into the hotel without a word. The driver gave a little salute, and the car had already pulled out into the traffic as the thought occurred to Suzie that she might have been expected to give him a tip. She was still trying to work out just exactly what this job entailed, so for now, she thought it best to concentrate on the luggage. One of the porters waved towards the glass doors.

'Do please go on in, miss. We'll bring your luggage.'

Suzie climbed the half-dozen steps, hardly daring to touch the glistening brass handrails for fear of marking them. As she stepped through the doors into the lobby, she felt a total fraud. All her life, she and her parents had struggled with money and she had had to do two different

14

jobs to fund her three years of postgraduate study. Her work at the charity had been fulfilling, but her salary had barely covered the exorbitant cost of renting a tiny room in a crowded flat in south London along with three other girls. Now here she was, embarking upon a holiday of unlimited all-expenses-paid luxury, beginning with this iconic five-star hotel. She felt pretty sure the porters and the immaculate reception staff here would be able to see clear through her disguise. She wasn't a member of the privileged classes and they knew it.

Alexandra, on the other hand, definitely was, and she was used to getting her own way. As Suzie arrived at the front desk, she found her looking and sounding like thunder.

'No, we are *not* sharing a room. The reservation was for two single rooms.'

A dapper gentleman wearing a sober dark suit bearing a badge on the lapel indicating he was the Assistant Manager inclined his head towards her deferentially.

'If you'll just give me a moment, Lady Tedburn, I'll get this sorted out.' Seeing Suzie at Alexandra's shoulder, he gave her a little bow of the head. 'Doctor Cartwright, I presume. Welcome to the Ritz.'

Suzie was mightily surprised to be addressed with her full title. Presumably Lord Tedburn had asked his PA to make the reservation and had informed her of Suzie's full qualifications. She took heart; it wasn't as good as 'milady', but it was still better than plain old 'Miss Cartwright'. She gave him an answering smile and a nod, while Alexandra just stood there, looking stony-faced. As the Assistant Manager and two receptionists pored over the computer screen, Suzie glanced around apprehensively. Near them was a chubby, bald, middle-aged man speaking what sounded like Russian. Alongside him was one of the most beautiful girls Suzie had ever seen. Was she his daughter, his PA or something else? Doing her best to avoid going any further along that line of conjecture, she hastily turned her attention to the wonderful vaulted ceilings, highlighted with intricate plasterwork, the polished marble and the impeccably clad staff. It was another world.

In spite of her father's occupation, she wasn't a particularly religious person – probably as a result of overexposure to it all – but she did hold strong views on right and wrong. And she knew that this kind of life – pleasant as it might be for some people to be waited on hand and foot – wasn't right. Not while a staggeringly high percentage of the world's population didn't know where their next meal was coming from. Everywhere she looked in this place, she saw opulence and excess and this, she reminded herself, was only day one of her month-long trip. She hoped she would manage to reach a point where it didn't feel so weird but, at the same time, she told herself, she had better not get too used to a lifestyle she knew she would never experience again in all her life.

Within a few seconds, everything was resolved and the formalities concluded. As a stylish young lady led them towards the lift, Suzie thanked the reception staff and gave them a smile. Alexandra ignored them completely. In the lift, their guide, whose lapel badge indicated her name was Anna, informed them that their rooms were on different floors, and accompanied Alexandra to her room on the third floor first. As they got there, Alexandra turned back to Suzie.

'We'll meet in the restaurant at eight. After having something to eat, we'll take a taxi to the party. I don't want to arrive too early.' And she turned away with a dismissive wave of the hand. Suzie could feel her hackles rise at Alexandra's attitude and her tone, but she bit her lip and, for now, just nodded. Maybe her stroppy companion would mellow as the days went by. She certainly hoped so.

Tonight was to be Alexandra's going-away party with a group of her friends. Lord Tedburn had insisted that Suzie be invited along to keep an eye on his daughter and she had been dreading it. From Alexandra's reaction, it was pretty clear she resented the intrusion, and the journey up in the car had been conducted in almost complete silence. As far as Suzie could gather, these friends didn't fall into the 'undesirable' category in Lord Tedburn's eyes and she wondered why he felt her presence to be necessary. Clearly, so did his daughter.

The party was scheduled to take place in a wine bar in Knightsbridge and Suzie had no illusions as to what hiring a place like that would cost. Presumably these friends were all from the same sort of privileged, or rather overprivileged, background as Alexandra. Suzie gave a little sigh as she was shown to her predictably faultlessly elegant hotel room. She had hardly been out anywhere socially since Rob's departure from her life a year ago and wasn't looking forward to finding herself in the midst of a whole bunch of people who all knew each other. The fact that they would almost certainly be from a very different world from hers didn't help.

Not having had lunch, Suzie was feeling hungry by eight o'clock and the dinner here at the Ritz would have been wonderful, except for her dinner companion. Alexandra appeared wearing a remarkably formal black evening dress that screamed style and expense. It also screamed the obvious fact that Alexandra wasn't wearing a bra and the open front of the dress extended almost down to her navel. In comparison, Suzie felt positively shabby – although far more structurally secure – in her only decent dress, and the look she got from Alexandra only served to confirm that opinion. Although Alexandra didn't comment – indeed, she barely said a word all meal – her distain was evident. Suzie made a few attempts at conversation, but ended up consuming her beef Wellington with celeriac and Périgord truffle in complete silence. Even the exquisite white chocolate and coconut mousseline failed to bring a smile to her morose companion's face and it was a relief when they got up and set off for the party.

A smile did, however, finally appear on Alexandra's face once they reached the wine bar. The place was packed with people and the noise level high. As Alexandra was spotted, it rose even higher as friends descended upon her from all round the room, air-kissing her theatrically and gushing greetings. A few people even greeted Suzie, but as Alexandra didn't bother to introduce her to anyone, she soon found herself on her own. She helped herself to a glass of champagne from a passing waiter and took refuge in a corner, quite happy to observe the goings-on from afar.

As it turned out, she wasn't on her own for long. Barely a minute or two after taking up her position, she felt a tap on her shoulder and turned to find herself looking up into the face of a tall man with short-cropped fair hair.

'Hello, I saw you on your own. I hope you don't mind me coming over to say hi.'

'Not at all. Are you one of Alexandra's friends?' As she asked the question, she studied him a bit more closely. He looked as if he were in his late twenties – pretty much the same age as she was – and, apart from being tall, he was undeniably good-looking. Very good-looking indeed. As he leant closer to her, she realised that he was also extremely drunk.

'We're all Alex's friends here. I'm Tommy. Who're you?'

The individual components of the cocktail of alcoholic aromas on his breath were hard to identify, but the overall effect was highly toxic. Breath like that could most probably strip wallpaper, and she took a step back, only to feel her bottom bump into the wall as she backed into the corner. Turning away slightly to take a deep breath of unpolluted air, she summoned a smile as she looked back and replied.

'I'm pleased to meet you, Tommy. I'm Suzie.'

'Hi, Suzie.' Hemmed in as she was, she found herself unable to avoid the ensuing kisses on the cheeks she received from him but, mercifully, he didn't try to do anything more intrusive. He just took an unsteady step back and stared right into her eyes. 'You're gorgeous.'

Suzie felt the colour rush to her cheeks. She had never been very confident in social circles and she certainly had very little experience of tall, handsome – if plastered – men calling her gorgeous. She began a slow process of shuffling her way out of the corner so as to clear a way of escape, but she soon realised that she had little to fear from Tommy. He was so drunk, he was wobbling about, and it was probably only a matter of time before he keeled over. In spite of his current state he looked friendly enough, and she didn't want him to hurt himself so, spotting an unoccupied table, she made a practical suggestion.

'Would you like to sit down, Tommy?'

'Good idea...'

Unsuccessfully attempting to restrain a burp, he turned towards the table and stood there, swaying slightly. He looked uncertainly towards it as if he were trying to decide whether his legs were capable of propelling him over to it or whether it might magically come to him. Taking pity on him, Suzie caught hold of his arm and guided him across the room until she was able to pour him into one of the low armchairs. He subsided with a deep sigh and his eyes closed. She was trying to make up her mind whether to go off and leave him or whether to sit down across the coffee table from him when she was surprised to hear her name being called. She looked round and saw Alexandra coming over from the bar, a glass of champagne in one hand and an unexpected sparkle in her eye. This was just about the first time Suzie had seen Alexandra looking truly happy and relaxed and it totally changed her whole appearance.

'I see you've met Tommy.' She chuckled. 'Somehow, I think he's going to feel awful tomorrow morning.'

Suzie smiled back. 'He looks like a nice guy, but he's drunk as a skunk.'

Alex nodded. 'It's his birthday and I've got a feeling some of the other boys have been spiking his drinks. I think he needs to sleep it off.'

Both of them turned their eyes back to Tommy and it was eminently clear that he had already embarked upon that course. His eyes were closed and he looked as peaceful as a little baby – a very drunk baby. Then Alexandra surprised Suzie.

'Come and let me introduce you to some of my friends.'

Suzie was impressed. 'Of course. I'd like that.' As Alexandra led her across the room, she risked a direct question. 'Are these what your father would consider to be "suitable" or "unsuitable" friends?'

Alexandra gave her a wry smile. 'Suitable, I think it's fair to say.' She then lowered her voice. 'My father probably knows almost all the parents, and any whose families he doesn't know are friends who've been approved by my big brother.' The smile became more sardonic. 'Sanitised for my convenience.'

By this time they had reached a group of a dozen or so people, roughly half male and half female. The men were wearing anything from jeans and T-shirts to lounge suits, while the girls were all dolled up to the eyeballs and, incredibly, two or three of them were actually exposing more skin than Alexandra. Clearly, Suzie thought to herself, she was now firmly in the midst of the *if you've got it, flaunt it* brigade. She was introduced by Alexandra as 'Suzie, my friend from Devon'. Suzie could understand why Alexandra didn't want to broadcast the fact that she had been employed by Lord Tedburn to escort and supervise his daughter. She smiled and shook a few hands and was even on the receiving end of a number of kisses – not just from the men.

The evening wasn't as grim as she had been expecting and Alexandra's change in demeanour was both welcome and surprising. This newfound cheerfulness lasted almost all evening, but was marred towards the end. It was nearly midnight and Suzie had been surprised to find that Tommy had discovered a second wind. As a result, she found him at her side like a little lapdog, breathing alcohol in her face and repeating how gorgeous she looked. The compliments would have had more weight if his booze-befuddled brain had managed to come up with another adjective. In the end she got so fed up with the constant repetition of the word 'gorgeous' that she excused herself and headed for the Ladies. It was while she was in there, looking at herself in the mirror, absently thinking that it was high time she spent some of her newly arrived cash on a visit to a hairdresser, when the door opened and Alexandra came stomping in. Or at least, doing her best to stomp in high heels.

'Hi, Alexandra, what's up?'

Alexandra gave a heartfelt sigh. 'Just life…'

'Anything you want to talk about?'

There was a pause before the shutters came down across Alexandra's face and the familiar surly look returned.

'No.' There was a brief pause and then, to Suzie's delight, she added one more word: 'Thanks.'

So, Suzie said to herself, no breakthrough yet, but maybe very early signs that the ice maiden might be beginning to thaw.

Chapter 3

They landed at Venice Marco Polo Airport in the late afternoon the following day. As the aircraft flew in over the calm grey-green waters of the lagoon, Suzie peered out of the window in fascination and marvelled at the sight of Venice below them. The whole city was clearly laid out and she easily recognised the Grand Canal, St Mark's Square and the Lido – the long island that formed a natural breakwater between Venice and the sea. Beside her, Alexandra shot occasional glances out of the window and then relapsed into the same morose state she had been in all day. Suzie had just made one attempt to get her to talk about what had happened at the end of the party, but this had been met with stony silence and so she had stopped trying. Hopefully Alexandra would start to mellow once they got to Italy. As for herself, she felt a rising sense of excitement that she was going to see Venice for the first time and then, after that, her long-awaited Verona.

A sleek varnished water taxi took them across the lagoon from the airport to the hotel. This was right in the heart of the city, by the side of the Grand Canal, and Suzie knew it to be one of the most famous hotels in the world, frequented by celebrities from all walks of life – from real royalty to Hollywood royalty. And now it was going to be home to Suzanne Cartwright from deepest Devonshire.

The more she thought about it, the more surreal it felt. Her room was next to Alexandra's and both rooms looked right out over the water to the island opposite and the spire of San Giorgio Maggiore, the setting sun turning the sky beyond an ethereal pink. As the door closed behind the porter who had brought up her suitcase, Suzie stood at the window and surveyed the view. This was, without a doubt, one of the most romantic places she had ever visited.

Romance, she reflected, had been largely notable by its absence in her life so far. She had had a few boyfriends at university and sporadically since then, but her natural shyness and her concentration on her studies, and then her job, had restricted her social life to a minimum. Her one relationship of any length had been with Rob, the only man for whom she had felt any real lasting affection, but this had come to an abrupt end when he had been offered a job in Canada. He hadn't asked her to accompany him and she hadn't offered, so their relationship – such as it was – had just died a death. That had been at Easter the previous year and it had taken her quite a while to get over him. She couldn't really say she had been broken-hearted – somehow the depth of feeling between them hadn't reached that far – but it had been tough all the same.

She and Alexandra had arranged to meet downstairs in the hotel bar at seven o'clock and Suzie was surprised to find Alexandra already there, deep in conversation with a dark-haired Italian. A firm believer in first impressions, Suzie took an instant dislike to this suave, slick Latin lover with his stylish suit and his predatory eyes. He must have been at least ten years older than Alexandra, and Suzie didn't like the look of him one bit. Alexandra, on the other hand, clearly did. A lot.

In spite of Suzie's best efforts, Alexandra refused point-blank to join her in the restaurant for dinner and marched out on the arm of her Italian without a backward glance. Suzie had a light meal on her own and went back to her room, hoping Alexandra wouldn't do anything silly. The following morning over breakfast, up on the spectacular terrace overlooking the rooftops and waterways of the city, she did her best to warn her companion off and finally got the impression that her words might have got through.

It therefore came as a great disappointment to find Alexandra sitting in the bar with her Italian again that evening, hand in hand, in what was unmistakably a romantic tête-à-tête. Suzie marched across and took a seat at their table, hoping that her presence would be enough to cool things off between the two of them. Alas, all that this intervention provoked was a spectacular scene and some harsh words from Alexandra, after which she and her Italian got up and left.

Suzie spent another solitary evening and an uncomfortable night wrestling with her conscience before making one last appeal to Alexandra's common sense the next day. When this, too, was ignored, she had no choice but to inform Lord Tedburn that his daughter appeared to have involved herself with an unsuitable man. She sent the message with a heavy heart, but the fact was that she genuinely felt there was something not right about the handsome Italian. Maybe if she had approved of him, she might have given Alexandra the benefit of the doubt and omitted informing her father, but not in this case.

Her text message resulted in a phone call, not from Lord Tedburn, but from Alexandra's big brother, Rafe. This sent a little shiver down Suzie's spine when she realised who was on the other end of the line. Back when she was a teenager she had had a crush on Rafe, ever since first spotting him among the congregation of her father's church. Needless to say, as so often with her and relationships, it had remained unrequited, not least because he most probably hadn't even known she existed. Apart from his exalted position as future lord of the manor, he was probably at least three or four years older than her and evidently hadn't been in the least bit interested in the vicar's chronically shy daughter with her specs and the braces on her teeth. She hadn't seen him for years and it felt weird to hear his voice now after so long.

'Suzanne, we got your message.' He sounded serious and definitely displeased. 'Father and I have been speaking and I'll be flying over to see Alexandra tomorrow. Father's furious.'

He didn't sound any less angry himself and Suzie felt a pang of sympathy for Alexandra. 'Look, Rafe, don't be too hard on her. I had to tell your father, but she's only just met the man. It may come to nothing.'

'Father intends to make damn sure it doesn't come to anything.' Rafe's displeasure was unmistakable. 'Now, tell me as much as you know about him.'

Suzie sighed and did as she was told. 'He's Italian and his name's Carlo Moretti. He says he lives in Parma and he's got a company that makes top-of-the-range leather handbags, belts and so on. He's told Alexandra he's thirty-three, but I reckon you can add at least ten years to that.' She paused, searching for any other snippets of information. 'They met in the bar of our hotel the other night, but he isn't staying here. That's about all I know, I'm afraid.'

'Fine. I'll text you when I know my ETA tomorrow. Tell Alexandra she's not to see the man again until I get there.'

And that, of course, had been the last straw that had resulted in Alexandra's outburst at the dinner table and the shower of Prosecco.

Even so, despite the tantrums and insults, Suzie still felt sympathy for her. Maybe the extravagant clothes and five-star hotels were an attempt to compensate for the happiness she had lost. And the succession of 'unsuitable' men in her life had quite probably been attempts to find some sort of affection after the death of her mother when she was barely into her teens. No doubt a psychiatrist would be able to read all manner of things into the fact that this man she had started seeing here in Venice was so much older than her. Although Suzie had felt compelled to rat on her, she felt sorry for this girl whose life had provided her with everything she could possibly want – except love.

She spent the following morning walking around Venice on her own, gazing with awe at one irreplaceable architectural gem after another, and it wasn't until lunchtime that she received a text message from Alexandra.

See you in the hotel lobby at one. I need to talk to you. A.

Suzie went down to the lobby at ten to one and waited twenty minutes before the now familiar figure of Alexandra appeared from the lift. Today she was wearing the skimpiest, shortest, most revealing summer dress – yet another from her seemingly inexhaustible collection of designer clothes – and the elderly man who emerged from the lift behind her had his eyes out on stalks. Alongside him, his silver-haired wife's expression of disapproval was unmistakable. As the lift doors swished silently closed behind them, the old lady took a firm grip on her husband's arm and frogmarched him to the exit. Apparently unaware of the effect her choice of clothing had produced, Alexandra came across to where Suzie was waiting close to a large pot plant she intended to use as a primitive means of defence in the event of assault.

'You've heard that my brother's coming tonight, I suppose?' No greeting, but this didn't surprise Suzie. 'This is all your fault, you know.'

Suzie nodded, but felt she should clarify things. 'What was I supposed to do? I had to tell your father. That's what he's paying me to do and I promised him. You knew that. And I warned you enough times before calling him.' Making sure she kept the plant between them, she hurried on before Alexandra could retort. 'Listen, Alexandra, put yourself in my shoes. He specifically employed me to look after you, and one of the things he insisted upon was for me to inform him if you got involved with any unsuitable men. You heard him say it.' She took a deep breath. 'And, to be totally honest, I thought… think Carlo is unsuitable. Maybe if it had been a different man, but I'm sorry, there's just something about him that isn't right.'

Alexandra didn't start screaming or launch herself into an all-out assault. Instead, her eyes dropped to the floor and she said nothing for a full minute before finally looking up again. This time there were tears in the corners of her eyes.

'Have you eaten, Suzie?'

Taken aback at the unexpectedly gentle tone, Suzie found herself shaking her head as Alexandra pointed across to the bar.

'Shall we go and see if they can do us some sandwiches? Rafe will want a full-blown dinner with all the trimmings tonight, I'm sure, but I haven't eaten since yesterday lunchtime and I'll fall over if I don't have something.'

Suzie nodded and followed her across the lobby. The elegant bar was nearly empty and they sat down side by side on a leather sofa, well away from anybody else. No sooner had they done so than a waiter arrived, and Suzie recognised him as the same one who had given her a napkin to mop her face in the restaurant. If he was surprised to see the two of them sitting together pacifically after last night's pyrotechnics, he didn't show it. Alexandra ordered ham and cheese sandwiches and a bottle of mineral water and Suzie did the same before sitting back in silence and waiting for several minutes before her companion began to talk.

'I'm sorry about throwing my wine all over you, Suzie. That was inexcusable.' Alexandra sounded as if she meant it. 'I was just so furious, but it wasn't really with you. It's with everything.'

Suzie got the impression Alexandra didn't do a lot of apologising, so she did her best to shrug the incident off.

'Don't worry about it. It was white wine anyway and it washed straight out.' She hesitated. 'So, what happens when your brother gets here? Is he going to go ballistic?'

Alexandra nodded. 'Maybe not ballistic – that's my father's prerogative – but he isn't going to be happy.' Her expression was sorrowful rather than angry – for now. 'I know you had to tell him about Carlo. My father made himself completely clear before we left. The thing is…' She paused and took a couple of deep breaths, the old familiar spark of annoyance flashing in her eyes. 'I'm twenty-five, going on twenty-six, for God's sake. Why does my father have to treat me like a child? I'm *not* a child.' Her voice rose in volume and pitch and a few heads turned towards them. Suzie gave her a little smile of comprehension. To her relief – and surprise – it appeared to do some good, as her companion's voice dropped back to normal volume. 'I'm sure your father doesn't tell you who you can and can't see.'

'My dad rarely raises his head from his reading – or the cricket – these days, but my mum always gives me the third degree when I come home, even though I'll be twenty-nine next birthday. And you know what comes after twenty-nine.' She was remarkably impressed at the way Alexandra's attitude had started to show signs of mellowing – although she had no doubt the fuse was still smouldering somewhere inside her – so she allowed herself to ask the question that had been on the tip of her tongue for the last three weeks since first meeting her, surreptitiously crossing her fingers behind her back as she did so. At least, she thought to herself, there were no drinks on the table yet to be thrown around. 'So why don't you just tell your dad to mind his own business? You're an adult. Surely you can do whatever you like.'

'You'd think so, wouldn't you, but it doesn't work like that in our family, for a variety of reasons.' Alexandra ran her fingers through her hair and sat back in frustration. 'Apart from anything else, the trouble with having money is that you get used to having it. My father has decided that I need to marry somebody "suitable".' Her acidic tone made clear what she thought of her father's choice of adjective. 'In the meantime I get my allowance, but only if I play by his rules. And that means effectively having all my friends – male and female – vetted by him. Why do you think you were employed? It's because he doesn't trust me.'

At that moment, the waiter returned with the drinks and two plates of immaculate triangular white-bread sandwiches without crusts, arranged with mathematical precision and accompanied by some decorative sprigs of watercress. Suzie gave him a smile and a '*Grazie.*' Alexandra totally ignored him. As he retired again, Suzie tried to give her a bit of support.

'Maybe it's not so much a lack of trust as the desire to protect you. Maybe this is just because he worries about you.'

Alexandra snorted and took a big bite of a sandwich. Suzie did the same – but without snorting – realising she, too, was hungry in spite of having had a big meal the previous night. The next thing Alexandra said came as a considerable – and welcome – surprise.

'To be honest, I'm not going to see Carlo again anyway.'

Suzie looked up from her plate. 'Is that you just being pragmatic, or is there some other reason?'

Alexandra gave a heartfelt sigh. 'After I left you last night, I phoned him and he came to meet me. I thought he'd take me out for dinner somewhere, but he took me to his hotel. We were halfway up the stairs when I came to my senses. I like... liked him a lot, but there was no way I was going up to his room so soon after I'd just met him.'

Suzie nodded approvingly. 'Quite right, too.'

'That's not what he thought. In fact, he got quite objectionable and then he caught hold of my arm and I didn't think he was going to let go until, luckily, a couple came down the stairs and he had to release me. It was really quite scary for a minute or two. As the other people came past, I turned and walked out alongside them and made a run for it.' She looked up with an attempt at a smile. 'When I got back here, I imagine you were still in the dining room, but I didn't want to bother you with my troubles.'

'But you should have. Besides, the food was very good.'

'I'm sure it was, Suzie, but I didn't feel in the mood for food.' Her lips were trembling as she fought back tears. 'Now, as a result, my father's furious with me, and my brother's been sent to read me the riot act – all because of some man I'm not even seeing any more. But you were right, Suzie. There was something wrong about Carlo.'

Suzie felt genuinely sorry for her and reached out to lay a hand on her arm for a few seconds. 'Look, Alexandra, I'm sorry you've got into this mess, but we'll get you out of it.' The beginnings of an idea occurred to her. 'Rafe and your dad don't need to know what happened last night with Carlo. What I think you should do when your brother gets here is to apologise profusely and tell him you immediately dumped him as soon as you heard your dad didn't approve. You know – roll over and play the obedient little girl, and they'll both be so pleased, they'll let you get on with your life. It doesn't always have to be confrontation, you know.'

Alexandra didn't reply for a while, concentrating on her sandwich. When she finally raised her face towards Suzie once more, she was looking perplexed. 'But surely you're duty-bound to tell them what happened between me and Carlo. Aren't you…?' Her voice tailed off helplessly and Suzie grinned at her.

'I've done my duty by telling them about his existence. How he disappeared from your life is totally up to you. No, Alexandra, you tell them you dumped him because you didn't want to displease them and I promise I'll back you up all the way. Okay?'

Alexandra began to look happy for the first time that day. 'You would do that for me?' Her smile broadened. 'And do please call me Alex. That's what all my friends call me.'

Chapter 4

When Rafe arrived, he was immaculately and formally turned out in a dark suit, collar and tie, and Suzie had to admit that he fitted into the five-star surroundings perfectly. As Alexandra had predicted, he wasted no time in taking them to the upstairs dining room for dinner. From there they had panoramic views out over Venice as the sun set and the lights gradually came on below them. Under other circumstances it would have been a charming and romantic view, but not tonight. Suzie braced herself for the explosion to come as they were shown to their seats alongside a huge picture window.

However, prepped by Suzie, Alexandra attacked first to deflect his anger. Also on Suzie's advice, she had replaced the revealing dress she had been wearing at lunchtime with a rather conservative – but still most elegant – dress with a modest neckline and hemline. Suzie sat back and did her best not to smile as Alexandra launched into a fulsome apology and told her brother quite clearly that nothing had happened between her and Carlo and, out of deference to their father, she had already dumped him. She assured him she only intended to do what her father wanted and he could trust her to behave sensibly.

Rafe's expression went from confrontational, through surprised, to pleased. However, as Alexandra brought her apology to a suitably emotional conclusion, he looked over at Suzie for confirmation.

'Is this all true, Suzanne? Is it all over between Alex and this Italian?'

Suzie adopted a suitably trustworthy expression as she replied. 'Absolutely. He's history.'

Rafe nodded, unaware of the surreptitious smile that Alex flashed across the table at Suzie. 'Excellent.' He returned his attention to his sister. 'Well, I'm glad you saw sense, Alex, not least as I've had somebody looking into Mr Carlo Moretti. I'm sure his wife would be very happy to know that you're not interested in him.'

'His wife?' Alexandra looked genuinely gobsmacked and Suzie felt for her.

'Yes, Alex, his *wife*.' Rafe sounded rather pleased with himself. 'And his three daughters would also be relieved, I imagine.' Seeing the expressions on both their faces, he elaborated. 'I contacted a private investigation agency yesterday and I got their report on my way here from the airport. You may be interested to hear that he's forty-five, not whatever age he told you.'

Suzie glanced across the table and couldn't miss the expression on Alexandra's face. She looked shaken to her roots and Suzie's feeling of sympathy grew.

The atmosphere improved as the meal progressed and Suzie had to admit that it was without a doubt one of the best meals she had ever had. All three of them opted for the restaurant's antipasti selection and the different dishes on offer were exceptional, ranging from all manner of different salami and hams on a massive wooden platter, to homemade Russian salad, hot garlic prawns and porcini mushrooms in olive oil. Suzie helped herself to a little of each, but tried not to let herself get drawn into eating too much as she felt sure there would be a lot more to come.

As they ate, they chatted and Suzie was delighted to see both Alexandra and her brother loosen up and start to enjoy themselves. While the two siblings talked, Suzie had the opportunity to study them more closely. There was a definite family resemblance, mainly around the mouth and high cheekbones, and she remembered what it was she had seen in Rafe all those years ago when she had been a spotty teenager, peeking at him from the anonymity of the rear pews. His hair was darker than his sister's but, like Alexandra, his eyes were a light hazel colour, rather like a wild animal's eyes. Even the lines around them added to, rather than detracted from, his overall good looks.

Yes, she thought to herself, they were two very lucky people – good-looking and as rich as Croesus. Not a bad combination, not bad at all. She gave a little sigh to herself as she sat back and wiped her mouth with her napkin.

'So how long are you girls planning on staying in Venice?' Rafe took a sip of wine and swilled it round in his mouth as Alexandra answered for both of them.

'I haven't made up my mind. Probably another two or three days.'

'And then where are you heading?'

'Suzie, where would you like to go next?'

Suzie was quite taken aback to be consulted. This was just about the first time Alex had asked for her opinion on anything. Things were definitely looking up. She gave Alex a big smile as she replied.

'Before I went to university I spent some time in Tuscany but I've never been to this region. Venice is fabulous but – I don't know if your father told you – the place I've been dreaming of has to be Verona. After all, it's not that far from here.'

Rafe looked mildly surprised. 'Why Verona in particular?'

'All sorts of reasons; history, culture, scenery, but mainly Shakespeare.'

'Shakespeare?' Brother and sister responded in unison and Suzie found herself grinning.

'I've always been fascinated by Shakespeare and by the fact that he set no fewer than ten of his plays in Italy, not counting his ancient Roman plays like *Julius Caesar* or *Coriolanus*. And Verona pops up in a number of them, most importantly *The Two Gentlemen of Verona* and, of course, *Romeo and Juliet*. Who wouldn't want to visit the setting of what's been called the greatest love story ever told?'

A beaming smile spread across Alexandra's face. 'Then that's your answer, Rafe. Next stop, Verona.'

He was also smiling by this time. 'Excellent. A happy coincidence. Father was talking to James's father before I left and he's invited you to stay at their villa. It's on Lake Garda and he says it's less than half an hour from Verona. It's right by the water and there's a pool. Sound good?'

From the expression that appeared on Alexandra's face, this idea didn't sound good at all.

'Oh God, Rafe, do we have to?' The familiar petulant note was back in her voice. 'You know I'm trying to stay away from him.'

'Come on, Alex, you've known him for years. As kids you were inseparable. Besides, he'll be there with a bunch of your friends. You'd enjoy that, wouldn't you?'

Alexandra snorted. 'The thing is, you know what he's like. All he'll want to do is to proposition me again.' She glared across the table at her brother. 'I've lost count of the number of times he's asked me to marry him and I've said no. Most recently at my going-away party in London the other night. Everything was going swimmingly and then he comes up to me and tells me he can't live without me. It totally spoilt my night. Can't the man take a hint? Marriage is all he talks about, apart from when he's talking about sailing, shotguns and bloody pheasants.'

'Well, Father thinks it's a wonderful idea.' There might even have been a flicker of sympathy in Rafe's eyes now. 'You know he and James's father fully approve of the idea of the two of you getting together.'

'For God's sake!' Alexandra's snort of anger was loud enough to attract the attention of a number of other diners and Suzie glanced across at her with an admonitory shake of the head. It worked and Alex grimaced, but lowered her voice. 'Suzie, you might have thought that arranged marriages were just the preserve of the Indian subcontinent, mightn't you? Well, you'd be wrong.'

Suzie thought it best not to respond. She had been trying to remember which of Alex's friends had been introduced to her as James back in Knightsbridge, but there had been so many of them. Just about the only man's name she remembered was Tommy, the birthday boy.

'Don't be silly, Alex. He isn't trying to marry you off. He only wants what's best for you.' Even Rafe himself must have heard the insincerity in his own voice.

The expression on Alexandra's face made clear the disdain with which she chose to treat that comment. 'As long as it's what's best for *him*.'

Fortunately the uncomfortable silence that followed was interrupted by the arrival of a waiter bearing a silver platter piled high with risotto, laced with pieces of prawns and scallops. It tasted as good as it looked. As Suzie came to the end of her helping and refused the offer of any more, she decided to introduce a lighter note to the evening.

'Are you coming out for a walk around Venice with us before bed, Rafe? You're only here for such a short time, you need to see as much as possible.'

He looked up from his food and shook his head. 'Maybe a quick drink somewhere. I've got an early start in the morning and a long day ahead of me.' He glanced across at his sister. 'Father wants me to have lunch with his lawyers in London.' He finished his risotto and took a mouthful of wine. 'But, seeing as I'm not in Venice every day, then maybe I should at least have a quick look round.'

'I know, why don't we go for a cocktail at Harry's Bar?' Alex was looking and sounding more enthusiastic now. 'You know, the place where Hemingway used to drink. What about it, Suzie? Are you in?'

Suzie felt conflicting emotions. On the one hand, she was pleased to be included in the decision-making process, however, on the other hand, she had a feeling the Hemingway place might be posh and she wasn't sure if the dress she was wearing would be sufficiently smart.

'That would be lovely, but I'm not sure I look presentable enough.' She felt Rafe's eyes on her and flushed as Alexandra reassured her.

'Don't be so silly, Suzie. You look fine, more than fine.' This was the first time Suzie had heard anything even vaguely approaching a compliment emerge from Alexandra's lips.

'Yes, you do indeed.' Suzie's blushes intensified as she heard Rafe add his support. 'That's a beautiful dress, and you're looking lovely.'

'Well, if you're sure…'

The rest of the meal was as excellent as the first courses. Suzie and Alexandra refused any meat and chose turbot, cooked with lemon and coriander. Rafe, as predicted by his sister, opted for a massive T-bone steak and demolished it with obvious enjoyment. He drank Barolo, but he insisted upon ordering a bottle of really good white for the girls to have with their fish and Suzie couldn't fault his choice. It was a Soave from near Verona and Rafe pointed out that this was a very good sign. If the wine was this good in Verona, he informed them both, then it was definitely where they should go – James or no James.

By the time Suzie reached her dessert of pistachio soufflé with white chocolate ice cream and a mango coulis, she was beginning to regret agreeing to go to for a walk, having serious doubts as to whether she would be able to raise herself from her seat at the end of the meal after all she had eaten and drunk. But, with the aid of a strong espresso coffee, she managed it.

Outside, it was still warm, although night had fallen and a light breeze was blowing in off the sea. As they walked along the water's edge towards St Mark's Square, Suzie found herself smiling. Her stay in Italy looked like it wasn't, after all, going to be curtailed and, even better, her irascible companion was showing definite signs of warming to her. She breathed deeply as she looked across the waters of the Grand Canal towards the twinkling lights on the other side. Yes, it was good to be here and, before long, she would finally realise her dream of visiting the setting of the greatest love story ever told.

Chapter 5

Next morning, after a very light breakfast, Suzie decided to take the vaporetto across to the Lido and go for a swim. There was no sign of Rafe, and Alexandra hadn't surfaced yet, so Suzie texted her to say where she was going and went out. It was another fine, cloudless day and last night's breeze had died away completely. The trip across the lagoon to the long thin island between Venice and the sea was a delight and she spent the whole time at the stern of the ferryboat, looking back in awe at the jumble of terracotta roofs, cupolas and towers of this unique city on the water. The water itself was alive with all manner of craft from an absolutely massive ocean-going cruise ship to fishing boats, yachts and the iconic gondolas. Although she was still dreaming of going to Verona, she had to admit that Venice took some beating.

The southern side of the Lido was a long strip of sand and she easily found the immaculately raked piece of private beach belonging to the hotel. She was escorted to a sunbed and parasol where she slipped out of her dress and left it in the shade, tucking her glasses into her bag and pushing it safely out of the way inside the rolled-up towel. She hopped gingerly over the already hot sand to the sea where she was pleasantly surprised to find the water warm. There weren't many people about at this time of the morning and it was delightful to be able to wade in and float about lazily, swimming a few strokes and then lying back, gazing up at the sky.

As she was slowly making her way back to the shore another swimmer came out past her, head buried as he did a stylish front crawl that took him far out to sea. When she reached the shallows, she sat down with the water up to her waist, and settled back on her elbows, idly playing with little blue shells she retrieved from the sandy seabed.

Twenty minutes later, the man who had passed her returned from his energetic swim and waded the last few metres to the shore, emerging from the water. Without her glasses and with the sun behind him, she couldn't see the features of his face too clearly, but what she could make out of his body was impressive. She was surreptitiously counting the ridges of muscle across his abdomen as he came past when she saw him glance across at her, do a double take and then stop. Unexpectedly, he spoke to her in English.

'Good morning. You're the Prosecco girl, aren't you?'

Suzie blinked in surprise, feeling suddenly very exposed with just a few ounces of cloth covering her body.

'I'm not sure what you mean…' Although she did.

'The Prosecco-in-the-face girl, the other night in the restaurant. I was a couple of tables away from you and I saw and heard the whole thing.'

Suzie was unsurprised to feel her cheeks glowing – not just from the early autumn sunshine. 'That was me, all right. I hope the commotion didn't put you off your food.'

'Not at all. I was alone and bored. Your friend's exploits made me smile… although I imagine the same can't be said for you.' He hesitated before moving a few steps towards her and she took a better look at him, instantly registering that he was way out of her league. Apart from the fact that he was presumably a guest in their five-star hotel – which *she* most certainly couldn't have afforded under normal circumstances – he was tall and good-looking in a careless way and she felt sure he wouldn't have been interested in somebody as ordinary as her. Besides, she noted, there was a wedding ring on his finger. She nodded to herself. Like all the good ones, he was pretty clearly already taken. She suppressed a silent sigh and introduced herself.

'I'm Suzie. I'm here as companion to the girl who threw the wine over me.'

'Michael. I'm pleased to meet you.'

He leant forward and held out his hand. As she shook it formally, rather incongruously as they were both half-naked, she felt a little shiver of attraction run through her body that she immediately did her best to suppress. Apart from being in another league, he was a married man, after all. She did her best to keep the conversation low-key.

'Are you British? You sound it. And are you here on holiday?'

'Yes, and no. I *am* British, but I'm here on business.' He stepped back as if regretting getting so close and, for the first time, she noticed the dark rings and a network of lines around his eyes. Clearly something was bothering him and she felt an immediate spark of sympathy. He squatted down at the water's edge, a non-intimidating distance from her, and, after a few seconds, addressed her once more. 'And you and your companion? Business or pleasure?'

'Pleasure. We're on a four-week Italian holiday. And I'm pleased to be able to tell you that Alex and I have buried the hatchet and we're friends again.'

'So this means your holiday's back on track and you can settle down and enjoy yourself. I'm very happy for you. And the hotel we're in is about as good as it gets.'

'I know, but…' She turned towards him and concentrated on his face rather than his well-honed body, noticing that his eyes were the exact same pale-blue colour as the sea here by the shore. 'To be totally honest, it's all a bit much.' She hesitated, well aware that he was apparently living the good life every bit as much as Alexandra and her brother. 'I'm just not used to all this.' She waved vaguely back in the direction of the hotel. 'Forgive the pun, but I feel a bit of a fish out of water.'

A little grin spread across his face and it took years off him. Then he surprised her. 'You and me both.'

'You?' She couldn't keep the amazement out of her voice. 'But surely if you're staying in our hotel… How come you feel you don't belong?'

'Firstly, I'm only in the hotel because somebody else is paying for it. I shudder to think what it's all costing.'

'On business, you said? May I ask what it is you do?'

'I'm an artist. I've been commissioned to paint the portrait of a very beautiful lady at the request of her very wealthy fiancé. I'm afraid I'm not at liberty to reveal his, or her, identity. He chose the hotel and he's picking up the tab and I'm not complaining.'

One thought was uppermost on Suzie's mind. She was genuinely surprised that an artist could be doing so well. If the accommodation provided for him was five-star, goodness only knew how much he was being paid for the portrait. He must be very, very good at his job. She did her best not to sound too amazed as she replied.

'So we're both impostors. That does wonders for my self-confidence. I thought I was the only pauper here among the princes.'

'Don't you believe it. And we're not the only ones, I'm sure. Very few people have the money of my current employer or yours.' He caught her eye momentarily. 'Besides, you look like a princess, even if you haven't got the bank balance to match.' After speaking, he hastily looked away again, as if regretting the compliment.

As her cheeks coloured once again, Suzie felt a little shiver of disapproval. This was quite evidently flattery, and a little bit flirty at that, and he was a married man. And her sense of right and wrong knew what it thought about that. Maybe this handsome Englishman was no better than two-timing Carlo. Fortunately, before she got round to reacting, a shadow fell across them and she heard Alexandra's voice.

'Hi, Suzie. Is the water warm?'

Suzie looked up with a feeling of relief. The thaw in Alexandra's demeanour didn't appear to have dwindled overnight.

'Hi, Alex. The water's like a warm bath. This is Michael. He's staying in our hotel.'

As Alex made her tentative way into the shallows to shake hands with Michael, Suzie studied the bikini she was wearing in awe. It was tiny, really tiny, and it left little to the imagination. It wasn't that it was obscene, but to describe it as minimal was to overstate its dimensions. No doubt it had cost a fortune and Suzie found herself reflecting that the price of designer clothes, just like designer food, was often in inverse proportion to the quantities involved.

Seeing Alex dressed like this, leaning down to shake hands with Michael, suddenly aroused an unexpected feeling in Suzie. She could only explain it as jealousy. Why she should feel jealous about Alex and a married man they had only just met was something her subconscious refused to consider – at least for now – and she did her best to shrug the thought away as Michael replied.

'Good morning. Suzie's been telling me you two are on a wonderful holiday. Are you staying in Venice for long?'

Alex shook his hand and settled down into the water with an appreciative sigh. 'A few more days and then we're off to Verona.'

'Ah, my favourite city in all Italy.' Suzie was pleased to see him looking and sounding more animated. The worry lines around his eyes were smoothed by his smile and, whether he was married or not, Suzie couldn't help another surge of attraction. 'Have you been before?' Both girls shook their heads. 'Well, you've got a treat in store.'

'Michael's an artist. He's here to paint the portrait of somebody rich and famous, but he can't tell us her name. All very secretive.' Suzie saw renewed interest on Alex's face.

'How exciting. And where's your studio? Are you based in the UK or Italy?'

'Over here now. I've got a place in the hills a couple of hours' drive away – not far from Verona in fact.'

'That all sounds idyllic.'

'Idyllic, yes…' The bleak expression that appeared on his face for a split second was at odds with his words and was unmistakable. It was patently clear that all was not well with him. As if realising he had given himself away, Michael pushed himself to his feet and bade them both farewell.

'Anyway, I'm afraid I have to leave you now. I need to get some work done before this afternoon's session. I may see you again if you're planning on eating at the hotel tonight.'

Suzie saw Alex drag her eyes off Michael's body and glance across at her in mock desperation. 'Oh God, don't mention food after the massive feast we had last night. What do you think, Suzie? Shall we try the hotel restaurant again?' She grinned. 'I promise not to throw any wine around this time.'

Suzie smiled back and agreed, looking forward to seeing Michael again this evening, although she decided she had better warn Alex that he was married first just in case she had designs upon him. When all was said and done, she reflected, that ring on his finger would at least prevent her and Alex from coming to blows about the same man – although if it were to come to a contest, Suzie knew she wouldn't stand a chance anyway. It was hard to compete with unlimited wealth, beauty and a bikini as tiny as hers.

'I look forward to it. Goodbye, Michael.'

'It was good to meet you, Suzie.' For a second their eyes met. 'Really good.'

After he had left, Alex waited until he was out of earshot and then gave Suzie a broad grin.

'I thought you said Verona was the city of love. Venice seems to be working well for you. I wonder what Juliet would have made of your Michael.'

Before Suzie could respond, Alex jumped up and splashed out into the sea for a little swim. When she returned to the shallows she sat down beside Suzie and looked across at her.

'Anything special you want to do today?'

Again, Suzie was greatly cheered to be asked. 'Nothing in particular. Whatever you feel like. I was wondering about maybe taking the boat over to the island of Burano. I've never been there and it's supposed to be very picturesque. It's the one with all the brightly painted houses. You must have seen the photos.'

Alex nodded. 'That sounds like a great idea, although I was thinking about something a bit more mundane first, if you don't mind. I really need to get my hair done.' She glanced across at Suzie who had, in fact, been thinking that very same thing earlier.

'Me too. Mine hasn't been cut properly for God knows how long. That sounds like a good idea. Let's do that first.'

'By the way, I got an email from my father this morning confirming what Rafe said about James inviting us to his villa. Father absolutely insists we go.'

Suzie couldn't help speaking out. 'Can't you just tell your father you don't want to? Or that it's not convenient? I know, maybe we could change our plans and go somewhere else first, and make Verona our final destination in the hope that James has left by then? Padua's supposed to be lovely and that's pretty much in the opposite direction from Verona. Or Bologna?'

Alex shook her head ruefully. 'I'm afraid we're going to have to grin and bear it. Father and Lord Witchampton are big buddies and it sounds as if it's all been stitched up between them.'

'Lord Witchampton?'

'James's father. The Witchamptons own half of Dorset.' She gave Suzie a resigned look. 'And the way my father's pushing, it might end up being my future home.'

'You'd really marry somebody you don't love, just because your dad says so?'

'I don't know.' There was exasperation in her tone. 'To be quite honest, Suzie, I don't dislike James. No, that's unfair; I actually like him a lot. I've known him for years and we get on very well – give or take his sailing and his bloody pheasants. The thing is, I refuse to let myself get pushed into marriage like some medieval princess. It's bloody barbaric!' Her voice began to rise but Suzie was pleased to see her stop, hesitate and then resume in more normal tones. Definitely signs of personal development. 'We live in the twenty-first century now and I should be the one to make that sort of decision, not my father. If my mother was still alive, I know she'd understand. It's maybe a bit unfair on James, but they all need to know that I'm my own person, not some kind of chattel.'

Suzie looked at her with pity in her heart. So Alex liked the man, but was refusing his advances because of her father. The words 'cut off your nose to spite your face' came to mind, but Alex was looking so dejected, she held her tongue. Not for the first time she thanked her lucky stars that she came from a relatively 'normal' family.

Chapter 6

After a morning spent at an expensive salon, they emerged at lunchtime and surprised themselves to find they were hungry again after all. Back at the hotel they took up their familiar spot in the bar and ordered sandwiches once more. As Suzie ate, she couldn't stop looking at her finger-nails in wonder. After a bit of prodding from Alexandra, she had agreed to have a manicure and a pedicure, and now boasted painted nails on her fingers and toes for the first time in her life – everything, including the trim and shape to her hair, unwittingly paid for by Lord Tedburn on his daughter's gold card. She looked over at Alexandra and saw her grinning.

'Getting used to them, Suzie?'

Suzie shook her head. 'It'll take time. I keep thinking I've spilt something on my hands.'

'They look great, though. Wait until your Michael sees them this evening.'

'He's not *my* Michael. I only met him a few minutes before you turned up this morning and apart from anything else, he's married. So even if he was interested in me – which he isn't – I wouldn't dream of getting involved with him.'

'Well, married or not, he seems like a nice guy, although he didn't look a hundred percent happy. I wonder what's troubling him…'

'I was wondering that myself. It surely can't be money if he's working for this super rich client. It has to be something more personal.'

Alex gave her a cheeky grin. She was looking and sounding so much better since they had cleared the air between them. 'Maybe he's lovesick. You know, recently struck by Cupid's arrow, hopelessly besotted by a mysterious English girl with a ponytail and nails that needed a manicure. He probably wants you to pose nude for him. You know what they're like, these artists.'

Suzie found herself blushing. 'No chance of that, Alex. More likely he's got trouble back home, or maybe he's just a moody artist. As you say, you know what they're like.'

'Art's sort of my thing, really. I've painted pretty much all my life.'

Suzie blinked at this revelation. 'What? For a living?'

Alexandra gave Suzie a very old-fashioned look. 'You've got to be joking. Nobody makes a living out of painting… well, almost nobody. Maybe your Michael. No, I paint just for myself. I wanted so badly to do a degree in Fine Art, but my father wouldn't hear of it.'

'What was the problem?'

'The problem was the same as it's always been. He has absolutely no interest in my happiness.' The smiles were now long gone and Alex's voice was once more rising in anger. So much so that the waiter glanced across at them from the behind the bar. Suzie reached over and gave her a gentle tap on the wrist.

'Surely not. Any father would want his daughter to be happy.'

Alex managed a weak smile and when she continued, her voice was back to normal volume. 'Not this father. He told me art was a waste of time. He wanted me to do something "useful" for the estate, so I ended up doing Ecology and Conservation at Brighton and just scraping a pass. Don't get me wrong. I love the animals and the plants, but I hate the science. Besides, I can't add up to save my life.'

Suzie was genuinely amazed – partly that Alexandra was obviously so passionate about art and also that her insensitive father could have stood in the way of her dreams. Surely with all their money, it wouldn't have hurt to let his only daughter follow her instincts and maybe find a bit of happiness? She sighed to herself as she swallowed her last piece of sandwich.

'Have you ever had any training? Surely since doing your Ecology degree, you could have gone on to do an art course?'

Alex shook her head again. 'Art colleges are dens of iniquity as far as Father's concerned. He's convinced himself I'd be led astray and would probably end up pregnant and living in squalor in an opium den or some such. He let me have some private lessons at the manor, but the tutor was a man, and father got suspicious that I was spending too much time with him and it was getting too intimate.'

'And was it?'

Even just twenty-four hours earlier, the idea that she could ask Alex such a personal question would have been unthinkable. Now, Alex didn't bat an eyelid. Certainly this marked considerable progress in their relationship, which had started out so precariously.

'To be totally honest, yes, but only in my mind. The guy was obviously much too scared of my father to lay a finger on me but, if he had done, I wouldn't have said no.' She smiled across the table. 'So, fair enough, in this case my father was right, but what harm would it have done?'

At that moment, Suzie looked up and was confronted with a very unwelcome sight. Standing in the doorway, scanning the faces of the guests, was none other than Alex's erstwhile suitor, Carlo Moretti. He spotted them and a smile spread across his predatory features. Suzie turned hastily towards Alex.

'I'm afraid we've got company.'

Alex looked up and Suzie saw her face flush with anger. She laid a restraining hand on Alex's arm as Carlo came across to where they were sitting. Ignoring Suzie, he addressed Alex.

'Alessandra, how wonderful to see you. I've been looking for you for two days now. You disappeared so suddenly the other night and I was worried.' Without being asked, he pulled up a chair and sat down opposite them.

Suzie saw Alex raise her hand and call the waiter.

'A glass of Prosecco for the signore.'

As the waiter went off, Suzie found herself wondering if this might, after all, indicate a rapprochement between Alex and her Italian. It wasn't long before she found out. As the waiter returned with the glass of Prosecco, Alex took it from him and surprised all three of them by throwing the contents full into Carlo's face.

'Here, Carlo, this is for you. I'm sure your wife will be able to wash it out for you.'

He jumped to his feet, thoroughly soaked, an expression of shock and anger on his face. 'What do you think you're doing...?'

Suzie found herself smiling. Alex's aim had been excellent and the wine had hit him square in the face and was running down his front. Even his trousers were soaked and Suzie restrained a giggle as it looked as though he had wet himself.

'Go away, Carlo. Go back to your wife and your three daughters, and leave me alone.'

The Italian blanched. 'How did you...? What...?' His anger had swiftly been replaced by an expression of guilt and no little anxiety.

'You heard me, Carlo. Just go. All right? And don't bother me again or I'll talk to your wife.'

By this time he was as white as a sheet – a very damp sheet. Without a word, he turned and beat a hasty retreat. As he did so, Alex looked up at the waiter, who was still rooted to the spot.

'I do apologise for that, but I'm afraid it was necessary.' She was sounding remarkably calm. 'Let me know if there are any costs involved.'

A grin spread across the waiter's face. 'No, signorina, that's perfectly all right. You managed to get all the wine onto that gentleman, rather than the furnishings.' He retrieved the empty glass from her hand and straightened up again, still smiling. 'You're getting very good at this.'

Suzie grinned up at him. 'Practice makes perfect.' After he had left, she looked over at Alex with newfound respect. 'That was brilliant, Alex. You handled that just perfectly.'

'Horrible, cheating bastard! I should have ordered a pint and flung it at him, glass and all.'

'No, I think that was just right – a refined response and definitely well-justified. And I'm sure that's the last we're going to see of Mr Moretti.'

That evening they went up to the restaurant where they were in for a surprise. On the far side, at a discreet table far away from the door, was Michael the portrait painter, and sitting opposite him was a stunningly beautiful woman with a mass of glossy black hair pinned up on her head, exposing earrings that sparkled in the light. Suzie reflected that if they were real diamonds, they must have been worth a fortune. She and Michael appeared engrossed in each other's company and didn't notice the two girls as they were shown to the same table by the window where they had dined with Rafe the previous night. Once seated, Alex looked across at Suzie and grimaced.

'Michael's wife is quite a doll, isn't she?'

'You can say that again.' Suzie did her best to keep any disappointment out of her voice. Why should she feel disappointed, after all? She barely knew the man and he was married. She tried to sound blasé. 'Of course, it might be his mistress – remember your friend Carlo. Maybe there's something in the Italian air.'

Alex's grimace intensified as she shuddered. 'Good riddance to Mr Moretti. But you're right, Venice is such a romantic place... I wonder what Verona will be like.'

Suzie was glad of the change of subject. 'Physically not that different, apart from the water. Verona, Vicenza, Padua and Venice were all part of the Venetian Republic, so I imagine the architecture's similarly gorgeous in all of them. As for romance, don't forget Romeo and Juliet.' She summoned a grin and Alex grinned back.

'How could I forget? Although by the sound of it, the closest to romance I'm going to get is fighting off the advances of a pheasant-fancier.'

Their meal was excellent, although they limited themselves to far less than the previous night. On Suzie's advice, they both chose fritto misto, a mixture of octopus, squid, prawns and whitebait, lightly dusted in flour and fried to perfection. Accompanied by a mixed salad and a bottle of the local, slightly fizzy white wine, this provided an excellent dinner and they both declined the offer of dessert. Instead, they decided to go out for a stroll and a coffee afterwards. As they left the restaurant, Suzie could see that Michael was still deep in conversation with his beautiful partner and didn't see them go. Secretly, she was quite pleased not to have to make small talk with the wife of a man she rather fancied – even though she was the first to acknowledge that a relationship with a married man hadn't been going to happen anyway.

Last night's visit to Harry's Bar had been a bit disappointing. Expecting somewhere luscious, stylish and decorative, they had been surprised to find themselves in a crowded bar that didn't look dissimilar to an English pub – and a fairly plain one at that – apart from the prices which were astronomical. Consequently, tonight, as they got down to the main lobby of the hotel, Suzie went over to the porter's desk by the door for advice. The immaculate porter in his sober grey waistcoat had no hesitation.

'If you haven't tried it already, you really should go to Caffè Florian. It's close by in St Mark's Square and it's the oldest coffee house in Venice, if not the whole of Italy… or even the world.' He winked. 'Although that claim is contested.'

St Mark's Square was busy, but not as crowded as during the daylight hours, and they easily made their way across to the arches on the far side and found the cafe. Inside, it was stunning. The tables were marble, the seats covered in red velvet and the walls a delightful mixture of gold leaf, murals and mirrors. It was very busy, but they managed to find a table, ordered coffees and sat back to admire the view. There were people of all nationalities in here, some in shorts, some more formally dressed, among them even a cluster of what looked like gondoliers in stripy shirts. Then, ten minutes later, a familiar face appeared and broke into a smile as he spotted them.

'Good evening, ladies. Fancy seeing you here.'

Suzie looked up and returned his greeting, and his smile. 'Michael, good evening.'

She kept the smile on her face as she transferred her attention to the stunningly beautiful woman at his side. The girl was probably a few years younger than her – maybe the same age as Alex – and the sleek red dress she was wearing fitted her like a glove. Her lustrous mass of black hair was piled up on her head in the sort of careless style that takes an age to achieve and costs a fortune. And the earrings and the matching diamond ring on her finger looked a million dollars. If he had bought them for her, could it be he was secretly a millionaire after all, in spite of what he had said? As she was still pondering this, Michael made the introductions.

'Frederika, this is Suzie from England and her friend Alex. I'm sorry, I don't know your surnames.'

Suzie was quick to respond. 'Good evening, Frederika. I'm Suzie Cartwright and this is Lady Alexandra Tedburn.'

'Good evening, I'm pleased to meet you.' Frederika's English accent was almost perfect, with only the slightest hint of what might have been German in the background. Beneath the glossy exterior, she looked like a friendly person and Suzie found herself thinking that somebody as beautiful as this was, without doubt, a far more suitable partner for a handsome and successful man like Michael than she would have been – particularly if he turned out to be a secret millionaire.

'So how do you know each other?' There didn't appear to be even so much as a hint of jealousy in Frederika's tone, so Suzie answered easily, deciding to leave out the Prosecco incident.

'We just met this morning on the beach. We got talking, but that's it. I'm afraid I don't know your surname either, Michael.' Annoyingly, she felt her cheeks begin to burn.

'Turner, like the artist. I told you I was a painter, didn't I? And, before you ask, no, I'm not related to the great man, I'm afraid. I just share his surname.'

This was followed by a slightly awkward pause while Suzie found herself wondering if she should ask them to sit down at their table but then, fortunately, Michael made the decision for her.

'Anyway, don't let us disturb your evening. We just dropped in for a coffee after dinner. I'm glad I've run into you as I wanted to give you this before I leave tomorrow.' He reached into the top pocket of his smart linen jacket and produced a business card. 'If you run into any trouble or, indeed, if you just want a chat while you're in Verona, these are my contact details. I'd be very happy to see you both again.'

'That's very kind of you, Michael.' Alex reached over and took the card from him. 'If all goes well, we should be there in a few days' time. It's good to know we've already got a friend in the area.'

Suzie added her thanks and he gave her a little smile before bidding them both good night and heading towards the rear of the cafe. As they disappeared from view, Alex handed the card across the table to Suzie with a grin.

'That was nice of him, wasn't it? And isn't she beautiful? That was a Stella McCartney she was wearing.' She shot a knowing look across the table. 'And they don't come cheap.'

Suzie had no doubts on that score. If anybody knew the price of designer clothes, it was Alex.

'I like your Michael, Suzie. Now that's what I call a very handsome man!'

Suzie knew she was blushing again, but there was nothing she could do about it. 'Like I keep telling you, he's not *my* Michael, Alex. He's married, remember?'

Alex shook her head. 'To the German girl? I don't think so. Did you notice anything peculiar about her, by any chance?' There was a cheeky sparkle in her eye and Suzie felt a little flash of happiness that her companion was definitely cheering up.

'Peculiar?' She cast her mind back, but couldn't think of anything special. 'I don't think so. She looked pretty perfect.'

Alex was quick to help with a prompt. 'Did you see the engagement ring on her finger?'

'Engagement? I saw a whopping great diamond on her finger. It matched the earrings.'

'And did you see the wedding ring?'

'Um, no. Was there one?'

'Precisely!' There was triumph in Alex's tone. 'There wasn't one. She's somebody's fiancée, not his wife.'

Realisation dawned on Suzie. 'Of course, if she's not his wife and she's not his mistress, she must be the girl whose portrait he's painting. He said she was engaged to some immensely rich guy, but their identities were secret. That's why he didn't tell us her full name.'

'So that explains it. She wasn't his wife, after all. Maybe the wife's back in England or maybe she's gone off with the milkman.'

'There aren't any milkmen any more. Besides, why would he keep the ring? I don't think so. Anyway, Alex, we'll probably never see him again, so what's the use of trying to speculate?'

'Who says we won't meet him again? You make sure you keep that card safe, now, won't you?'

Suzie glanced down at his card. It just said, simply, *Michael Turner, Artist*, followed by an email address and two Italian telephone numbers – one a landline and one a mobile. As she tucked the card safely into her purse, she found herself wondering if they would ever see him again and had to admit that – married or not – she rather hoped she would.

Chapter 7

They travelled by high-speed train from Venice to Verona at the end of the week. The journey took barely an hour and when they arrived, they found James on the platform waiting for them.

As soon as Suzie saw him, she remembered him from the leaving party in London. He was a good-looking man with broad shoulders, lush dark hair and a stubbly beard that made him look unexpectedly hunky. Suzie definitely approved. At least Alex's father wasn't trying to marry her off to Jabba the Hutt. He was wearing an impeccable light-blue polo shirt and tailored shorts and there was a beaming, welcoming smile on his face. Alongside him was a man with a trolley and Suzie felt an immediate sense of relief. Although she only had one medium-sized bag, Alex's two massive suitcases were jam-packed with clothes and weighed a ton. Leaving the porter to deal with manhandling the luggage out of the train, James advanced upon Alex, arms outstretched.

'Alex, how good to see you. You're looking great.'

Alex's smile as she hugged him and kissed him on the cheeks didn't look forced, but of course he and she went back a long way as friends. 'James, how wonderful to see you, too. And thank you so much for the invitation to your place by the lake. We're so looking forward to seeing it, aren't we, Suzie?' She broke out of his embrace and pointed. 'James, you remember Suzie from the party last Saturday, don't you?'

James smiled politely and extended his hand in Suzie's direction. 'Of course. Good to see you again, Suzie.'

Although Suzie seriously doubted whether he really had noticed and remembered her, she shook his hand and thanked him in turn for his offer of hospitality, desperately hoping she wouldn't find a whole bunch of his overprivileged pals already ensconced at the villa. By this time James's man had piled the cases onto his trolley and was awaiting orders. Taking a grip on Alex's arm, James set off down the platform towards the exit. Suzie let the two of them walk ahead of her and hung back alongside the man with the trolley. As they made their way out through the crowds, she took the opportunity to exchange a few words of Italian with him and he looked pleased to be addressed in his own language.

'Are you from Verona?'

The porter smiled and nodded. 'Born and bred.'

For the first time Suzie registered that he wasn't wearing a uniform. Maybe station porters didn't wear uniforms here in Verona, but it was unlikely. She took a guess.

'Do you work for James?'

She was right. He nodded. 'My wife and I are responsible for the Villa Magnolia, Lord Witchampton's house on Lake Garda.' He shot a little smile at her. 'I'm Roberto. I would shake your hand, but I might drop all your luggage if I do.'

Suzie grinned back at him. 'Hello, Roberto, I'm very pleased to meet you. My name's Suzie and I'm travelling with Alexandra. So do you live at the villa?'

'Yes, but my parents and my three brothers live in Verona so I spend quite a bit of time here.'

'What's Verona like as a place to live?'

Before he replied, he skilfully weaved the trolley around a nun fiddling with her iPhone. 'It's my home town, so I think it's the best place in the world.'

That sounded good. 'And what do we absolutely have to see while we're here? Juliet's House, maybe?'

He gave a dismissive shrug. 'If you like, but don't go there expecting too much. It's just a tourist trap these days.' He followed James out into the oppressive heat of the midday sun, narrowly missing a couple of backpackers who suddenly chose the middle of the concourse to stop and settle down on their packs. 'No, the most important thing you have to see is the Arena. That certainly wasn't dreamt up recently. The Romans built it, and it's still in use today. Mind you, Lake Garda and the Villa Magnolia are also beautiful. I'm sure you'll love it there.'

In the clammy heat, they made their way to the car park and Suzie was taken aback to see an enormous open-topped Rolls-Royce waiting there, occupying a space and a half, the sun gleaming on the immaculate white paint-work. Clearly Lord Witchampton had no scruples about displaying his wealth. As Roberto loaded the suitcases into the cavernous boot, Alex caught Suzie by the hand and dragged her into the back, relegating James to the front. As he took his seat with an expression of barely disguised pique, Alex shot Suzie a wink and the two girls almost dissolved into fits of the giggles.

Roberto took the wheel and as he set off, many heads turned to follow the progress of the extravagant white limousine. Suzie, cheeks glowing with embarrassment, perched in the back of the car and wished she could disappear into the hand-stitched seams of the soft cream leather upholstery. As the car sped up and her embarrassment dwindled, she looked around at the city she knew to be a UNESCO World Heritage Site, but was disappointed to see just modern residential blocks and commercial buildings. Evidently, the old part of Verona was in a different direction.

Less than twenty minutes later, they crested a rise and Lake Garda appeared before them. In spite of her reservations as to what, or who, might await her at the Villa Magnolia, Suzie gazed in awe at the panorama that opened up before them. Although the sunshine made the view a bit hazy, it was still mightily impressive. The blue waters, dotted with colourful sails, sparkled in the autumn sunshine. Steep mountain slopes – some carpeted with greenery, some bare rock – dropped down on both sides and far away at the head of the lake to the north, the peaks of the high Alps were visible above the haze. Only the edges of the lake showed signs of habitation and the overall impression was one of peace and tranquillity. Suzie instantly fell in love with the place.

Little more than five minutes later they were down by the lakeside and here the sensation of tranquillity was less evident. The narrow strip of relatively flat ground by the water's edge was lined with houses, the road suddenly became a lot busier and their progress slowed drastically. This didn't last long as Roberto soon pulled the big vehicle off the road into an impressive entranceway set in a tall stone wall. As the car came to a halt, a yellow light on the gatepost began to blink and the gates swung open automatically. As they drove in, Suzie saw the gates behind them silently start to close once more. James and his father clearly valued their privacy. The car crunched along a gravel drive, shaded from the sun by a magnificent selection of specimen trees, until they reached a circular parking area in front of the villa.

The villa was a delight. It wasn't anything like as enormous as Lord Tedburn's sprawling manor house back home in Devon, but it was a spectacularly beautiful building all the same. It probably wasn't terribly old, maybe nineteenth century or even early twentieth century, built in the style of a Renaissance villa, and it took her breath away. Three steps led up to double entrance doors set in the light ochre walls, with massive ornate terracotta urns on either side of the doorway, overflowing with fragrant trailing rosemary plants, covered in bright blue flowers. The scent in the air was almost overpowering. While Roberto dealt with the bags, James led the girls into the house, along a tiled passage to a living room whose wall-to-ceiling windows looked out over a well-tended garden set right on the lakeside. Alas, as they got there, Suzie's fears were confirmed.

'Alex, you're here! How super.'

Figures appeared from all sides, many of whom Suzie recognised from the party in London, and the noise levels rose. Hugs and kisses were exchanged as Alex was greeted by the others. Suzie found herself left on her own over to one side so, seeing that Alex was fully occupied with saying hello to the other guests, she slipped out of the French windows and onto the lawn. There was a pleasant breeze coming off the water and she breathed deeply. It was a gorgeous place and, whatever the company, she knew she was very privileged to be here. She had no idea how many millions a place like this might be worth, but whoever had chosen it had demonstrated some excellent taste. It was set in a stunning location and as she strolled through the grounds she saw that there was a boathouse, the swimming pool mentioned by Rafe and even a private jetty jutting out into the lake. The water in the lake was remarkably clear and looked very appealing so she slipped off her sandals and sat down on the edge of the jetty, dangling her feet in the water. She had been there for a few minutes, staring around at the scenery, when she heard Alex's voice.

'Suzie, here you are. I've been looking all over for you.'

Suzie turned towards her and smiled. 'Sorry, I could see you were tied up saying hello to everybody so I came for a little stroll around. It's a lovely place.'

Alex followed Suzie's example, stepped out of her shoes, sat down and joined her with her toes in the water. 'I'll introduce you to the others in a minute. Anyway, look, I came to give you the good news. Everybody's leaving in two days' time.' She glanced around and lowered her voice. 'And that includes James. They've already booked flights to California. There's a big wedding going on over there – I was invited some time ago, but I told them I couldn't make it because I was determined to be in Italy – and they can't stop talking about it. James said he'd cancel and stay on with us here, but I've said no, he has to go to the wedding. So this means I get him out of my hair and we can move into Verona proper on Monday.'

Suzie felt a wave of relief. 'That's great. Do you want me to book a hotel, or will you?'

'Leave it to me. I've heard there's an absolutely amazing hotel bang in the centre.' She glanced at her watch. 'Anyway, it's gone twelve and he said lunch will be at half past. Shall we go and see where we're sleeping?'

They stood up and let the sun dry their feet on the old wooden planks for a few minutes before putting their shoes back on again. As she stood there, Suzie noticed the quirky old house next door, just a little further along the lakeside from them. It was quite small, built in the faux-Gothic style, and the garden was rather overgrown. She was idly wondering if it was uninhabited when a first-floor window opened and a grey-haired lady in an apron began to bang a rug energetically on the wall outside, raising clouds of dust into the air. Catching her eye, Suzie gave her a little wave and received a smile and a nod of the head in return.

'Come on, Suzie. Let's go and see where he's put us.'

–

Suzie's room was on the top floor, right underneath the roof, and it was boiling hot, although she was relieved to see an air-conditioning unit above the window. She rather wondered if this had once been the servants' quarters as the furnishings, while perfectly adequate, weren't in any way as opulent as those she had seen elsewhere in the house. Alex's room, almost directly below her on the second floor, was a wonderful combination of marble, lace and silk. Still, Suzie told herself, her own room was still a hell of a lot more luxurious than most rooms she had ever occupied. It was all relative. Besides, the view out of the window across the lake to the mountains beyond was spectacular. She took a photo and sent it to her parents along with a message that all was going well.

As instructed by James, she dumped her stuff, washed her hands and headed straight back downstairs. As she emerged hesitantly from the corridor into the sitting room, she heard somebody call her name. This time it was a man's voice and she instantly recognised both it and its owner. She went across and shook his hand.

'Tommy, how nice to see you again.'

'Hello, Suzie. You're looking lovely. How wonderful to see you.'

She was impressed that he had finally managed to find an alternative adjective to 'gorgeous'. Seeing him now that he was sober, Suzie had to admit that he really was a very good-looking man: tall and slim with short fair hair and a ready smile. She wondered if he was also immensely rich. If so, with his looks and a pot full of money, she had no doubt he would be fighting the girls off – assuming he didn't get drunk too often. Certainly, today he was looking and sounding very different from the last time she had seen him.

'Listen, Suzie, I'm sure I owe you a massive apology.' Seeing the look on her face, he explained. 'I'm afraid I must have behaved pretty shabbily last week. It was my birthday, you see, and my so-called mates had been feeding me all kinds of spiked drinks all night and I was totally wasted. I hope I didn't do anything too awful. I can just about remember chatting to this gorgeous-looking girl, but then she disappeared and never came back. I wasn't too obnoxious, was I?'

He looked and sounded genuinely contrite and she was quick to reassure him. 'Not at all, Tommy. And you don't need to worry – you weren't too bad. I've known far worse.'

'Thank God for that. Anyway, look, I just wanted you to know that I'm not normally like that. I'm really quite a nice guy when you get to know me.'

Suzie gave him a smile. 'I look forward to getting to know you, Tommy.'

'That's great.' He looked genuinely relieved. 'So, how's your holiday?' He lowered his voice a fraction, although the background babble assured him of privacy. 'Getting along with Alex? She can be a bit hard going.'

'We're getting on really well, thanks. It must be the Italian air. And what have you been doing?'

'Oh, you know, just hanging out. A few of us have been windsurfing. James is mad about it and Lake Garda's famous for it.'

Suzie's ears pricked up. During her summer vacation work in Italy, back when she was at university, she had learnt to windsurf and had developed a real taste for it. By the third year she was teaching it to the kids. Her former boyfriend, Rob, had been fanatical about surfing, windsurfing and kitesurfing, and they had spent most weekends on the water. She hadn't been out as often as she would have liked since Rob's departure from her life over a year ago and the idea of getting back on a board had considerable appeal.

'Yes, I've heard that. Something to do with regular winds, I believe. Everybody says it's a Mecca for windsurfing and kitesurfing. Where do you sail? Direct from here?'

'Yes. There's all sorts of kit in the boathouse. I'll take you out and show you how to do it after lunch if you like.'

Suzie decided not to mention that she was already pretty competent and accepted his offer enthusiastically. Apart from anything else, it would get her away from the rest of the bunch.

Alex appeared and took her round the room, introducing her to the others – some of whom Suzie recognised and some new faces – and Suzie was relieved to find herself feeling a lot more comfortable than she had done a week earlier. Lunch was taken in the large dining room and she did a quick count of the people around the long table as they sat down. Including Alex and herself, there were fourteen of them, six girls and eight men. As far as she could see, a few of them were already paired off, and she was unsurprised to find that Tommy plonked himself down beside her and did his best to chat her up. Even more surprising was that she didn't mind that much. In fact, as the meal progressed, she found that she was enjoying his company.

The meal was served by Roberto – who, she discovered, spoke excellent English – and when Suzie complimented him on the excellent food, he told her it was his wife, Rosa, who was responsible. Suzie was seriously impressed; cooking for fourteen people twice a day couldn't be easy. When they reached the end of the excellent main course of roast lamb with rosemary and roast potatoes, Suzie collected a pile of dirty plates and followed Roberto out to the kitchen, ignoring his objections. In the kitchen she was introduced to Rosa and told her how much she had enjoyed the meal, taking an instant liking to this smiley, friendly lady. She stayed and chatted for a few minutes, delighted to have the opportunity to speak Italian, until the oven timer rang and Rosa had to spring into action.

That afternoon, after the big lunch, most people disappeared for a siesta or to sunbathe, and James soon monopolised Alex. Suzie decided she would sneak away for a quiet walk by herself. Roberto gave her the code so she could come and go through the electric gates and she set off. She soon found a footpath along the shore and strolled happily along, enjoying the view out across the lake to the hills on the other side. The number of small crafts, yachts, kitesurfers and windsurfers had increased considerably since the morning and they added spots of bright colour to the deep blue of the water.

After a while she sat down on a bench where she let her mind roam and found herself thinking of Michael, the artist. She wondered where he was and whether he had ever painted the lake. He had said he lived in the area, after all. For a moment she even thought about calling him for a chat, but decided against it. Maybe if she had something to ask him, but she couldn't just ring him and say hi. Besides, what if his wife were to answer?

Pulling out her phone, she did something she had been meaning to do for some days now. She googled his name, Michael Turner, and what she found confirmed her supposition that he must be well-known and successful. There were numerous pages with entries about him and his highly successful career, particularly for somebody who it turned out was barely four years older than her. Apart from a lengthy Wikipedia article about him, she found multiple references to galleries exhibiting his work and a series of news items. One headline in particular caught her eye and, as she read the article, the significance of his careworn expression and the ring on his finger became all too clear.

The article from the online version of the Milanese newspaper *Corriere della Sera*, dated the fifth of December three years earlier, was entitled *University Professor Dies in Horror Crash*. As she scanned down the page, it soon emerged that the university professor in question was called Grazia Varese and it mentioned the name of her husband as *Michael Turner, the renowned portrait painter*. She raised her eyes from the screen and let them roam across the water to the mountains on the far side as she reflected on the true awfulness of what must have happened that foggy winter's day on the Verona to Milan motorway. She could only begin to imagine what Michael must have suffered and must still be suffering, and a wave of compassion flooded over her, bringing tears stinging to the corners of her eyes.

She sat there for an age, her mind turning over and over the implications of the tragedy that had happened, before she gradually began to pull herself together. In a concerted attempt to change to a more cheerful train of thought, she took a few moments to consider how well things were going between her and Alex. Their final few days in Venice had been great and the two of them had spent a considerable amount of time talking. She had told Alex about Rob and in return had learned that Alex had had a lot of boyfriends, but no special one – apart, maybe, from James. It was pretty clear that she liked James a lot, although she stubbornly refused to let her interfering father railroad her into a relationship. It didn't take Suzie long to confirm that her original assumption that Alex's life had been irreparably blighted by the death of her mother was indeed correct. Growing up in that massive manor house, cut off from the real world by a 500-acre deer park, had taken its toll and Suzie was in no doubt Alex needed love... but then, maybe, so did she.

At four o'clock, she changed into her swimming things and went down to the boathouse. Tommy was already there, and he showed her where there was an amazing collection of windsurfing kit, including wetsuits. Over lunch he had revealed that he was James's cousin and he obviously came here often and knew his way around. Although the air temperature was high, Suzie was under no illusions as to how quickly she would lose body heat if she ended up in the cold lake water, so she chose a shorty summer suit and found it a remarkably good fit. It even still had the shop label inside. Evidently she was the first to wear it and she was very pleased about that, even though she had brought a protective vest just in case. As she knew from personal experience, old wetsuits were not the most appealing of environments. Ever since Rob had told her that the best way to warm up in a wetsuit was to pee in it, she had viewed other people's suits with considerable mistrust.

James and his father had clearly spent a lot of money on windsurfing kit and she found a good harness and strapped herself into it quite easily. Tommy was all in favour of setting her up with a bulky beginners' board and small sail, but Suzie chose a virtually brand-new lightweight board and race sail, in spite of his scepticism. The wind had picked up here at the waterside and she could see from the little wavelets further out that the wind strength way out in the lake promised to be exciting. She expressed surprise that James, allegedly a windsurfing fanatic, didn't want to come out and Tommy explained.

'He says he'd rather stay back at the villa with Alex.'

Suzie shook her head in wonderment. 'There's what looks like a good breeze out there. My old boyfriend wouldn't have had any qualms about dumping me if the wind was just right. Your cousin must be serious.'

'Oh, it's serious all right... on his part. You'd know better than me how *she* thinks about him.'

Suzie decided it wasn't her place to interfere in other people's love lives, so she shrugged her shoulders. 'I don't really know her that well yet, but they look good together.'

The two of them set off and Suzie was pleased – and mildly surprised – to find herself a little way ahead of him by the time they rounded the headland and came into the full force of the wind. This was from the south, but it was still cool so close to the high mountains and she was grateful for the warm wetsuit. As the sail filled, she hooked into her harness and leant back, relishing the acceleration as the board came out of the water onto the plane. It was like being in a sports car, accelerating away from the lights, and she had always loved the sensation. She took off across the lake like a scalded cat and when she finally gybed round to return, she found Tommy close behind her. As he came past, he gave her a big smile and she had no trouble smiling back at him. She did a few more long runs, feeling the board skitter and bounce as she hit larger waves, before finally turning back towards the shore. It was exhilarating and she hadn't had so much fun for ages. She was still smiling by the time she got back to the jetty. She dragged the board and sail out of the water and sat down, muscles screaming, for a rest on the warm timber.

She had only been there for a minute or so when she discovered she had company. Feeling she was being watched, she turned her head towards the shore and found herself face to face with a big black dog, barely a few feet away from her. It was only then that she suddenly realised that this wasn't the right jetty after all. Unwittingly, she had landed on the jetty belonging to the small house with the overgrown garden next door to James's villa and this, presumably, was the owner's dog. She liked dogs, but she wasn't sure how this one might react to a trespasser. She was just tensing her muscles, ready to jump into the lake, when the dog's tail began to wag, uncertainly at first, and then more enthusiastically. Relieved, she held out her hand, knuckles first, and adopted a friendly tone.

'Hello, dog.' It probably didn't matter to the dog that she had chosen to speak in English, but, just in case, she added a quick translation. '*Ciao, cane.*'

The dog came trotting across to her and nuzzled her hand with its cold wet nose. As it did so, she heard a voice and saw an elderly man approaching along the jetty. Unlike the dog, he didn't look friendly. He was limping heavily and leaning on a stick, but he stopped to brandish it in the air as he approached her.

'*Via, via! Qui é proprietà privata. Via!*' To her considerable surprise, he then looked down at the dog and addressed it directly. 'As for you, Dogberry, you're useless. Call yourself a guard dog!'

The unexpected thing was that he spoke to the dog in English and he was quite evidently a native speaker, with a soft Scottish accent. Suzie rose to her knees, by which time the dog had decided she was definitely a friend, rather than a foe, and had buried his head affectionately into her armpit, his tail wagging ever harder. She ruffled his ears as she replied to the old man – in English.

'I'm terribly sorry. I'm staying at the villa next door and I got my jetties mixed up. I'll go straight off again. My apologies once more.' She glanced down at the Labrador, who had now decided it was time to lick her face. 'I'm afraid your guard dog might need a bit more training.' Gently dissuading him from putting his big paws on her shoulders, she added an afterthought. 'Mind you, as an English scholar, it's always good to meet a dog with a Shakespearian pedigree.' Dogberry, the bumbling watchman from *Much Ado About Nothing*, had always been one of her favourite comic characters.

By this time, the old man's expression had softened. He came closer and lowered himself heavily onto an old bench as he did so. There was a sinister creak – presumably from the bench, rather than the old man – and Suzie found herself hoping it wouldn't collapse underneath him.

'So, you know your Shakespeare, eh?' There was definitely the hint of a smile on his face.

Suzie grinned. 'Well, I know enough to recognise the name of my favourite character from *Much Ado*.'

'I called him Dogberry because I got him from a Sicilian lady.'

Suzie nodded. 'Of course, the play's set in Messina.'

'Very good.' The smile broadened. 'So, what brings you here to the lake?'

Suzie gave him a brief summary of her background, the collapse of the charity where she had been working and how she had been engaged to accompany Alex to Italy.

He nodded along with her account and suddenly looked up as she mentioned her doctorate in English.

'May I ask the subject of your doctoral thesis?'

'Um, Shakespeare, actually.' Seeing distinct interest in his eyes, she spelled it out for him. '*A fresh appraisal of Italian influences in the works of Shakespeare.* You know, whether he ever made it over here, or whether he got it all out of books or from other people who had visited Italy. It *is* pretty suspicious, after all, that so many of his works are set in Italy.'

'Well, well, well.' The old man held out an unsteady hand towards her. 'In that case, my dear, I am even more pleased you chose my landing stage rather than Lord Witchampton's. Dennis Macgregor-Brown. I'm very pleased to make your acquaintance.'

Suzie straightened up so suddenly the dog who had been leaning up against her almost lost his balance and came close to toppling into the lake. She steadied him with one hand and then stroked his ears while she shook the old man's hand with the other. 'Did you say Dennis Macgregor-Brown… *Professor* Dennis Macgregor-Brown of Oxford University? That's who you are?' She was truly astounded. 'I've read every book you've ever written and your seminal work on Shakespeare in Italy formed a major part of my research. A dog-eared copy of *The Foreign Travels of Shakespeare* accompanied me wherever I went. I'm truly honoured to meet you in person, Professor Macgregor-Brown. Somehow, I feel I already know you so well.'

He gave her a modest little bow of the head. 'Thank you for your kind words, but it's *formerly* of Oxford

University. I've been retired for a good while now. But I'm sorry, I didn't catch your name.'

'Of course, I'm so sorry. My name's Suzanne Cartwright. Everybody calls me Suzie.'

'Dogberry and I welcome you to our home, Doctor Cartwright... Suzie. It's a very happy chance that has brought you here.' He hesitated. 'If you can spare the time, I'd be delighted to see you again, maybe when you are fully clothed.' The smile returned to his lips and the familiar red patches to her cheeks. 'I'm no longer an evening person, but I'd be very pleased if you felt like coming for lunch one of these days. Paolina, my house-keeper, is an excellent cook.'

'I would really love that, Professor, but I'm only here until Monday. I don't know if you're free tomorrow, by any chance.'

'I'm always free these days, Suzie.' There was a more melancholy note in his voice. 'Dogberry and I don't exactly enjoy a scintillating social life. Tomorrow will be perfect.'

'Thank you so much, but I wouldn't want to intrude.'

'Absolutely not. But a word of warning – once I start talking about Shakespeare, it's very hard to get me to stop.'

Suzie laughed. 'That's something we have in common. It could be a long afternoon. Now I'll get out of your hair. My apologies again for the intrusion.'

When she got back to James's jetty, she found a little group waiting for her. Tommy surprised her by coming over, grabbing her hand in both of his and pumping it up and down.

'Suzie, you're great on a board. You should have told me you were a star.'

'Suzie's not one to blow her own trumpet. That looked fantastic, Suzie.' Alex was beaming proudly at her and James even managed to drag his eyes off Alex long enough to pay her some other compliments. Inevitably she found herself blushing and she hastened to tell them that not everything had gone smoothly by recounting her choice of the wrong landing stage upon her return to the shore. When she mentioned the old man and his dog, James gave a snort.

'Bad-tempered old sod. He keeps sending emails to my father complaining about us making too much noise. And that bloody dog got into our garden a few days ago and we found him in the pool swimming around as happy as you like.'

Suzie grinned at the image and related her connection with Professor Macgregor-Brown and her invitation to lunch. James looked positively astounded at this.

'He's invited you for lunch? What, in his house? Not even my father's been in there.'

'Your father's not a pretty girl, James.' Alex gave Suzie a smile. 'Suzie, you look really good without the glasses, you know.'

Sensing another flush of embarrassment coming on, Suzie hastily disappeared into the boathouse to return the windsurfing kit, after which she slipped unobtrusively back to her room and ran a hot bath. As she lay in the water and relaxed, her mood was bittersweet. Part of her was happy after the exhilarating sail and the chance meeting with one of her academic idols, while she still couldn't shake off the image of a horrific accident on a foggy motorway and a heartbroken husband. Life could be so terribly unfair sometimes.

Dinner that evening was excellent and she was feeling quite sleepy by the end of it. The others, not so. James announced his intention of driving down to a nightclub at the southern end of the lake and most of his guests decided to accompany him. Among these was Alex. Suzie, in spite of being barely a year or two older than many of them, felt like an old maid when she told Alex she thought she would give the nightclub a miss. Her conscience pricked her as she found herself wondering whether Lord Tedburn would have expected her to stay by Alex's side, so she had a quiet word in her ear.

'Would you like me to come along, Alex? I will, if you want.'

'Not if you're tired.' Alex gave her a grin. 'And I promise I'll be a good girl – although in fact if I end up in James's bed I expect my father would approve. But that's definitely not going to happen.'

Suzie grinned back. 'That's the spirit. Anyway, if you're sure you don't mind, I think I'll head upstairs. Have a good time.' A sudden thought occurred to her. 'How are you all going to get there? The Rolls-Royce can't take that many people.'

'That's no problem. James says they've all rented cars, so we'll be quite a convoy.'

An image of the fatal crash flashed before Suzie's eyes for a moment and she reached out to touch Alex on the arm. 'Well, you make sure James drives safely. I wouldn't want anything to happen to you.' As she spoke, she realised that she really meant it.

For the very first time Alex leant across and gave her a peck on the cheek. 'You are so sweet. I promise we'll take care. Besides, I've got James eating out of my hand. If I tell him to drive all the way in first gear, he'll do it.'

As Suzie climbed the stairs to her room, she reflected on that spontaneous sign of affection from Alex and she was still smiling when she reached her room.

Chapter 8

Very few of the other guests surfaced before mid-morning the following day and Suzie had time to go for a long walk by herself. A stronger breeze was blowing through the branches of the trees and there was something strange about the lake this morning. Unlike the brilliant blue of yesterday, today the colour was a sinister deep grey-green, not dissimilar to the colour of the lagoon in Venice. As she looked up, she could see ominous dark clouds massing over the hills and she felt sure a storm was on the way. She sighed, but couldn't really complain. They had been in Italy for a week now and had hardly seen a cloud in the sky. Autumn was drawing on, however, and it was inevitable the weather would change sooner or later. From what she could see around her, it looked like that was definitely going to be sooner, most probably today.

There was a shop in the nearby village where she bought a bottle of good whisky as a gift for the professor and chatted to the owner who confirmed that a storm was indeed on its way and advised her not to stay out too long. When she returned to the villa, Alex had just appeared and Suzie sat and had a coffee with her while she ate her cornflakes. She heard all about the trip to the nightclub and James's attempts to take things to the next level, and was interested to hear what was maybe a wistful note in Alex's voice as she reported that she had rejected him. She also related how sorry Tommy had claimed to be when he had discovered that Suzie had stayed at home. She gave Suzie a knowing look and a wink.

'You see, all you have to do is take off your glasses and the men will come running.'

'I'm quite happy with my glasses and without any man at the moment – running or not.' She set down her cup. 'But listen, I'm afraid I have some awful news. I didn't get the chance to tell you yesterday.' She went on to tell her what she had read about the road accident and the shattering effect it must have had on Michael. Alex was appalled.

'Oh, good God, how terrible. Poor lady, and poor Michael. Little wonder he was looking troubled.' She laid her napkin on the table and sat back. 'Mind you, it's been almost three years now, so don't you think it's about time you cheered him up?'

'Me?'

'Absolutely. It was pretty obvious he's attracted to you. Why don't you give him a ring and arrange to meet him?'

Suzie shook her head in bewilderment. She hadn't noticed anything. Besides, she barely knew him. 'I was thinking about calling, but I think I'll wait until we have something to ask him. It'll sound a bit lame otherwise. And I can hardly just call him and say how sorry I am about his wife. That way, he'd know I'd been checking him out. Anyway, we'll be in Verona tomorrow night and I'm sure we can come up with a plausible reason for the call.' She hesitated. 'But wouldn't you like to be the one doing the cheering up?'

Alex grinned. 'I know when I'm beaten. Anybody could see you're the one for Michael.'

Suzie's cheeks were still burning an hour later when she let herself out through the main gate and went along to the house next door. There was a bronze panel on the gatepost with a bell push marked 'Macgregor-Brown'. She pressed this and a minute later heard footsteps. The gate opened and she saw the friendly grey-haired lady she had spotted at the window the previous day. No doubt this was Paolina, his housekeeper and cook.

'*Signorina, buongiorno.*' She gave Suzie a welcoming smile and beckoned her inside. As Suzie stepped through the gate, she was greeted a second time, this time much more effusively, almost floored by a familiar, friendly black Labrador. She knelt down to pet him.

'Ciao, Dogberry. How are you today?' She looked up at Paolina and smiled, addressing her in Italian. 'I believe he speaks English.'

Paolina smiled back. 'He's a Labrador. He's only interested in his stomach. If you offered him food in Chinese, I'm sure he'd understand.'

With the happy dog bouncing along at her side, Suzie followed Paolina up the gravel drive to the front door. The garden was indeed fairly overgrown, filled with flowers, bushes and trees of all descriptions, and a gorgeous mixture of scents wafted past her nose as they walked up to the front door. Inside the house itself, on the other hand, everything looked neat and tidy. It was charming and spotlessly clean, with ornate floor tiles, high ceilings and some excellent and unexpectedly modern paintings on the walls. A wonderful aroma of food filled the air and Suzie had a feeling she was going to eat well today.

'Suzie, welcome to my humble home.' Professor Macgregor-Brown appeared and ushered her into a fine, long living room overlooking the lake. The trees and bushes in the garden were being whipped about by the steadily increasing wind and the grey clouds almost obscured the sun. It was patently clear that the lady in the shop had been right – a storm was now imminent. She turned back with a smile to the elderly man and held out the bottle of Scotch.

'It's really good to see you again, Professor Macgregor-Brown. Here, a little drop from the land of your fathers.'

'How very kind of you, my dear. You shouldn't have. And please stop calling me Professor Macgregor-Brown. It's such a mouthful. My friends call me Mack and I'd be delighted if you would do the same.'

'Of course… Mack. Thank you.'

'Now, what can I get you to drink? A glass of Prosecco? This is the good stuff from Valdobbiadene.'

The professor opened the bottle with a practised hand and poured two glasses of Prosecco. They sat by the windows, gazing at the increasingly threatening weather outside, and chatted. At their feet, the dog sprawled on the fine old rug and snored. As they talked, Suzie discovered, among other things, that the professor was eighty-four years old. When she told him her own age, she saw him give a weary smile.

'Ah, to be twenty-eight again. Your whole life before you. I envy you that. And I'm sure you'll make a success of whatever you choose to do.'

'Like you've made of yours.'

'Thank you, my dear, but I'd willingly exchange my academic career for the chance to be twenty-eight again. Now, do, please, tell me about you.'

The conversation flowed easily and when Paolina arrived to tell them that lunch was served, Suzie was amazed to see that an hour had already passed.

As they sat down in the dining room next door, Paolina appeared from the kitchen with a steaming bowl of pasta. This consisted of really thick spaghetti, the diameter of straws, apparently known locally as *bigoli*, and the taste was excellent. The professor informed Suzie that this was his favourite pasta and that Paolina had made the sauce with speck, the wonderful smoked ham from the mountains, and fresh porcini mushrooms.

'It's high season for mushrooms at the moment and this year has been really good for porcini. I'm a lucky man because Paolina's husband, Giovanni, is an expert mushroom hunter and he keeps me well provided.'

'It's all superb... Mack.' Suzie was still finding it odd to address such an eminent academic in such an informal manner, but he appeared to relish it. 'I love pasta and I love porcini. This is delightful.'

A black nose appeared as if by magic from beneath the table and landed on her thigh, nostrils flared. Clearly, Dogberry shared her opinion, but she obeyed the professor's instructions not to feed him at table.

The main course was equally good. Paolina had chosen to do boiled beef with a thick, green parsley sauce. As they ate, the professor offered her some of the local red wine, but Suzie drank sparingly. Having the opportunity to exchange ideas with such a colossus in the world of English literature was too valuable to spoil by getting tipsy.

They returned to the lounge for coffee after the meal and no sooner had they sat down than the heavens opened. By now it was so dark outside it felt almost like dusk, instead of early afternoon, and when the rain started, it came in almost horizontally, smashing against the windows with such ferocity that Dogberry jumped to his feet and started barking. As the professor stroked him and tried to calm him down, Suzie went over to the glass and looked on in awe as the rainfall reached biblical proportions. Puddles the size of ponds formed on the ragged lawn, trees were bent double and she saw one sizeable branch break off and crash to the ground. It was an apocalyptic scene and the noise was almost deafening. She even found herself eyeing the panes of glass in the windows apprehensively, wondering how solid they really were.

When she looked back round again, Dogberry was lying on the floor at the professor's feet. His eyes were wide open and his head cocked to one side, but the barking had stopped and he even wagged his tail as Suzie went over, crouched down and made a fuss of him. Then, barely a minute or two later, the rain suddenly stopped as abruptly as it had started and the ensuing silence was almost unnerving. Finally reassured, the dog relaxed, stretched out and gave a huge sigh. As Dogberry closed his eyes, Suzie glanced up at the professor.

'When it rains here, it really rains, doesn't it? I can see why the dog was worried.'

'This whole area gets quite a bit of rain compared to the rest of Italy, but luckily these violent storms are relatively rare.' He smiled at her as she took a seat opposite him. 'Still, after a long, hot summer, the garden needs a good drink.' He pulled himself laboriously to his feet, gripped his cane and headed towards the door. 'Now if you'll just excuse me a moment, there's something I need to do.'

As he left the room, Paolina arrived with a tray. On it was an old Moka coffee pot and two small cups, along with a plate of delicious-looking pastries. She set it down and came over to Suzie.

'I'm going off back to my husband now and I wanted to say goodbye to you first. It was so nice of you to come to see the professor.' She glanced round and lowered her voice. 'It's so good to see him smiling and happy. He rarely goes out nowadays and he hardly talks to anybody apart from me or my husband and I'm sure your visit has done him good. Thank you.'

Suzie gave her a big smile. 'I feel immensely honoured to be a guest of such an illustrious academic. And such a kind, friendly man. And thank *you* for a delicious meal. You're such a good cook. I wish I could stay here and take lessons from you.'

Paolina blushed at the compliment and they shook hands. '*Arrivederci, signorina.* I do hope you'll come back and see him again.'

'I'd love to, and please call me Suzie.'

A minute or two later, the professor returned with a present. It was a hardback copy of his book, *The Foreign Travels of Shakespeare*, and it was in mint condition. He sat down heavily and rested his stick against the arm of the chair.

'You said your copy was getting dog-eared, my dear. Do, please, let me replace it for you.'

He produced a fountain pen and laboriously scrawled a dedication on the first page. Over lunch she had already noted how unsteady his hands were. Finally completing his task, he pushed the book across the coffee table to her and she picked it up reverently. Although his handwriting was erratic, she could easily read what he had written.

> *To Suzie. From one Shakespeare scholar to*
> *another. Wishing you every happiness and success.*
> *Dennis Macgregor-Brown.*

As she read the dedication she felt incredibly touched so she stood up and went across to give him a hug and a kiss on the cheek, her eyes stinging with emotion. As she returned to her seat, she wiped her eyes and thanked him profusely.

'I don't know what to say… Mack. I will cherish this for the rest of my life, just like I'll cherish the memory of today. I'm so amazingly lucky to have met you. Thank you from the bottom of my heart.' She hugged the book to her chest. 'If there's ever anything I can do for you, just say the word.'

'Just stay in touch, my dear.' He produced a visiting card and handed it to her. 'I look forward to hearing about your future career. By the way, have you ever considered university lecturing? I'm sure you'd be good at it.'

'Lecturing positions in the Humanities are few and far between these days, I'm afraid. They say there are a hundred applicants for every post on offer at UK universities – and they only come around very rarely.'

'I'm sure a bright girl like you will soon fall on your feet.' He gave her a little smile. 'Thinking about it, there *is* something you might like to do for me, though. I wonder if you'd be willing to let me read your thesis. It is my chosen field, after all.'

Suzie was stunned. This was a rare honour indeed. 'Of course, but only if you have time…'

'Time, my dear? Dogberry and I have got all the time in the world.'

Chapter 9

Over the course of the afternoon the storm pushed through and the clouds disappeared along with it, leaving increasingly large patches of clear blue sky once more. The lake took longer to settle and a strong wind was still producing sizeable waves as Suzie returned to the villa. She was just sitting down to read in the sitting room when she was interrupted by the arrival of James with an unexpected suggestion.

'Hi, Suzie. Fancy a windsurf? I've been out in these conditions a few times and they can be awesome. I saw you yesterday and I know you're up to it. I wouldn't ask you otherwise.'

Tommy appeared at his shoulder to add support. 'I'm going to give it a go as well, and you're a lot better than me. Come and watch me make a fool of myself.'

Suzie folded the corner of the page and looked up, a smile forming on her face. 'You know something? I'd love to. Just give me five minutes to get changed.'

'Great.' James sounded as if he meant it. 'I'll go and start getting the boards out. I think a 4-metre sail or so should be all you want today. It's blowing a hoolie out there.'

'You're the expert.' Suzie normally used a 6- or 7-metre sail, but the stronger the wind, the smaller the sail, and extreme conditions demanded specialist kit, so she was happy to agree.

As James disappeared through the door, Tommy paused and glanced back at her. 'I was sorry you didn't come to the club with us last night. I missed you.'

She gave him a little smile, but didn't reply. Hurrying up to her room, she stowed her precious book in her bag and changed into a bikini along with a vest to protect her inside the wetsuit. After taking off her glasses, she wrapped a towel around herself and ran back down the stairs again. As she reached the bottom, she almost bumped into Alex.

'Hi, Suzie. Going for a swim?'

'A windsurf. Your boyfriend's just asked me to go out with him… on the water.'

'Boyfriend? Whoever can you mean?' Alex gave her a wink. 'You be careful. It looks like it's blowing a gale out there.'

By the time Suzie had squeezed into her wetsuit and harness, James had rigged his sail and hers and Tommy had brought out her board. She noticed that James had chosen a very specialised and very expensive race board for himself. This was definitely not a toy for a beginner and she looked at him with newfound respect as they set off. The first few hundred metres were fairly easy going, apart from the choppy, chaotic waves, but once they reached the headland, all hell broke loose. The wind, as predicted by Alex, was definitely close to gale force and Suzie needed all her skill and all her strength to stay upright as the board powered away like a rocket, taking sudden evasive action as Tommy was flattened by a gust right in front of her. Somehow she managed not to follow suit and as she did so, she saw James come flying past, lying back almost level with the water and, as he cut in front of her, she heard him bellow with delight and drop his head back into the waves for a second, emerging to shake himself like a dog.

In all, they were probably only out for less than an hour, but Suzie was close to exhaustion by the end. She had ended up in the water half a dozen times – mainly as a result of jumps that didn't quite come off – and, although she had been able to waterstart again quite quickly, it had been really hard work fighting the force of the wind and the sizeable waves. When she finally got back to the jetty, James and Tommy were already waiting for her and gave her a hand getting her board, her sail and herself out of the water. As Tommy obligingly carried her rig into the boathouse, she slumped down wearily on the warm planks and James came and crouched beside her.

'You were bloody brilliant, Suzie.' He sounded really impressed. 'I'm sure I saw you jump at least your own height out of the water a few times.'

She gave him a happy smile. 'I'm not in your league, James.' She meant it. He was even better on a board than Rob used to be, and that was saying something. His gybes and jumps had been something else entirely and on one occasion she had seen him do a full forward loop, landing upright and intact. 'That was a real masterclass. Thanks for inviting me along and letting me use your gear.'

They sat there for a good few minutes, chatting, exchanging experiences and slowly regaining their breath before he turned the subject away from windsurfing and onto more personal matters.

'Suzie, could I ask you something? You know Alex pretty well now, don't you? Tell me, what do you think my chances are? I'm crazy about her, but I really can't make her out.'

Suzie had to stop and think. It wasn't her place to discuss her companion's personal life, but she felt a bond with James now that hadn't been there before, and after all his hospitality she owed him a favour, at the very least. She had been thinking quite a bit about what Alex had said about him, how she liked him, but was deliberately not letting things develop as she resented her father's interference. The more Suzie was getting to know James, the more she was coming round to thinking that he would make a pretty good boyfriend for Alex. Even without this declaration of his now, she had already realised that he was potty about her, so, after a long pause, she threw him a bone.

'I don't know her that well, James, but, if you want my opinion, I think the two of you would make a nice couple.' She saw his eyes sparkle. 'She likes you a lot, I'm sure of that. To be totally honest, I don't think you're the problem. I think it's her father.'

Out of the corner of her eye she saw Tommy emerge from the boathouse, register that she and James were in a close conversation and diplomatically opt to leave them to it. He picked up Suzie's board and carried it off for her. Catching his eye, she gave him a little smile of thanks and he smiled back. There was no doubt about it: without all that drink in him he was a really nice guy. Returning her attention to James, she continued.

'If you want my advice, I'd say take it slow and give her time to sort her head out. She hasn't had an easy time of it since her mum died, you know.'

He nodded. 'She's probably told you we've known each other pretty much since we were both toddlers. She was very close to her mother and I know how tough it was for Alex when she died. Her father's a good man – although he can hide it well on occasions – but he isn't a mother. She lost out big time with her mum's death, and her father's attempts to replace her have just resulted in his interfering too much.' He reached across and caught hold of Suzie's arm for a few seconds. 'I know all that and I understand. I just wish she'd give me a chance to talk it through with her, but she always clams up as soon as I try.'

Suzie gave him a big smile. 'If at first you don't succeed… Like I say, James, give her time.'

He smiled back. 'Thanks for the advice, Suzie. I owe you.'

'You owe me nothing, James. It's the other way round. Now, if I can find the energy to get to my feet, I'm going for a hot shower.'

He jumped up remarkably nimbly and leant down to catch her by the hands and haul her to her feet. 'We've got hot showers at the pool. That's only just over there. Come on.'

Together they crossed the narrow strip of lawn to the bushes that masked the pool and formed a natural wind-break and found most of the other guests either in the water or lying around it on sunbeds. As Alex saw the two of them, she sat upright and raised her sunglasses onto the top of her head. She was wearing her tiny bikini once more and Suzie didn't need James's earlier comment to sense the upsurge of attraction from him.

'So, slinking back in together after spending the after-noon all on your own, eh? And looking hot, sweaty and distinctly rumpled. You must have had a good time.' Alex was clearly joking, but Suzie saw James go red in the face all the same. Before he could make a fool of himself, she jumped in. Seeing James's embarrassment made her feel unexpectedly relaxed so, instead of her usual attack of the blushes, she managed to smile back at Alex and latch onto her joke.

'What a ride! I'm exhausted, Alex. He's worn me out.' She saw a few of the others look up with interest. 'He's got amazing stamina and some really good moves.' Giggling, she collapsed theatrically onto a sunbed alongside Alex and set about removing her wetsuit.

'So was she good, James? Did she rock your world?' Alex was also close to giggles, but James still looked embarrassed. However, Suzie was pleased to see he was quick to recover.

'Not like you do, Alex. You know that.' The emotion in his voice was clear for all to hear.

This time Alex was the one to blush and Suzie smiled into her wetsuit as she hauled it off and then pulled her rash vest off over her head. It was only after she had removed the vest that their roles were reversed and she heard Alex's voice, barely choking back the laughter.

'Suzie, you do realise you've removed the top half of your bikini along with your vest, don't you?'

Suzie blushed furiously and scrabbled for her towel. She couldn't miss the expression on the face of Tommy, now installed only a few feet away from her. He grinned and winked, and her embarrassment went into overload. Retrieving the offending garment, she clipped it back on again before dropping the towel and looking back at Alex.

'Touché. Now I really need a long hot shower.'

By the time she returned to the poolside, she was feeling pleasantly relaxed and she stretched out on her towel on one of the sunbeds. She had been there for a while and had even dozed off when she felt a gentle tap on her bare shoulder. She opened her eyes and looked up. It was Alex. She pulled herself upright and noticed that the pool area was now empty.

'Come on, sleepyhead. Everybody's going in for champagne and cake. As it was Tommy's birthday last week, it's his treat.' As Suzie stirred and climbed wearily to her feet, Alex leant closer to her. 'Did you hear what James said? Or rather, did you hear the way he said it? What's that all about?' Her voice dropped to a whisper. 'Has he said anything to you?'

Suzie nodded. 'Yes, but all good. He told me he was crazy about you and—'

'He said that?'

'He certainly did, and he said he wants to talk to you, but you keep changing the subject.' She gave Alex a little smile. 'I told him not to give up.'

Alex was looking unusually unsure of herself now. 'So do you think I should sit down with him and see what he says?'

'It couldn't hurt.'

–

That evening turned out to be a lot of fun. Tommy had not just laid on a case of very good champagne and a wonderful cake in a Harrods' box, but either he or James had somehow managed to book an amazing three-piece band. As soon as another of Rosa's feasts had been finished, the band started playing and Suzie found herself dancing, in spite of her aching limbs. She wasn't surprised to find Tommy asking her to dance with him. She was pleasantly surprised to see him drinking sparingly, and he was remarkably well-behaved.

Fortunately the music was not outrageously loud, but even so she had a horrible feeling James's father would be on the receiving end of an email from Professor Macgregor-Brown next morning. The thought of the old man brought a smile to her face. She had enjoyed her day with him and his lovely dog. She would miss them when she and Alex set off for Verona the next day. Before going windsurfing she had sent him a copy of her thesis, along with a thank-you email, and she knew she would await his verdict on her work with considerable anxiety.

She finally got to bed at about one o'clock, but the music was still drifting up the stairs as she went off to sleep. She woke once at around three o'clock and all was quiet, so presumably the other guests must have eventually called it a night.

The next morning she was the first down for breakfast, but that didn't surprise her. It was barely eight o'clock and no doubt they were all still in bed. As she nibbled one of Rosa's homemade biscuits, she found herself wondering how things had gone between Alex and James and whether they had had their talk. She looked forward to hearing from her later on. As it was, she was feeling excited, knowing that today she would be going to Verona at long last. Of all the Italian places mentioned in Shakespeare's plays, Verona was the one that had always held a special fascination for her.

Her period of peaceful reflection didn't last long as the others started to appear and the noise levels in the dining room increased. Apparently they were all heading off to the airport soon to catch their flight back to London and from there onward to Los Angeles. Suzie hoped they were all sober enough and rested enough to drive their hire cars safely. Two of the last to appear were James and Alex, who arrived suspiciously together. Suzie was unable to read anything much into their expressions or body language, but the fact that they sat down and had breakfast together had to be a positive sign. It was clear that their conversation – if, indeed, they had been able to have one – hadn't blown up in their faces. She felt pleased for both of them.

The house emptied rapidly as the morning progressed until only James, Alex and Suzie were left. Before leaving, Tommy came over to say goodbye and to give Suzie his contact details. She gave him a smile and kissed him on the cheeks in return and wondered if she would ever see him again, reflecting that she rather hoped she would. She found she liked him quite a bit – and there was no doubt he was a very attractive man – but as she had told Alex repeatedly, she wasn't interested in finding herself a man. The inescapable fact, however, was that the recurring image of Michael, the artist, stubbornly remained in her head. Somehow, he had made a remarkable impression on her and, although she knew she was unlikely to see him again either, she couldn't stop thinking about him. And his poor, dead wife.

Roberto had been designated to take James to the airport in the Rolls-Royce, dropping Alex and Suzie in the centre of Verona as he did so. The drive was smooth and fast and Suzie made a point of sitting alongside Roberto in the front this time, leaving the back seat to the other two. As she chatted to Roberto, she felt a rising sense of excitement that the big day had finally arrived – she was going to the city of her dreams. When they reached Verona and emerged from the modern part of town into the old centre, it was a squeeze to get the big vehicle through the traffic in the crowded streets leading to their hotel and, as James was running late, their farewells were brief. Nevertheless, Suzie thought she saw definite affection in the kiss Alex shared with him. As the luxury car whispered away, he gave them both a cheerful wave, but there was a wistful look in his eyes. Turning back to Alex, Suzie was interested to see a more uncertain look on the face of her companion. She was about to start manhandling the heavy cases towards the door when a uniformed doorman materialised at her side and took over. She was very happy to leave him to it.

The hotel was in a fabulous position, right on the edge of the *centro storico* reserved for pedestrians, within a couple of hundred yards of the massive bulk of the Arena. Suzie just stood and gaped at it for a full minute until Alex grabbed her by the arm and led her towards the hotel entrance. She had seen pictures and even videos of Verona, but somehow they hadn't prepared her for the sheer scale of the Arena. She knew that this huge amphitheatre had been built by the Romans way back in the first century, and as Roberto had told her, she knew that it was still in use to this day for concerts and opera. It looked for all the world like a slightly less ambitious – but still enormous – version of the Colosseum in Rome and was set in a long, wide piazza complete with a park, fountains, trees and a never-ending selection of restaurants. The whole area was full of tourists, even at this time on a late September morning. There was a vibrant buzz to the whole place and Suzie felt sure she was going to enjoy exploring the city the Italians referred to as the city of love.

The hotel was a grand affair, probably built back in the days when all this part of Italy had belonged to the Austro-Hungarian empire, and redolent of old-world luxury and refinement. The entrance lobby was paved with black and white marble and the staff were all immaculately turned out in white tops and smart dark suits and waistcoats. The air-conditioning was working well and it was cool in there among the leather sofas and exotic pot plants. They were escorted up to their rooms in a modern lift by a smiley lady who spoke to them in excellent English. Suzie's room was every bit as large and luxurious as her room in Venice had been, with the added bonus of a private rooftop terrace that she shared with Alex's room. Once they had settled in, they met up on the terrace, looking out over the Arena in one direction and the red terracotta roofs of the old town on the other side of them, the skyline punctuated by spires, towers and cupolas. In the distance was a green hill with what looked like a fortress on top. It was breathtaking and Suzie couldn't wait to start exploring the place. But first, there was something she wanted to know.

Once they were seated, she asked the burning question.

'So, how did it go with James last night? Did the two of you get the chance to sit down and talk?'

Alex leant back on the wicker sofa with a sigh and stretched her legs. 'Yes, and no.'

Suzie didn't press her for an explanation. She didn't need to. A few seconds later, Alex elaborated.

'We did a bit of dancing like everybody else and then, around midnight, or maybe later, we went outside and walked down to the jetty. There's an old bench there and we sat on it to talk. It was really rather romantic, with the moonlight on the lake. He told me – just like he told you – that he's crazy about me and I told him I liked him a lot. But it all comes down to my father in the end.'

She paused for a few moments but, again, Suzie didn't interrupt her train of thought. Alex's eyes were on the jumble of ancient rooftops spreading out beyond the edge of the balcony towards the distant outline of the mountains as she carried on.

'My father, I'm sure, has no idea at all that he's behaving in a way that's outdated or unfair. He just naturally assumes he has the right to dictate what happens to me, and it really annoys me. It's so patronising.'

Alex gave another sigh – this time of exasperation – and Suzie very nearly got up and went over to give her a big hug. Instead, she offered a bit of verbal support.

'But does it matter, Alex? As long as you and James are happy together, who cares if that also happens to be your dad's bidding? From what I could see, you and James were getting along fine and the more I've got to know him, the more I've come round to thinking he could be the one for you.'

Alex lowered her eyes from the rooftops and nodded slowly, her expression now one of blank frustration. As she turned her gaze towards Suzie, there were tears in the corners of her eyes.

'That's pretty much what I was coming round to thinking, but it's not as simple as that. You see, Suzie, I ended up in James's bedroom last night.'

'So? You said yourself your dad would probably approve.' She couldn't work out why Alex's expression was so deflated. 'Was there a problem?'

In response, Alex just nodded and reached for a tissue to wipe away the tears. Suzie didn't know what to do. Although there was no doubt she and Alex were really getting on very well now and she genuinely considered Alex as a friend – and a good one at that – she still didn't feel she knew her well enough to reach out and give her the big hug she so patently needed. Even so, she was about to go across to her when Alex started talking again.

'Yes, there was a problem, a hell of a problem. You see, it just didn't work.'

Suzie was puzzled. 'What didn't work?' An idea occurred to her. 'Do you mean he couldn't…?'

Alex shook her head violently. 'We didn't get that far. We didn't even kiss properly. The problem wasn't with him, it was with me. It felt weird, I just couldn't do it. You see, James and I have known each other since we were tiny. We've played together, been on holiday together, built sandcastles together, gone riding together and I've probably spent more one-to-one time with him than with Rafe or my father. We're almost like brother and sister, and much as I like him – and I do – I just don't see him in anything but that light. Feeling his hands on me actually made me physically sick.' Angrily, she rubbed the tears from her eyes. 'I mean it. I threw up.'

'What, all over him?'

'Not quite, thank God. No, I made it to the bathroom, but the very thought of going back to him sent waves of nausea through me over and over again. In the end, I told him I was feeling awful and had to go back to my own room, and left.'

'Wow! And do you think he realised why you were being sick?'

'I don't think so. This morning he was considerate and caring, asking if it was something I'd eaten. If he'd realised what it was all about, I'm sure he'd have acted differently. No, I reckon he's gone off to the States confident that he and I are now an item.' She cast a pleading look in Suzie's direction. 'So what the bloody hell do I do now?'

This time Suzie did get up and go across to sit down alongside Alex on the wicker sofa. She reached out and caught hold of her hand and squeezed it reassuringly, doing her best to sound positive.

'The first thing you've got to do is to stop crying. You were sick, so what? People get sick and, for all you know, it might have been those prawns last night.' Ignoring Alex's attempt to disagree, she ploughed on. 'James is away now for, what? A week?'

'Ten days.' Alex sniffed and wiped her eyes with her free hand.

'Even better. That gives you ten days to get over the shock of it all and to work out the kindest way of explaining to him what happened. When all's said and done, the problem is that you like him too much. He can hardly feel rejected because of that. So, come on, try to cheer up and let's see if the city of Romeo and Juliet manages to work its magic on you.'

Chapter 10

They spent the day walking round the lovely historic town, starting with Via Mazzini, a pedestrian-only road lined with shops – many of them big names – boasting some amazing clothes and accessories on sale. Where there were prices, Suzie soon worked out that buying clothes here in the centre wasn't going to be cheap – maybe not quite as expensive as Venice, but not far off. This didn't appear to worry the numerous people all around them carrying shopping bags bearing the names of famous fashion houses. The road itself was paved with slabs of marble, worn smooth and shiny by the passage of countless pairs of feet. Fascinating-looking narrow lanes led off to the left and to the right, and churches, chapels and historic buildings appeared in endless succession as they strolled along. The atmosphere was happy, busy and redolent with history. Suzie found herself wondering if Shakespeare really had ever walked here and rather hoped he had.

As they wandered through the narrow streets and magnificent piazzas, Suzie felt an overwhelming sense of relief. Somehow, after so many years of dreaming about this moment, there had been a nagging doubt lurking at the back of her mind that the reality might not match up to her expectations. Instead, she felt as if she had belonged to this place all her life. The medieval heart of the city was surprisingly small and the atmosphere was homely and intimate, in spite of the hordes of tourists wandering aimlessly around. Much of the *centro storico* was pedestrian-only and it was wonderful to be able to walk about without fear of traffic. The only traffic to watch out for, she soon discovered, were the bikes. Clearly the mode of transport of choice of the Veronese – irrespective of age or sex – was the bicycle, and both girls soon got used to the ringing of bells and the rattle of battered bikes on the cobbles and paving slabs wherever they went.

Neither of them felt like lunch, but they stopped for an ice cream around mid-afternoon and sat at a table under a parasol in the long, thin Piazza delle Erbe, looking straight out along the beautiful square towards the imposing buildings at the far end with statues lining the parapets. There was a market in the centre of the piazza and from what Suzie could see, the stalls specialised in T-shirts, sunhats and sunglasses, aimed directly at the throng of tourists passing by. They had chosen their ice creams from an open-topped fridge with a magnificent selection of flavours, piled up in colourful swirls and embarrassing them with choice. After a lot of deliberation Suzie had opted for a mixture of meringue, strawberry and banana, while Alex chose vanilla, pistachio and dark chocolate. The ice creams, topped with whipped cream and thick wafer biscuits, arrived in tall glasses with long-handled spoons and looked sumptuous. They bought bottles of sparkling mineral water to wash them down. It all tasted as good as it looked and Suzie found herself smiling into her glass.

Suzie had been doing a lot of thinking about what Alex had told her. She herself was an only child and had never had a brother or any really close male friends when she was growing up so she had no standard of comparison, but it was clear that Alex had a problem. No doubt James would be in touch with her as soon as he reached California and Alex needed to have at least an idea of what she was going to say to him.

Alex's thoughts, too, must have been running along similar lines. After a minute or two, she brought up the pressing subject without Suzie needing to prompt her.

'So what the bloody hell do I do about James?'

Suzie didn't reply straight away. To give herself time to think, she took a spoonful of the delicious ice cream and let it melt in her mouth, deliberating the right course of action, her eyes coming to rest on the beautiful frescoes painted high up on the walls of the old building opposite them. They were doubtless very old and utterly charming, but they did little to help solve Alex's dilemma. Finally she gave her opinion. Fundamentally, the way she saw it, there was no alternative.

'You've got to tell him. And I mean tell him everything, just like you've told me. You owe him that.'

'What, over the phone? Isn't that terribly cruel? It's not like he's done anything wrong. In fact, he's done everything right. I'm the one who's screwed things up.'

'Nobody's screwed anything up. In fact, not to put too fine a point on it, but it's probably just as well you didn't do any of that last night. If you had had sex with him and then had to tell him you didn't want it to go any further, think how much worse he might feel. You know, wounded macho pride and all that. No, as it worked out, nothing happened, and I'm sure that's for the best.'

Alex just nodded vaguely while Suzie took another spoonful of ice cream for moral support.

'But I'm sure you're right, Alex. It's not a conversation to be had on the phone. You need to have it out with him face to face. For now, over these next ten days while he's in America, if he contacts you, I think you should just be nice and friendly like you always have been with him. If he brings up what happened last night, just apologise for how it ended and try to avoid getting his hopes up too much. Keep it cordial, but stay vague. Do you think you can do that?'

'I can try.' Alex looked up from her ice cream. 'The thing is, I know James and I just know he'll come straight back here as soon as he gets back from the States. In fact, he might even cut short his stay over there and come back sooner.' Her voice began to rise in panic and Suzie was quick to leap in and pour oil on troubled waters.

'Hang on there. When's the wedding? He can hardly come back before that.'

'On Saturday.'

'Today's Monday so you know you've got at least all this week before he might turn up here. That's bags of time for you to rest and recuperate and work out exactly what you're going to say to him. Now eat your ice cream before it melts and then let's go and look for Juliet's House. We can do the Arena tomorrow. It's too hot for walking around in the open. At least here in this maze of streets we can find some shade.'

Juliet's House was absolutely heaving with tourists. The road outside and below the famous balcony was packed, and the walls of the covered area were solid with graffiti, presumably declarations of undying love left there in the same way that people sometimes carve their initials in the trunk of a tree to immortalise their existence. Suzie felt a little shiver of disapproval and found herself in danger of becoming very nerdy. She took Alex by the arm and dragged her to one side, pointing up at Juliet's balcony.

'Although Verona town council do their best to conceal the truth, there's something these people either don't know or, if they do, it doesn't bother them. There isn't an ounce of proof that Romeo and Juliet ever existed, nor that Shakespeare ever visited here. The origins of the play are most probably in a long, rambling poem that surfaced in England in the middle of the sixteenth century, and much of that was borrowed from a couple of earlier Italian works of fiction. In the play, there's no mention of a balcony – remember the line, "But soft! What light through yonder window breaks"? No balcony, just a window, and I can tell you for a fact that the balcony up there isn't even original. It was tacked onto the building back in, I think, the Thirties, for the sake of the tourists.'

Alex looked round at her and grinned. 'Calm down, Professor. Everybody'll be able to hear your outraged academic tone and you'll get us lynched. So what if they never existed? So what if it's a phoney balcony? It doesn't alter the fact that it's become a romantic Mecca. I was reading on the train the other day that the city has to employ a team of secretaries to answer all the love letters left for Juliet. Let the people have their dreams. If I wasn't trying to avoid a relationship at the moment, I'd probably write something myself.'

Suzie smiled back at her. 'All right, all right, I promise I'll be good, but just let me say this. Even the house doesn't work. In the play, Romeo is hiding in the garden below Juliet's window, not in the middle of the bloody street!'

'So what? It's the principle of it that counts. He loved her so deeply, he was prepared to kill himself when he thought she was dead. And she loved him so much she did the same when she found his body. That's some pretty powerful love, Suzanne, my friend.'

–

That evening, as Suzie was waiting in the lobby for Alex to come down from her room, she cast her eyes over the collection of leaflets and brochures on the information desk, anxious not to miss anything while they were here in this wonderful old city. Among the adverts for historic buildings, museums and concerts, one pamphlet caught her eye. It was for a private academy offering art courses. As Suzie turned it over in her fingers it occurred to her that this might be the perfect way to take Alex's mind off her worries about James. As far as she could see, the courses were short, one-week affairs at this time of year, with full academic year diploma courses starting early next month. The place was here in central Verona and it all looked very nice, but she didn't want to suggest something to Alex that might turn out to be a rip-off. She needed somebody knowledgeable about art to tell her whether it was any good or not.

There was, of course, just such a person.

Realising that this was the perfect excuse for calling him, she dug out Michael's visiting card and went out onto the pavement in front of the hotel, returning the greeting from the uniformed doorman as she did so. She leant against the hotel wall, still warm from the day's sunshine, dialled his Italian mobile phone number and waited, feeling unusually nervous. He answered almost immediately and she couldn't ignore the little spark of pleasure that buzzed through her at the sound of his voice.

'*Si, pronto.*' His accent was so perfect, for a moment she thought she might have got the wrong man.

'Michael? It's Suzie. You know, we met in…'

'Suzie, how lovely to hear from you. Where are you?'

Suzie told him where they were staying and heard him whistle.

'Blimey, Alex likes the good life, doesn't she? That's supposed to be one of the hundred best hotels in the world.'

'It's lovely all right, but listen, Michael, you said to call you if we needed help. It's nothing drastic, but I need your advice as an artist.'

'Fire away.'

Suzie told him about Alex's interest in art and how she had been unable to pursue it until now. She mentioned the leaflet she had found in the lobby and asked him what he thought of the idea. His reply was enthusiastic.

'The Academy's very, very good. They offer high-level courses, but inevitably, they're picky about who they accept. A lot of it'll depend on how good she is.' There was a brief pause while he considered the best course of action and when he continued, Suzie felt a little surge of excitement. 'Listen, how about this? We could meet up and I could take a look at what Alex is capable of producing. Maybe she's got some photos of stuff she's already done and I could get her to draw or paint a few bits and pieces for me. If I think she's got what it takes, I could have a word with a few people I know at the Academy and see whether they could squeeze her in. Their courses aren't cheap, but I don't suppose that would be a problem for her. What do you think?'

'I think that would be wonderful. Thank you so much. To be honest, I haven't mentioned this to her yet as I didn't want to disappoint her if you had told me the place was no good. Let me talk it over with her this evening and call you back. Would that be convenient? You're not going to be tied up or anything?'

'Call me any time, and Suzie, it would be good to see *you* again.' She felt her cheeks colour as she picked up the unmistakable emphasis. 'I'm pretty free tomorrow or Wednesday if it suits. Let me know.'

Suzie thanked him warmly and there was no getting away from it – she hoped Alex would go for it, and not just for the sake of her artistic ambitions.

Alex leapt at it.

The two of them sat down at a table among the magnificent plants and trees in the courtyard of the hotel and ordered glasses of Prosecco. Remembering what the professor had said, Suzie specified that the Prosecco should be from Valdobbiadene and saw the waiter give a nod of approval. As Suzie started to lay out her proposal and Michael's offer, she saw the gloom on her friend's face swept away by a burgeoning wave of optimism. Within a matter of minutes, Alex was pleading with her to call him back and set it up. Suzie didn't need any persuading.

'Michael. Hi, it's me again. Alex thinks it's a fabulous idea and she says thank you so much for offering to help.'

'Terrific. Listen, I've been thinking. I reckon the best thing is for me to collect the two of you and bring you out to my studio. It's barely half an hour from Verona and it's quiet and peaceful. All the materials are here and we won't be disturbed. If you're free tomorrow, I could pick you up at, say, nine o'clock, or is that too early? You're not going out clubbing tonight or anything?'

'Very much the opposite. An early night for both of us, I'm sure. Thank you so much, Michael. Alex is really looking forward to it.'

As she returned the phone to her bag, Alex gave her a grin. 'I notice you said "Alex is looking forward to it", not you. That's no way to get your man, you know.'

Inevitably this set Suzie off on another of her attacks of the blushes before she could pull herself together and explain.

'You've seen him, Alex, he's still grieving. I don't think for a moment he's got any interest in doing anything for us except giving you a hand with your art. No, we may be in the home town of Romeo and Juliet, but I don't think we're talking romance.' She glanced up at Alex. 'Besides, I know my limitations.'

'What's that supposed to mean?'

'Look at him, Alex. He's obviously talented, he's successful, he's amazingly good-looking. Would he really be interested in somebody like me?'

'There are moments, Suzanne Cartwright, when I feel tempted to repeat my Prosecco-throwing trick on you. Take a look in the mirror, would you? You're tall, you're very attractive, your hair looks really good – and if you ever felt like discovering a thing called make-up, you could look stunning. And, even more important for a man like Michael, you've got a brain.' She reached across the table and tapped the back of Suzie's hand with her fingers. 'And you're a good person, and I really mean that.'

This did little to calm Suzie's blushes so she sought solace in alcohol – always a risky business. In this case, it involved swallowing half a glass of Prosecco in one and erupting into a fit of hiccups as a result. However, by the time she had recovered enough to see straight and breathe again, she had got over her embarrassment – at least for now.

'Time for dinner?'

They left the hotel and walked up to the massive space that is Piazza Bra. A line of restaurants stretched out before them, the buildings a colourful mixture of pinks, yellows and sun-bleached ochre. Tourists thronged the area and there was a real lively atmosphere as they strolled around. Battered bikes rattled past carrying an amazing mix of humanity, from elegant ladies and formally dressed gentlemen to students, children and even a pair of nuns. After the storm the previous day the weather had returned to clear, cloudless skies and, although the air temperature had dropped a couple of degrees, it was still very comfortable to sit outside under an awning, with the unmistakable mass of the Roman Arena right before their eyes.

Alex opted for a risotto to settle her stomach while Suzie chose what the menu referred to as *insalata Veronese*. This turned out to be a massive plate of mixed salad with slices of ham, speck, various salami, walnuts, chestnuts, olives and cheese. Accompanied by the lovely local bread and a bottle of slightly fizzy local white wine, it made an excellent meal.

As they ate, they chatted and Suzie thought she should explain the interesting name of the square.

'In case you were wondering, Bra in Italian is a place name. The article of clothing is a *reggiseno*, so the name of this piazza doesn't strike the Italians as funny, although I'm sure it gives the tourists a giggle.'

'Although I couldn't help noticing a lingerie shop on the corner as we arrived in the square.' Alex was definitely giggling.

Suzie was delighted to see her looking and sounding much more cheerful now. They chatted readily and after a while Suzie asked her what work she did back at the manor house. She knew they opened parts of it to the public in the summer months and she wondered if Alex was involved. The answer was a bit depressing.

'I don't do much, to be honest. Father and Rafe take care of virtually everything and they certainly make all the decisions. My degree in Ecology doesn't get used at all. It was a total waste of time.' She looked up from her risotto. 'I suppose the truth is that I'm just treading water, really. If I disappeared, nobody would miss me.'

'Don't say that. I'm sure you do important stuff.'

All she got in reply was a little shake of the head and her heart went out, once more, to this unhappy girl who was the living proof that money doesn't buy happiness.

Chapter 11

Next morning they emerged from the hotel into the street at five to nine to meet Michael. Although they were deliberately early, he was already there, waiting for them in his car, and he gave them a wave and jumped out to open the doors as soon as he saw them. Before Suzie could do anything, Alex jumped into the back seat and slammed the door, meaning that Suzie was left with the seat alongside Michael. As her door closed, he hurried round and slipped into the driver's seat, started the engine and moved off immediately, glancing round at them with an apologetic smile as he did so.

'Sorry for the rush, but the local police are on the prowl. This whole area's a no-waiting zone and the fines are punitive. Anyway, hello to you both. It's really good to see you again. What've you been up to since we last met in Venice?'

As he concentrated on navigating his way through the streets of the old centre, some little wider than the car itself, Suzie surreptitiously studied him. He was wearing shorts and the sight of his muscular legs close by her was rather stimulating, as were his strong forearms, clad in soft brown hair and protruding from a well-worn T-shirt. As much for a displacement activity as anything else, she launched into a description of what they had done during the last few days of their stay in Venice and then went on to tell him about the weekend at James's villa. When they mentioned the lake, his interest appeared to increase. When Suzie told him the name of the little village next to the villa where she had bought the whisky, his eyebrows raised.

'Little did we know it, but we were neighbours. I also live in Bardolino, barely a kilometre or so further along the lake from where you were. In fact, I even know the villa where you were staying.' He grinned. 'It's a small world.'

They retraced the route they already knew and subsequently even found themselves driving past the entrance to James's villa. As Michael had said, only a minute or so later he turned off and they climbed up a narrow winding road for another couple of minutes as the houses thinned out and they found themselves surrounded by olive trees and rows of meticulously trained vines. At a corner, he swung through an open gateway into a courtyard and stopped.

'Here we are. Welcome to the Old Stables, *La Vecchia Scuderia*. The house isn't very big but what sold it for me was the barn. You'll see, it makes a magnificent studio – although it's bloody freezing in winter.'

'How lovely.' Alex climbed out of the car and looked around appreciatively. Suzie joined her and they gazed at the view. The rows of vines behind the house sloped away right down to the houses by the lakeside and the broad panorama across the water to the mountains beyond was even more spectacular from up here than from James's villa. 'How long have you lived here, Michael?'

'We bought it seven years ago, but it took well over two years to get all the permits and then to get the work done.

It was almost derelict when we bought it and it needed a hell of a lot done to it. I did some of it myself, but even so we had the builders here for nearly a year. Anyway, do come in.'

Suzie couldn't miss his repeated use of the pronoun 'we' but she made no comment. She intended being as tactful as possible and taking her time when it came to the mention of his wife and the accident. He led them into the house and they could immediately see that it had once been a stable. The walls of the surprisingly large open-plan room were bare stone and there were even fan-shaped metal baskets – now containing dried flowers – bolted to the walls where the fodder for the horses would once have been. The floors were newly tiled although the beams supporting the ceiling were clearly ancient. Over to one side was a very modern kitchen area with a massive farmhouse table, while further along were armchairs and a long sofa. It was a delightful place and Suzie instantly fell in love with it. Unlike the grandeur of James's villa, this place felt like a home.

'So do you live here all the time or do you get back to the UK much?' Suzie went over to a huge glazed archway at the end and peered out. The whole lake was laid out before them. 'It's such a beautiful place. If I owned it, I'd spend my whole life here.'

'That was the plan.' He supplied no explanation and, again, Suzie didn't press matters. 'I must admit I've spent most of my time here in Italy over the past few years. Not that I don't like England, but this is a pretty nice place. Now, can I offer you a coffee, a cappuccino or some tea? I've got real English tea if you want it. My mother still sends me food parcels every now and then.'

As he filled the kettle to make the tea he glanced back over his shoulder at Alex. 'Have you got any photos of your work you can show me, Alex, or are we going to have to start from scratch?'

She pulled out her iPad. 'Give me a minute. I'll see what I've got on here.'

As she was doing that, Suzie caught a movement out of the corner of her eye and an enormous grey cat appeared from the hall and jumped languidly onto the worktop beside Michael.

'No, cat, get off. Go and say hello to the nice ladies.' He lifted the monstrous beast easily and set it down on the floor. Giving him a scornful look, it immediately jumped onto the table and sauntered across to where Alex was swiping her screen.

'Wow, that's one hell of a big cat.' Alex was impressed. 'What do you feed it?'

'Surprisingly little, but he's got at least another household or two on the go, and so I bet he gets half a dozen meals a day. He's not even our cat. He just pitches up when he feels like it. He belongs to the people down the hill from here. When we first saw him a few years back, he was a scrawny little thing. Just look at him now.'

'What's his name?'

'We just called him Cat. If you're holding food when you say his name, he appears to recognise it. He's probably got a different name in each of the households he graces with his presence.'

He returned to the table with the teapot and mugs and brought a glass milk bottle out of the fridge.

'Real milk? Not the usual stuff out of cartons? How wonderful.'

'I get it from the farmer just up the hill, along with really good wine and olive oil. He's talking about trying his hand at making cheese next and I'm looking forward to that.'

Suzie studied him as he busied himself pouring the tea and handing the mugs round. The dark rings under his eyes were still there, but he was looking and sounding quite cheerful and she felt happy for him. After the horror of what he had lived through, he deserved some happiness.

'Right, Alex, show me what you've got.'

He took a seat alongside her and together they began to flick through the pictures. While they concentrated on that, Suzie found herself selected as a suitable resting place by Cat, who wandered across the table towards her, hesitated and then jumped down onto her lap with a thud and set about the usual feline bread-kneading movements with his paws as he softened up her thighs before deigning to lie down on them. She stroked his head and back and he started purring loudly as he relaxed and she did the same.

By the time she had finished her tea, the other two had completed their browse through Alex's photos and Suzie vowed to get a look at them herself later on. She hadn't seen any of Alex's work yet and she was intrigued to see what her stuff was like. Swilling the last of his tea, Michael stood up.

'Next stop, the studio, if you don't mind. Alex, I'd like you to do a few sketches for me. Suzie, just make yourself at home – unless you want to come and do some painting as well.'

'I'd love to see the studio, but I'll leave the artistic stuff to you two. There's just one problem, though. I'm not sure I'm strong enough to get up with Cat on my lap.'

'No problem.' Michael reached into the fridge and emerged with a half-empty tin of what looked like pilchards. As he did so, Cat rose to his feet like magic, stretched and jumped surprisingly lightly onto the floor, leaving Suzie feeling a good few kilos lighter. As Michael tipped the fish into a saucer, the cat settled down to what was in all probability his second or third breakfast of the day. Evidently Cat was no fool.

They crossed the yard to the long building on the other side and Michael unlocked a pair of hefty wooden doors. Downstairs was a jumble of building materials, tools and bits of what looked like two or three different bikes along with two sets of skis. Once they climbed up the old stairs to the first floor, however, things looked very different. Michael's studio was a single long room with a wooden floor made of wide old floorboards, worn smooth and shiny with age. Huge beams spanned the width of the room every few metres, supporting equally ancient-looking angled timber trusses that in turn supported the roof. A series of windows had been set in the pitched ceiling and the whole place was bathed in light as a result.

All around were trestle tables, at least three big easels and a low cupboard presumably housing his equipment. The lingering smells of turps and linseed oil filled the air and almost every horizontal surface was cluttered with pots, jars, vases and even a galvanised bucket containing paintbrushes of all shapes and sizes. At the far end of the room, a picture window had been inserted into the gable and the view from here down across the vineyards to the lake and beyond was breathtaking. Directly in front of the window was an old sofa and Suzie headed for it while Michael set Alex a series of tasks. As she walked around the room, she noticed a number of canvases resting against the wall, so she stopped and glanced back.

'Michael, do you mind if I take a look at your paintings?'

'Do, by all means, although most of the stuff there is either old or unfinished or both. If you like I'll show you some of my more recent stuff later on. In fact, I've got Frederika's portrait over in the house, waiting to be framed, if you like.'

The paintings were a mixture; all unframed canvases. Some were what looked like early studies for portraits, while others were very different – some abstract, some almost photographic. One painting in particular immediately caught Suzie's eye. She lifted it from the floor and blew the dust off it. Clearly it had been resting here for some time. She set it on a table against the wall and sat down in a battered old armchair opposite it, letting her eyes roam across the canvas. There was no doubt about it; although it was little more than an initial sketch, it was unmistakably the old house by the lake belonging to Professor Macgregor-Brown. As she raised her eyes to the huge picture window and looked out, she realised she could actually see the roofs of James's villa and the professor's house from here. She was gazing out at the stunning view of the lake when she heard a plaintive miaow and looked down.

'Hello, Cat. Finished your breakfast?'

In response the big beast jumped effortlessly onto the arm of the chair beside her and from there quickly installed himself on her lap, purring happily as he set about licking his sleek furry coat. She was just settling back under his not inconsiderable weight when she heard Michael's voice at her shoulder. She glanced up with a smile.

'Looks like you've made yourself a friend, Suzie. You're particularly honoured. It's quite unusual for him to sit on anybody's lap, let alone somebody he's just met.'

'I've always liked cats, and dogs for that matter. Maybe he can tell. How's your student doing?'

'I've asked her to do a couple of charcoal sketches; a still life and landscape. She's only got half an hour to do both of them, so I've left her to it.' As he sat down on the sofa opposite her, she pointed to the painting of the Professor's house.

'You know what you were saying about it being a small world, Michael? Well, it might surprise you to know that I had lunch in that very house on Sunday.'

'So you know Mack, then?' He did sound surprised.

Suzie nodded and explained. 'I only met him on Saturday, but we pretty soon discovered we share a common interest.'

Michael's face broke into a grin. 'No prizes for guessing what, or rather, who that is. So what's your connection with Shakespeare?'

Suzie told him about her studies and her job with the charity and he looked impressed. 'So it's *Doctor* Suzie Cartwright? *Complimenti*, as they say over here. So you're between jobs at the moment? What's on the horizon when this holiday finishes?'

'Not a lot, and to be honest, I'm beginning to panic. The charity was a bit of a one-off, really. We were responsible for restoring damaged manuscripts – you know, resulting from fire, vandalism, flood or even warfare. As you can imagine, it's going to be difficult to find something similar. The Professor... *Mack* thought I should try lecturing, but there are very few jobs going round.' She hesitated. 'And, to be honest, I'm not sure how good I'd be in front of a class. You've probably noticed by now that I do have a habit of blushing at the least provocation.' To underline what she was saying, her cheeks duly reddened as she spoke.

Michael gave her a gentle smile. 'You'd soon get used to it. I'm sure a bright person like you'll find something and, if you don't, you can always sit down and write the definitive book on Shakespeare. He's always popular – especially in a town like Verona.'

'How do you know Mack?'

'I'd come across him on and off over the years via various charities, and then we rented a house he owns in the centre of Verona while all the work was being done on this place here. As a result I got to know him pretty well. He's got a reputation for being a bit grumpy, but we always found him charming. In fact, I painted a picture of his house as a little present to him when we left. This one here was an early study.'

'What a nice idea. I think he's a sweetie. In fact, I'm looking forward to hearing from him or even seeing him again sometime soon. He's currently reading my doctoral thesis and I'm scared stiff of what he might say. It would be like Rembrandt taking a look at your paintings. Professor Macgregor-Brown is a legend in the Shakespeare world.'

'Well, if you need any moral support when you go to see him, just say the word and I'd be happy to come with you. I haven't seen him for a while. Is Paolina still looking after him?'

'Yes, and she's a fabulous cook.'

'If she ever went off and left him I don't know what he'd do. She's been looking after him ever since I've known him.'

They chatted about all sorts of things from art and literature to this beautiful part of Italy, but he made no mention of his personal circumstances and she avoided the subject. As and when he felt like bringing the subject up, she knew she would offer all the support she could, but it was going to have to come from him. She found talking to him very easy and she enjoyed his company. From the smile on his face, she definitely got the impression he was enjoying himself as well and she was mildly surprised when he glanced at his watch, looked back towards the other end of the studio and raised his voice.

'Time's up, Alex.' He gave Suzie another little smile and stood up. 'Right, I must go back and see what my student's been able to produce. If you're happy here, fine, but if you want to do anything else, like go for a walk or make yourself some tea or whatever, just do it.'

'That's an idea. Would you like another cup of tea, or something stronger?'

He grinned. 'A cup of tea would be great. Artists, as you may know, have a reputation for drinking a lot. I made a decision years ago to limit myself to tea or coffee when I'm working. Otherwise, it's a slippery slope. Wine and a steady hand don't mix.'

After persuading the cat to relinquish her lap for the warm cushion beneath, Suzie left Michael and Alex to their discussions and headed back down the stairs. The door to Michael's house was unlocked and she reflected how trusting he must be. Mind you, she thought to herself as she filled the kettle, this place was very much off the beaten track so it was unlikely there would be any casual sneak thieves passing by. As the kettle boiled, she wandered round the room, stopping to study the half-dozen paintings on display. One of them, in particular, stopped her in her tracks.

It was a fine painting of a beautiful, dark-haired nude. She was seated on the floor, resting forwards, clutching her knees modestly, her eyes looking straight at the artist, an expression of such joy and love on her face that Suzie felt a wave of emotion sweep over her. There was no doubt in her mind that this had to be Michael's poor dead wife and she felt tears in her eyes as she stood there and contemplated the full horror of what had happened to her and her heartbroken husband.

It was a good while later before she roused herself and reheated the now lukewarm water in the kettle to make the tea. As she loaded three mugs onto a tray and carried them across the yard, one thought was firmly lodged in her head. However much she might feel attracted to Michael – and she couldn't deny that she did – she felt sure it would be a long, long time before he could possibly even begin to think about restarting his life after something so cataclysmic. The irony of finding herself in an equally frustrating situation to the one Alex faced wasn't lost on her. Alex was haunted by the memory of James as a child-hood friend, while Michael was doubtless haunted by the memory of his one true love. Either way, the result was that neither she nor Alex looked likely to form a romantic relationship any time soon. As she climbed the stairs to the studio she reminded herself with a little sigh that romance wasn't really her thing anyway.

Afterwards, she spent a delightful hour walking round the nearby vineyard in the warm sunshine, stopping to chat to an old woman working among the vines. Once Suzie had explained that she was a friend of Michael's, the lady became very chatty and told her all sorts of interesting facts about the process of winemaking here at Bardolino and insisted she accompany her to her nearby cantina to taste last year's wine. As they walked back through the rows of vines, she informed Suzie that this year's grape harvest, the *vendemmia*, was due to start in a little under a week and she pointed out the bunches of grapes, already looking full and luscious.

At the cantina, Suzie ended up tasting not only red, but also white and rosé wines, and she had to fight to keep the lady from filling her glass to the brim each time. As for the notion of tasting the wine and then spitting it out, the old lady was having none of it. Wine was made to be drunk, and that was that. As a result, when Suzie got back to Michael's studio where he and Alex were deep in conversation, she settled down happily on the sofa and drifted off to sleep, accompanied by Cat.

Michael and Alex broke for lunch very late. In fact, when Suzie managed to extricate her arm from beneath the sleeping cat and consult her watch, she saw that it was almost three. She looked up to see Michael standing beside her and she gave him an apologetic smile.

'Sorry, I must have dozed off after my walk.'

He smiled back. 'I have a feeling you might have bumped into Giuseppina or her husband when you were out on your walk. Am I right?' Michael's tone was gently accusing. 'There's a drop of what looks suspiciously like red wine on your top.' He grinned down at her as she blinked sleepily. 'They do make good wine, don't they?'

Suzie glanced down and spotted the incriminating red mark on her right breast and, inevitably, felt her cheeks colour as a result. Still, she managed a little grin as she slid the somnolent cat off her lap and stood up. 'Their wine is far too good, I'm afraid, and I'm just too weak-willed. I can see why you insist on only drinking tea when you're working – all I wanted to do was sleep. So, how has it gone? What do you think of Alex?'

'I've just been telling her how much promise I see in her work. I need you to back me up here, please. She's accused me of bullshitting her and I swear I'm not. Come and take a look at what she's produced. I think she's really got something.' He swung his head round towards Alex. 'Alex, you have to believe me – you're good.'

Together they walked back up to where Alex had been working and Suzie surveyed the two charcoal sketches and one painted canvas. Michael was right. Alex really was good.

'Blimey, Alex, these are great! Really. No bull. I love the still life in particular. You've got the curve of the glass and the ripple on the surface of the water down to a T. Quite amazing.' She looked at Michael. 'So, maestro, what's your advice? Should she sign up for a painting course?'

He nodded vigorously. 'No question. In fact, I've just been trying to persuade her to enrol for a full year and do the diploma course. She's good enough and it'll add so much to her art. I reckon I should be able to convince them at the Academy to take her, even if they say they're full. And she doesn't even need to worry about it being in Italian – they speak all languages there.'

Suzie looked at Alex. 'That sounds very positive. Are you going to do it, Alex?'

'I'd love to, you know that, but there's just one teensy-weensy little problem: my father. If he wasn't prepared to let me go to art school in England, imagine how much he's going to hate the idea of letting me go to one overseas.'

'But surely it's your decision, Alex?' Michael sounded as bewildered as Suzie had been before Alex had explained the weird dynamic of the Tedburn family. 'Would you like me to talk to him? Tell him how good you are?'

Alex hung her head and Suzie reached out to take her by the arm and give her a little shake.

'Michael's right, Alex, if you're that good, you need to take it further. Talk to your dad and maybe he'll see sense. And, like Michael, I'd be happy to talk to him as well if it helps.'

'I don't think it would help, but thanks for the offers. You don't know him like I do. Once he's made up his mind about something – like the fact that I'm a lazy waste of space – there's no changing it.' She looked up at Michael. 'Thank you so very much, Michael, for taking such a lot of time and trouble over me, but I'm afraid it's almost certainly been a waste of time. He'll never say yes.'

Chapter 12

They got back to Verona in the late afternoon and although Alex did her best to get Michael to let her buy him a slap-up meal to say thank you, he excused himself, pleading an important prior engagement. As they watched him drive off again after dropping them at their hotel, Suzie felt an acute sense of loss. She glanced across at Alex.

'Nice guy.'

'Very nice. I'll say this, Suzie, you've got very good taste in men. Impeccable, in fact.'

'A fat lot of good it's going to do me.'

Together, they walked into the hotel and took the lift up to their rooms. As they got there, Alex announced her intention of having a little lie-down to give her time to think. Suzie on the other hand had already had a snooze today so she decided to check her emails and then go for a walk around Verona. The result of the email check was disappointing. She had applied for an interesting job a few weeks back and she was saddened, if unsurprised, to find an email from the British Museum Archive informing her that the position she had applied for had been awarded to somebody else. She knew enough about how these things worked to wonder whether they had already had a candidate in mind all along, but it didn't help. With a sigh, she deleted it and headed back out of the door.

She walked around the city, doing her best to let the beauty of the town offset her disappointment. She made her way through the centre to the old castle and the handsome bridge leading away from it across the river. The bridge itself was for pedestrians only and was crowded with a cosmopolitan mass of them. It was lined on both sides by the characteristic splayed red-brick crenellations found on fortresses all over this part of Italy. Suzie paused in the middle, looking out over the wide sweep of the River Adige, its waters a milky brown colour, and wondered if anybody had fought a real battle here. She recalled there had been ferocious fighting in the First World War just a bit further to the north and the east of here. And then, towards the end of the Second World War, the retreating Germans had blown up all of Verona's bridges. As a result, although skilfully rebuilt, the present-day bridges were all replacements. It might look like a delightful quiet tourist destination now, but this whole area had seen more warfare over the years than most places.

As she was resting on her elbows on the brickwork, her phone started ringing. It was a familiar voice.

'Hi, Suzie. It's me, Tommy, calling from the US. I hope you don't mind. I got your number from Rafe.'

'Hello, Tommy. Good to hear from you.' And she realised that it was. 'How's California?'

They chatted for some minutes and she wondered if there was any special reason for the call. This emerged towards the end of their chat.

'Um, Suzie, I just wanted to tell you I've been thinking about you. A lot.'

She was mildly surprised. She now knew, through Alex, that his family lived in a castle and he was another

132

extremely wealthy member of the aristocracy – apart from looking like a film star. What interest might he have in her?

'I hope you were thinking nice things.'

'Yes. In fact, Suzie, I just wanted to say once again how sorry I am about my behaviour back in London. I'm really not a bad guy. Please don't hate me.'

'Of course I don't hate you, Tommy.'

'Would you mind if I see you again sometime?' He sounded remarkably meek and it was hard to believe that this was tall, handsome Tommy with all his wealth. 'If I were to come over to Italy again sometime with James, would it be okay for me to see you?'

'Tommy, of course it would. I look forward to it.'

'That's great.' The relief in his voice was palpable.

At the end of the call, as she put her phone away safely in her bag, she found herself reflecting on what he had said. Could it be that he wanted to take things to the next level with her? And if he did, how did she feel about it?

Her mind still mulling this over, she circled round, walking down by the riverside where ducks swam in the water at her feet and cypress-clad hills rose above her on one side, with the wonderful buildings of old Verona on the other. It was a very romantic view and she felt, in her bones, that she could so easily have let romance sweep her away, but the more she thought about it, the more she realised that the only romantic interest in her life at present was an artist she barely knew who was crushed beneath the weight of his grief. Nice as it was to hear Tommy expressing his interest, the object of her affections was Michael, but he was a forlorn hope. Even an espresso in a little cafe in a delightful cobbled square did little to cheer her up. Despite being surrounded by lovely old buildings made up of row upon row of red bricks alternating with horizontal strips of cream-coloured stone, she barely registered their beauty and she was feeling quite low by the time she got back to the hotel.

It was almost seven by this time and she realised she was feeling hungry. That afternoon Michael had given them bread, local cheese and huge, tasty, home-grown tomatoes, apologising that his intention had been to take them to the nearby trattoria, but that he and Alex had lost track of time. Washed down with a glass of good red wine it had been fine, but now Suzie knew she needed something more substantial.

She collected Alex and together they went out into the street and wandered around until they were attracted by the entrancing aromas emanating from a friendly-looking pizzeria in a narrow back lane near the riverside. As they ate, they talked.

'Weren't Michael's paintings amazing?' Alex looked up from her plate of seafood antipasti. 'If I could ever get to be even half as good as him, I'd be delighted.'

That afternoon, after the snack lunch, he had shown them a selection of his work, including the newly finished portrait of Frederika the Austrian. It was a stunning likeness and the level of intricate detail, right down to the light reflecting in the diamond earrings and the hint of a smile on her face, was a tour de force. There was no hiding the fact that it had been painted by a master and Suzie had been reminded of some of the great portrait painters of the past. Maybe, she thought to herself, her mention of Rembrandt earlier had not been so far off the mark. He had then shown them other canvases but he stayed away from the end of the sitting room where the painting of his wife was hanging.

Suzie had no doubts about Alex and her art. 'I really think you should do the art course at the Academy, you know, Alex. Just think what it would do for you as an artist – and as a person.'

Alex nodded morosely. 'I know, I can't stop thinking about it, but I know what my father's going to say. What's the point?'

There was a brief interval while the waiter appeared with two enormous pizzas and removed the remains of their starters. After he had left, Suzie looked across the table at Alex, still thinking about the resigned note of defeat in her voice.

'Alex, can I ask you something? Something personal? If you don't want to answer, please don't, but I know I need to ask.'

'Whatever you like.' Alex sounded intrigued.

'The reason you always do what your father says is because he might turn off the money tap. Is that right, or is there more to it than that?'

Alex took her time before replying.

'Of course the money's important. I'd be lying if I said it wasn't, but you're right, there's more to it than that.' She took a mouthful of sparkling mineral water. 'It's my mother. Before she died, when she was in the hospice, she made me promise to do exactly what my father said. She said he would know what was best for me. A few days later, the cancer finally killed her and it was an awful time for me. I was barely into my teens and my mum had been my best friend in the whole world. I felt completely lost.

There was Rafe, of course, but he was older and he was away at school most of the time anyway.

'I was all alone at home with my father, but he's not the sort of man who shows his emotions or goes in for open displays of affection. I'll always remember him taking me to one side before my mother's funeral and telling me it was my duty – he actually used the word "duty" – not to cry in the church. We were Tedburns and we didn't do that sort of thing.' She paused for a few deep breaths. 'Well, I cried my eyes out all the way through the service and I'm not sure he's ever forgiven me. After that, he sent me off to school and our relationship, if you can call it that, has remained at arm's length.'

Suzie nodded slowly. 'So you're still accepting his control over your life because of a promise made when you were thirteen?' She glanced up. 'That's a long time ago, Alex.'

'I know, but a promise is a promise, isn't it?'

Suzie carried on eating her pizza, turning over in her head what she had just heard. Deep down she felt sure that the very best thing for Alex would be for her to study art, and she could sense her indecision. After a while, she had another go.

'But surely your mother just meant while you were growing up? Now that you're an adult, I'm sure she would have wanted you to do what makes you happy.'

Alex just nodded vaguely, but didn't reply as Suzie carried on.

'Deep down, your father must want what's best for you, too. And I'm certain he also wants you to be happy. Don't you think so?'

'I suppose so, but the fact is that he's convinced that all I need to make me happy is a whole heap of money and a husband chosen by him.'

'Have you tried talking to him about it?'

'Have I tried?' Alex snorted into her mouthful of *quattro stagioni* pizza. 'Time and time again, but it always ends up the same way. He knows best and he refuses to hear my side of things. So, gradually, I've drifted into being what he wants – a spoilt little rich girl.' She made an attempt at a wry smile. 'Tough life, eh? Nothing to do, and all the money in the world.'

Suzie sat back from her pizza and took a mouthful of water. After the wine she had drunk during the day, she had decided to stay off alcohol tonight. 'Does he love you?'

Alex looked up abruptly. 'Of course he does. He's my father.'

'And you love him?' Suzie didn't wait for a reply. 'Then, if you love each other, I think you need to sit down and have a serious talk. Maybe not in that formal study of his, but somewhere neutral.' A sudden thought occurred to her. 'I tell you what, why don't you invite him over here for a day or two? When's the last time he had a holiday?'

'Him, a holiday? Hardly ever. He says the estate's his life.'

'But he could get away?'

'I'm sure he could. After all, he's got Rafe there to keep an eye on things.'

'Well, go on then. Give him a call and see what he says. Don't mention the art course on the phone. You can pick your moment for that once he's over here.'

The result of the long phone call Alex made to her father later that evening came as a surprise to both of them. After a lot of cajoling, he finally agreed to come to Verona on Friday and stay until Sunday, and Alex declared herself amazed.

'This'll be his first time out of the country for ages. Come to think of it, it'll be just about his first time out of Devon for a good long while, too. I never thought he'd agree.'

'That's got to be a good sign. Now all we've got to do is to make sure you know what you're going to say to James and you're away.'

'Oh, bugger, I'd almost forgotten about him. One thing's for sure, I'm not mentioning anything to my dad about my being unable to marry James until he's agreed to let me stay here and study art.'

'And it might also be a good idea to tell James you can't take things to the next level with him first, before letting your father in on the secret.' Suzie gave her a little smile. 'All in all, you're going to have your work cut out over the next week or two.'

'You can say that again.' Alex gave her a look of desperation before breaking into a little smile. 'And it's all your fault. If you hadn't agreed to come to Italy with me and if you hadn't taken a liking to Michael, I'd still be sitting back home looking out over the deer park without a care in the world.'

'Without a care in the world? Really?'

'As long as I didn't think about my life, my future or my ambitions…' Alex smiled again, but it was bittersweet.

'And now where would you rather be?'

'No question – here.'

Alex sent a text to Michael telling him what was going to happen and he replied saying he would speak to the people at the Academy about her anyway. That way she would hopefully know if there was going to be a place for her before her father came to Verona.

Apart from that, over the course of the next few days, they set about visiting Verona properly, starting with the Arena itself. Inside, it was even more impressive, with seating in its heyday for thirty thousand spectators who would have come from all over the Roman Empire to watch sports, games and bloody combat. The central area had now been transformed into comfortable seating and a stage, while cheaper seats were all around on the stone terraces. Sadly, they were informed that the summer opera and concert season had finished only a few weeks earlier, so they weren't able to sample the famous acoustics that made it one of music's great venues – with performances over the years from musical legends ranging from Pavarotti to Pink Floyd.

They were at the end of September by now and Suzie wondered how much longer the fine weather might last. Sooner or later it was bound to change and she felt sure that the winters here, so close to the mountains, would be harsh. As the thought crossed her mind, she found herself wondering where she would be and what she would be doing from the middle of October onwards when her contract to accompany Alex came to an end. And that was little more than two weeks away.

Every evening, she had been scouring the Internet ever more feverishly for possible jobs, but without any great success. Following on from what Professor

Macgregor-Brown had suggested, she had sent off CVs to a handful of universities, but without much hope, not least as the academic year would be starting any day now and most of the positions would already have been filled. On Thursday afternoon she did, however, receive a very welcome text message of a different kind.

> Hi Suzie. I gather from Alex that she's got her dad coming tomorrow. I imagine that'll mean you'll be on your own that night. I've got tickets to a special concert if you're inter- ested? Michael

Suzie rocked back on her heels and headed out onto the terrace where Alex was filing her nails. She held the phone under Alex's nose and waited until she had read the message.

'What do you think?'

Alex beamed. 'You want to know what I think? I think you should say yes and then make yourself look as good as possible. And a clothes shopping trip wouldn't do any harm either. After all, he does say it's a "special" concert, doesn't he? That almost certainly means dressy.' She was looking positively animated now. 'I'll come shopping with you. I'd better find something fairly conservative for my father's benefit.'

Suzie shook her head uncertainly. 'I don't know. I don't want it to look as if I'm throwing myself at him, after all.'

'But, given half a chance, isn't that exactly what you'd like to do?' There was a note of triumph in Alex's voice.

'Well, yes, but...'

'No buts. This time let me be the one giving the advice. Let him see just exactly what he's been missing.'

Chapter 13

Michael had agreed to meet Suzie at the hotel at six o'clock and by that time she was a bag of nerves. Alex, with the imminent arrival of her father in an hour or two, was little better. The two girls sat uncomfortably on the terrace, watching the sun sink towards the distant hills, both immersed in their own thoughts.

Suzie also had something else to worry about. She was now wearing a frighteningly expensive dress that Alex had insisted on buying for her with her gold card and she was terrified of creasing it or even ruining it. She was also more than a little worried that it might be too revealing. She had never had a dress with such an open neckline before and, although Alex and the shop assistant had laughed at her fears and had assured her that she was anything but indecent, she kept on glancing down in terror to check that everything was as it should be.

And as if she didn't have enough to worry about, her contact lenses – also worn at the insistence of Alex – were making her eyes sting. She made a silent resolution to stick to glasses from now on.

When the bells of at least three different churches starting ringing to announce that the long-awaited hour had come, Suzie stood up, straightened her dress and went over to give Alex a hug.

'Good luck with your dad. Maybe best to stick to trivia at first and let him settle in. A bottle of wine probably wouldn't hurt either.'

'Good luck to you, too, Suzie. You look gorgeous. You'll probably have to fight him off.' She giggled. 'That's if you want to put up a struggle.'

Downstairs, Suzie had the unaccustomed pleasure of seeing a man do a double take as she appeared. Michael was standing by the information desk where she had found the leaflet about the Academy of Art and as he turned towards her there was no mistaking the impression her appearance made upon him.

'Suzie, good evening. Wow, you look amazing.' He sounded as if he meant it and, needless to say, she found herself blushing.

'Hi, Michael. Thanks for the compliment. You're looking very good yourself.'

And he was. It was a warm evening and he was wearing a simple white cotton shirt, with a light blue jumper slung over his shoulders. As she walked across and shook hands with him, she couldn't help noticing that the jersey was the exact same shade as his eyes. She wondered idly if he had bought it himself or if this might have been a present from an admirer. His wife? She didn't have much time to ponder this as she could see him looking puzzled and shot him an enquiring glance.

'Something wrong, Michael? You're looking a bit bewildered.'

He gave a little shake of the head as the penny finally dropped. 'It's the glasses. Of course, you aren't wearing your glasses. And with your hair up, you look like a film star.'

'Stop it, or I'll be blushing all evening. The contact lenses are because Alex bullied me, but they make my eyes sting, so next time you see me, you'll have to put up with the glasses again. Anyway, because you said in your text that it was going to be a special concert, Alex took me to the salon this afternoon where they ganged up on me and insisted on putting my hair up.' She glanced down briefly. 'And then she got me this dress.'

As she looked up again, she saw his eyes had followed hers and were now trained on the revealing neckline. This did nothing to calm her embarrassment. What he said next didn't help.

'That's my mistake, I'm afraid. To be totally honest, I should have been more specific. It's a special concert because it's being put on by the kids of a special school that I'm a trustee of. It'll be hard chairs in the gymnasium, I'm afraid. Sorry if I didn't make myself clear.'

Great, Suzie thought to herself. Now she was going to look ridiculous, all dressed up to the nines in the midst of a bunch of parents and teachers. Her embarrassment grew.

They walked out into the evening air and she took a few deep breaths. High above, she could hear the high-pitched cries of gangs of swallows as they wheeled in the sky, which was already flushed red as sunset approached. Down at street level the shadows were deepening and she was glad she had managed to resist Alex's encouragement to wear heels – not least if they were going to be in a gymnasium with a delicate wooden floor – as they set off on foot. As she and Alex had already discovered, the pavements weren't always perfectly flat here in Verona, often with patches of cobblestones, and she had no wish to trip and end up flat on her face.

The school was barely ten minutes from the hotel and she enjoyed the walk – not least as it gave her blushes a chance to retreat. Michael exchanged a few words with her, in particular the news to be relayed to Alex that if she decided to do the art course at the Academy, they would almost certainly be able to offer her a place. For the most part they walked in silence, but it wasn't an awkward silence by any means. In fact Suzie was surprised by how comfortable she felt just being with him. What he thought of her, she was unable to guess.

The school, housed in a charming Renaissance building, turned out to be for children with learning disabilities and she was impressed to see that the students were doing everything from collecting the tickets to ushering the audience to their seats. As Michael had said, these were in a huge gymnasium, complete with wall bars and basketball hoops. A stage had been prepared at one end and she was mildly surprised to see a wide selection of instruments ranging from a grand piano to a full drum set waiting to be played. A little girl with a delightful smile pressed a plastic beaker of what looked like orange squash into her hand and Suzie was acutely conscious that she no doubt looked more than a little silly sipping this while decked out like a Hollywood diva. She was also immediately terrified she might spill the drink on her new dress and held it very, very carefully at arm's length.

As they made their way through the rows of chairs to their seats, Michael paused every now and then to say hello to some faces he recognised among the other members of the audience. Suzie caught a few curious glances from some of the ladies – and looks of a different type from some of the men – and she had little doubt that they were wondering who she might be. No doubt in other years Michael had been accompanied by his wife and a lot of their expressions registered sympathy. She kept a smile plastered on her face and tried not to think of anything but the forthcoming concert.

They sat down in the seats they'd been allotted and chatted sporadically as they waited for the concert to begin. She sensed that Michael was tense and wondered if he, too, was thinking of his wife. He told her that this charity was something he had been involved with for a number of years. He didn't go into detail and Suzie felt pretty sure this would have been something dear to his wife as well – after all, she had been a teacher. She didn't press him, sensing his hesitation. They exchanged a few snippets of conversation after that, but stuck to generalities, and it came as quite a relief when the lights were dimmed and the concert began. By this time she had finished her orange drink and she stowed the empty cup under her chair, relieved she had managed to avoid any disasters.

The concert was remarkably good. In particular, there was a young violinist who played quite beautifully and the pianist who accompanied him, although probably barely thirteen or fourteen, was of a high standard. The choir were excellent and, altogether, the result was a concert of real quality. When it ended, just before eight o'clock, Suzie joined the rest of the audience in giving them all a standing ovation. As the lights came back on again, she was quite relieved when Michael took her arm and steered her out of the gymnasium without stopping to talk to any of the other audience members. Emerging into the dusk, he released his grip on her arm and she almost grabbed him back again in support as she sensed that he was struggling with some internal conflict. Instead, in an attempt to get a casual conversation going, she made a suggestion.

'Alex and I had a lovely meal in Piazza Bra the other day. Would you let me buy you dinner there to say thank you for tonight and for lunch with you the other day?'

He hesitated before answering and, although she couldn't see his face very clearly, she could tell he was deliberating what to do. Finally he must have come to a decision.

'Absolutely not. You're my guest tonight and dinner's on me. I've actually booked a table in a little place I know well. It's not very sophisticated, but the food's really good.' His tone warmed. 'If I'd known you'd turn up looking like you've just stepped off a film set, I'd have gone for somewhere far posher.' Now she could hear him smiling, even if she couldn't see him in the dark. 'If you don't mind slumming it, it's only a ten-minute walk from here.'

'Anywhere you like is good with me, but I still think it should be my treat.'

But he wouldn't hear of it. He led her through the pedestrian zone where they mingled with the crowds. Even though it was nearing the end of September, the tourist trade was quite evidently still booming here in Verona and there was a friendly, happy air to the place and the people. She hoped it would extend to him. For her part, the combination of this beautiful, historic city and this handsome, generous man was everything she could have wished for. Above them, the swallows had been replaced by bats in the night sky and they wheeled and turned around the street lights. There was a smile on her face as they made their way through the gathering dusk towards his chosen restaurant.

The restaurant was charming. It was outside the main tourist area, located down a broad, tree-lined avenue on the other side of the river and, as he had said, it wasn't flashy. In fact, unlike so many establishments here in Verona, the name also had nothing to do with either Shakespeare or Romeo and Juliet. It was simply called Da Beppe. Beppe, the owner, was a broad-shouldered man with grizzly stubble covering his chin. He greeted them with a welcoming smile and a friendly handshake for her, and a bear hug for Michael. The two men obviously knew each other well and Suzie listened in awe as Michael switched into faultless Italian with more than a hint of the local accent. This was the first time she had ever heard him saying more than a few words in Italian. Of course, she reminded herself, with an Italian wife, spending most of his time over here, it was natural he should have learnt the language well. He introduced her simply as 'Suzie', although she couldn't miss the interrogative look she received from Beppe before he led them to their table. No doubt this restaurant was also somewhere that Michael used to come to with his wife.

Confirming what Professor Macgregor-Brown had said, there was a big wicker basket on the counter, full of gorgeous-looking porcini mushrooms. The scent of the forest filled the air; a mixture of dry leaves, moss and wild herbs. There was no doubt this was high season for mushrooms. Above the bar were bottles of liqueur, and one whole shelf was filled just with different types of grappa, ranging from transparent, indistinguishable from water, to some a rich golden colour and some with what looked like herbs in them. Suzie knew this powerful spirit of old and determined to do her best to avoid having more than a sip. While working over here in Italy back in her student days, she had tasted some good grappa and a lot of very bad grappa, but one thing was certain: there was no such thing as weak grappa.

As she sat down, she was interested to see a recurring theme in the pictures on the walls. Quite clearly, Beppe or somebody in his family was mad keen on windsurfing. There were photos of windsurfers racing, jumping, relaxing by the water and collecting medals and cups. To her considerable surprise, a black and white photo on the wall across the room from where they were sitting was unmistakably of three men on a podium receiving prizes, surrounded by a crowd of cheering people. The man in second position was none other than Beppe, but the surprise was the fact that the man on the top step of the podium, his wetsuit unzipped and hanging loose in front of him, exposing a muscular chest, was without a shadow of a doubt Michael. She suppressed a guilty little shiver of desire as she glanced back towards him and pointed across the room.

'A man of many talents.'

For a moment he looked puzzled and then, as his eyes alighted upon the photo, he looked positively uncomfortable. 'Oh God, I'd forgotten. I wouldn't want you to think I'd brought you here just to show off.'

'Not in the least. But I'm fascinated that you're a windsurfer.' She then went on to tell him about the sail she had had with James at the weekend, and it was his turn to look surprised, and impressed.

'You went out after the big storm on Sunday?' He saw her nod. 'Then you really must know what you're doing on a board. The conditions were pretty extreme.'

'Were you out on Sunday?'

He nodded. 'Beppe and I were out for almost three hours. As a result, I could hardly lift my arms on Monday. It was awesome.'

'You and he are big buddies, then?'

Michael smiled. 'He's my best friend.' But then his expression became more serious. 'He's been a real rock.' At that moment Beppe returned with the menus and Michael returned a smile to his face as he broke the news that Suzie shared their interest in windsurfing. Beppe beamed.

'He doesn't always win gold, you know. I've beaten him loads of times.'

'Three times, but who's counting?' Suzie was delighted to see Michael looking and sounding so animated. He glanced across at Suzie with an open, natural smile on his face and she found herself smiling back, happy for him. 'One of the things I love most about living here is the windsurfing on the lake.'

'And the other is my cooking.' Beppe clapped him on the shoulder and left them to the menus.

On Beppe's recommendation, they opted for a salad of raw porcini mushrooms and local salami as a starter, followed by steak. As they ate, they chatted – at first hesitantly, but both of them relaxed as the evening progressed, helped in no small part by their shared interest in windsurfing and a bottle of Bardolino. The food was excellent and the steak, when it arrived, turned out to be a single massive T-bone between the two of them that Beppe carved vertically into strips. This was served with fresh rocket and slivers of Parmesan and the result was exquisite. Then, as Suzie reached the point where she couldn't eat any more, Michael said something that took her mind right off food.

'Suzie.' There was something so compelling in his tone, she looked up immediately. 'I need to tell you about my wife.'

He hesitated, searching for words, and the desolate expression on his face said it all. As he cleared his throat apprehensively, she decided to help. Reaching across the table, she took his hand in hers. When she spoke, it was in hushed tones.

'Michael, I know.' As he looked a bit confused, she explained. 'You see, I was so keen to find out more about this famous artist I'd just met that I googled you, and I saw the dreadful news about your wife.' She gave his hand a squeeze. 'I'm so terribly sorry. I can't even begin to think how you must feel.'

He dropped his eyes, but didn't remove his hand from her grip. He set down his fork and sat there, immobile, for a couple of minutes, maybe more, before finally looking up.

'It's been awful, really awful.' He was in control, but only just, and her heart went out to him. 'We'd been married for almost five years and we were so very close, and then, in an instant, she was gone.'

'I'm so, so sorry, Michael. I don't know what to say.'

'You're very sweet. I really mean that.' He summoned a weak smile before dropping his eyes again until he was staring down at her hand holding his. 'This is the first time I've been out alone with a woman – apart from business

– since it happened. That's almost three years now. Like I say, Beppe and I are very close and I often come here to eat, but I always eat on my own or with a group of friends.'

She saw him take a big mouthful of wine before resuming. This time it was with another attempt at a smile at her. 'Suzie, the thing is, I like you a lot and I knew I'd enjoy your company, but this evening's just brought home to me all the more poignantly so much of what I've lost. The concert, this place, just sitting at a table for two and looking across at a beautiful woman; they all bring the memories pouring back.'

She could see his eyes were wet with tears, but he refused to let them run. She could feel her own eyes stinging now, and this time she knew it had nothing to do with her contact lenses.

'Like I say, Suzie, I really like you and I have done from the very first moment I saw you back in Venice with Prosecco dripping off the end of your nose, but it's no good. It's all still too raw. I don't know how you feel about me, but it's only fair that you should know where I stand.'

Suzie's experience tonight had, to a great extent, already prepared her for this, but the disappointment she felt was palpable all the same. Still, doing her best to hide her regret, she gave his hand another little squeeze.

'For what it's worth, I like you a lot as well, Michael. I think you're kind, you're generous, supportive and very talented. I had a longish relationship that ended a year ago, but not in anything like such tragic circumstances, and I haven't even thought about dating again. Like I said, I can only begin to imagine how grim life must have been for you over these last few years and I totally understand it's going to take time before you can even begin to think of moving on – if you ever can.' She mustered an encouraging smile. 'But I do know one thing, Michael Turner. I'd like to keep you as my friend. Good friends are so very hard to find.'

She read relief on his face. 'Thanks, Suzie. You can always count on me as a friend. I promise.'

Determined not to give in to her disappointment, she picked up her glass and held it out towards him. 'Let's drink to it.'

He took his glass, clinked it against hers and managed a little smile in return. 'To friendship.'

Chapter 14

Suzie got back to the hotel feeling dejected. It was all very well telling herself she was only going to be here in Italy for another couple of weeks, so there wouldn't have been time for anything much to develop apart from, maybe, a fleeting holiday romance, but she knew herself well enough to recognise there could so easily have been more to it than that. He was kind, he was generous and his involvement with the special school and its pupils had endeared him to her even more. He was caring, talented and bright and there was no possible doubt about the fact that she found him very physically attractive. Under other circumstances, she knew she could so easily have fallen for him, and she couldn't get away from the realisation that she had never felt quite like this about any man before – not even Rob. It was, therefore, with a heavy heart that she walked into her empty room and closed the door behind her. Without putting on the light, she opened the French windows and went out onto the terrace.

Although it was almost eleven o'clock, it was still warm, although as October approached there was no longer the sultry heat of summer in the air. Before long, autumn would bring cold winds down off the mountains and the leaves would fall from the trees. Where she would be, and what she would be doing by then, was still the great unknown. She leant on the balustrade and looked out over the flickering lights of this city she was growing to love and felt tears in her eyes. She told herself she was crying for poor Michael and his tragic loss, but, deep down, she knew she was crying for herself as well. Here she was, nudging thirty, and her life was still far from settled. She had no job, no home – apart from her parents' home in Devon – no direction, and she had no special someone at her side. In spite of the beauty of the view over the rooftops, she felt low.

Finally rousing herself, she went back inside and the first thing she did was remove her disposable contact lenses. She wasn't used to wearing them for any length of time and it was a relief to throw them in the bin and reach for her glasses once more. Her eyes were a bit red but, tonight, that wasn't necessarily the fault of the lenses.

However, she received a much-needed boost to her flagging spirits when she went back into her room and checked her emails. To her delight, there was one from Professor Macgregor-Brown and it instantly brought a smile back to her face. He informed her that he had read her doctoral thesis and had only the highest praise for it. He was very complimentary and he finished by asking if she might like to join him for Sunday lunch once again, in just two days' time. She didn't hesitate. Alex's father would be here until Sunday afternoon and no doubt the two would be together, so she would be a free agent. She replied immediately, thanking the professor for his kind words and accepting his invitation.

Next morning, she went down to breakfast not expecting to see Alex until later on and was surprised to find her already sitting in the elegant dining room. As she looked up, Suzie could see at once that all was not well.

'Hi, Suzie, how was your date?' Suzie could see she was trying to sound cheerful.

'It was a lovely concert and then we went to a super restaurant and had a great meal. I'll tell you all about it in due course, but first, tell me how it all went with your father.'

Alex shook her head. 'It didn't. I took your advice and waited all the way through the meal until he had relaxed and appeared to be enjoying himself. Finally, as we were walking back to the hotel, I brought up the subject of an art course…'

Her voice tailed off and Suzie had to prompt her. 'And…?'

'And he said what I thought he'd say.' Her voice was flat and heavy with disappointment.

'He said no?'

'He said no.' Alex hesitated. 'Well, to be precise, he said he'd think about it, but I could tell from his tone what his answer's going to be.'

Suzie tried to offer encouragement. 'So he hasn't actually said no yet?'

'No, but…'

'Give him time. You never know. And Michael gave me a message for you: if you do decide to do the course, it looks like the Academy will be happy to take you.' Determined to cheer Alex up, she changed the subject. 'What are your plans for today? Want to do something together?'

Alex glanced at her watch. 'Father's already finished his breakfast and he said he was going for a walk. He's got hold of a guide book and he's keen to see as much as possible. I'm meeting him at ten.'

'Do you want me to come along? I will, if you think you need a bit of moral support.'

Alex hesitated. 'Probably not this morning. I'd better stick by his side by myself. But he said he wants to take both of us out for dinner in some famous restaurant this evening, so why don't you do your own thing until then?' She gave Suzie a conspiratorial wink. 'Maybe meet up with Michael?'

'Not going to happen...'

Suzie went over to the buffet and helped herself to a bowl of fresh fruit salad and a croissant, ordered a pot of English Breakfast tea from the waitress and returned to the table. Once she had sat down, she gave Alex a full account of what had, or rather hadn't, happened with Michael the previous night and she read great sympathy on her friend's face.

'I'm so sorry, Suzie... for you both. It's an awful situation, but maybe it's for the best.'

'For the best?'

'Well, we're going home in two weeks' time so maybe it's better for nothing to happen, or you might end up back in the UK and heartbroken.' She gave Suzie a little smile. 'Better to be hurt a little now than hurt a lot then, don't you think?'

Suzie didn't know what to think. She had struggled to get off to sleep last night as her brain tried to digest what Michael had told her. Although his promise of friendship and the professor's encouraging email had cheered her somewhat, she hadn't been able to shake off a lasting feeling of regret for what might have been. When they had separated after dinner, they had made no plans to meet up again. When or whether he would contact her was something she just didn't know and, while the optimistic part of her brain was hoping he would, her more pragmatic side told her she had quite possibly seen the last of Michael Turner, Artist. She took a spoonful of the wonderful fruit salad and looked across at Alex with a shrug of the shoulders.

'Not a brilliant prospect for either of us, is it? What are you going to do back home if your father says you can't study here? Try applying to art schools in the UK?'

Alex shook her head sadly. 'Like I've told you before, that would just be a waste of time. He'd never countenance it. No, if I can't paint, I suppose I'll just go back to the estate and wait for an arranged marriage to James or somebody else to be signed, sealed and delivered.' Her expression suddenly changed from glum to worried. 'Oh God, it's Saturday. The wedding in California's today. James might be on his way back here tomorrow.'

'I quite like James, you know.'

'So do I, Suzie, but just not in that way.'

'So have you prepared what it is you're going to say to him?'

'Um, sort of.' Alex grimaced. 'But I'm not looking forward to it.'

Suzie left the hotel just before ten and spent the day winding in and out of the maze of little streets of the *centro storico*, constantly coming upon one historic marvel after another. The shopkeepers were just beginning to open up in readiness for a busy Saturday and tantalising smells wafted from shops selling gorgeous pastries as well as savoury focaccia and pizza. Having just had breakfast, she was able to fight temptation, but she had no doubt it would be easy to pile on the pounds here if she wanted. From the look of some of her fellow tourists, a good number of them already had.

After a while she turned left into Piazza delle Erbe. This really was the throbbing heart of the city and the market stalls were already set up, with tourists browsing the souvenirs on display. As she knew by now, when evening came, the market would disappear and the square would assume its other function as Verona's principal meeting place, home to bars and restaurants all along its length. She made a point of looking up as she walked along and realised that no two buildings ringing the square looked the same. Some were older, some younger, some tall, some not so tall, some red, some yellow and many ochre or red brick with dusty brown or green shutters at the windows. There were arches, turrets, crenellations and towers all around. Piazza delle Erbe claimed to be the most beautiful square in Italy and, although there was considerable competition for this honour, she felt sure it had to be right up there alongside other iconic squares like Piazza Navona in Rome or Piazza della Signoria in Florence.

After lunch, she climbed the never-ending steps to the vantage point on the hill above the town, Piazzale San Pietro. When she reached there she was glad to be able to rest on the wall and catch her breath as she looked out over Verona, the town centre framed by the meandering loop of the river. Directly below her was a Roman amphitheatre and beyond that the castle. A sea of red-tiled roofs, punctuated by spires, cupolas and towers stretched out before her, making for a spectacular panorama, and she took a number of photos and sent them home to her parents.

For a few moments she even wondered about sending one to Michael with a friendly message along the lines of 'perfect subject for one of your paintings' or some such, but then decided not to bother him. She would leave it to him to contact her if he so desired. And she really hoped he would. From the hill she made her way slowly back to the hotel by a circular route – via an amazing ice cream shop – and reached her room feeling quite weary. She decided against going out on the terrace in case Alex's father was there, so she lay down on her bed and very easily drifted off to sleep, not waking until almost six.

Showered and dressed, she tapped on Alex's door at seven and they went down the stairs together to meet Lord Tedburn. As they walked, Alex informed Suzie in a deadpan voice that her prediction had been correct – her father had said no.

'He refuses to believe that art can be a subject worth studying, and he refuses even more strongly to believe that I would be capable of applying myself seriously, even if he let me do the course.'

'Would you mind if I talked to him tonight?'

'Be my guest, but you'll be wasting your time.' Alex shook her head sadly as they rounded the last corner and walked down the broad flight of steps to the lobby. 'Once he's made up his mind about something, there's no dissuading him.'

Lord Tedburn – wearing a formal suit, collar and tie – was waiting for them and he greeted Suzie very cordially. A taxi took them to a magnificent Renaissance villa on the outskirts of the city, set in its own formal park, where they were ushered into a swanky restaurant with frescoes on the ceiling and glittering chandeliers made of Murano glass. Forewarned by Alex, Suzie had put on not only the expensive new dress, but even her only pair of heels.

Unlike the special school concert, in this restaurant she most certainly didn't feel overdressed. There was more bling on display than at a footballers' wives' get-together and she felt decidedly uncomfortable. She and Alex had been getting on so well, she had even started to forget that they were staying in an exorbitantly expensive hotel, but this place brought back to her the fact that she was an insignificant speck of very ordinary cosmic dust at the edges of the glittering Milky Way inhabited by the rich and famous.

The meal was predictably excellent, although Suzie secretly felt that Beppe's had been better – but maybe that had been the company. The atmosphere around the table tonight was far from relaxed, even after they had disposed of a bottle of champagne while waiting for their antipasti. In fact, Suzie and Alex only had a single glass each, while Lord Tedburn had made short work of finishing the rest. By the time a bottle of frighteningly expensive Barolo had gone the same way, Alex's father had mellowed considerably and Suzie took the opportunity presented when Alex went off to the Ladies to plead her friend's cause.

'Um, Lord Tedburn, I wonder if I might be allowed to speak in support of Alex's plan to study art. She's got real talent, you know.'

Lord Tedburn glanced up in some surprise and studied Suzie for a few seconds before responding. When he did, she was surprised to hear not irritation, but sorrow in his voice.

'I'm sure she has. Her mother always enjoyed painting – as a pastime.' He added emphasis to the last word of the sentence. 'But there are two reasons why I think it's a bad thing. First, an art course isn't going to lead anywhere. At best it would give her a hobby.' He shook his head slowly. 'She'll never make a name for herself. We both know that. She'll only end up disappointed, and I wouldn't want that. But more importantly, she's still wet behind the ears, you know. I can only imagine how she might end up if she got in with the wrong crowd – and from what I've seen of her choice of friends so far, she would.'

Suzie felt she had to object, but tried to make it as diplomatic as possible. 'I've got to know Alex pretty well over the past few weeks, Lord Tedburn, and I really don't think she's as immature as you say. In fact, she's always displayed a surprising degree of maturity.' Give or take a glass of Prosecco in the face, she thought to herself, but did not voice it. 'And I've seen the artwork she's capable of producing, and it's very, very good.'

He shook his head. 'Besides, it's time she settled down. She's not getting any younger. Her mother was already married to me by the time she was Alexandra's age. No, I'm sorry to disappoint her, but it's for the best.'

Suzie had another couple of tries before Alex came back, but it was no good. As his daughter had said, Lord Tedburn wasn't the sort of man to change his mind once it was made up. All the way through the rest of the meal, she reflected on what he had said and the unfairness of it. She was ever more convinced that, if she had been in Alex's position, she would have put her foot down and done the course anyway. But then, she didn't have the added complication of a promise made by a child to a dying mother. She sighed surreptitiously into her panna cotta.

Chapter 15

On Sunday morning, Suzie took the Bardolino bus and got off at the stop directly outside Professor Macgregor-Brown's house. All along the way they had been held up by tractors and trailers as the grape harvest got underway. This had made her think of Michael, whose house was amid the vineyards barely a mile further on. She hadn't heard any more from him and, although she had prepared herself for it, this lack of contact came as a disappointment all the same. As she walked up to the professor's gate, she glanced along the road and was unable to see any sign of activity in James's villa, so at least it looked as though Alex wouldn't have to face that next emotional hurdle immediately. After the stressful weekend with her father, this was probably just as well.

She rang the bell on the gatepost and waited for Paolina to come and let her in. When the gate opened, Suzie greeted her warmly and gently fought off Dogberry's effusive welcome.

The professor was waiting in the living room, sitting in an armchair, looking out over the lake. As he heard the door, he struggled to get out of his chair and Suzie could see how hard he was finding it. Today he was looking all of his eighty-four years. She hurried over and caught hold of his arm, helping him to his feet.

'I'm delighted to see you again, Prof... Mack. Thank you so much for the invitation.' She kissed him on both cheeks and saw him smile.

'The pleasure is all mine.' He stepped back and caught hold of the armchair for support as he studied her. 'You're looking quite charming. I'm sure you'd much rather be out with people your own age.'

Suzie assured him she was delighted to be there and they sat down to chat. After a few minutes of small talk – mainly about the *vendemmia*, which promised to produce exceptional wine this year – she hesitantly asked him about her thesis and was greatly relieved to see him smile.

'Excellent, scholarly, impeccably researched and authoritative. I'm immensely impressed.'

Suzie gave him a beaming smile in return. 'Coming from you, that's high praise indeed – although a lot of it came from your very pen.'

'I have only one slight hesitation.'

Suzie's smile slipped a notch or two as she straightened up and braced herself for the critique she felt sure was coming.

'You appear to be firmly positioned astride the top of the fence.'

'The fence?'

'Tell me, are you a Stratfordian, an Oxfordian, a Baconian or a believer in some other candidate for the true identity of the man we know as William Shakespeare, the greatest playwright of all time?'

'I thought it best to leave the reader to make up his or her own mind. I presented the facts as best I could, but it's up to the reader to decide.' She went on to explain that her supervisor had been an unshakable believer in the plays having been written by the 'traditional' Shakespeare, the man with minimal formal education who at eighteen was married in a shotgun wedding to Anne Hathaway in Stratford-upon-Avon. Her supervisor had dismissed Francis Bacon, Christopher Marlowe and Edward de Vere, the seventeenth Earl of Oxford, just as he had scoffed at the idea of anybody else being responsible. As she explained, she read comprehension and sympathy on the professor's face.

'I understand, my dear. Indeed, when I wrote my doctoral thesis many, many years ago, I found myself in a similar position – having to tailor my findings to the expectations of the man who would ultimately decide my fate.' He lowered his voice theatrically. 'But now, *entre nous*, where do you stand? Who was Shakespeare?'

Suzie took a deep breath. One of the things she had discovered early on in her Shakespearian studies was the depth of animosity that existed between the Stratfordians and the so-called Anti-Stratfordians. It was quite remarkable how aggressive those who believed in the Shakespeare of Stratford could be against those who doubted his status and vice versa. To an outsider, this academic spat might look trivial and insignificant, but to the initiated, it was capable of generating depths of feeling that wouldn't have been out of place in some of the Bard's grittier plays. From her reading, she knew Professor Macgregor-Brown to fall into the Anti-Stratfordian camp, which was just as well, because so did she. She, however, actually went further and it was with some trepidation that she told him the truth.

'Much as I would like to believe that a young and relatively inexperienced man from rural England could be behind these great works, I have to agree with you that it's very unlikely. My own feeling is that it had to be somebody with a broader cultural background and intimate knowledge of, and a deep love for, Italy. It could have been any one of the men you mention but, although I don't have all the facts to support my hypothesis, since writing my thesis I've been coming round to thinking that the works of Shakespeare might even have been written by a woman.'

This time she distinctly read surprise on the old man's face and she hastily outlined her case for Shakespeare having fallen in love with an Italian woman: the 'dark lady' of his sonnets. Quite possibly the mystery woman had been living in London and it had been there that he had gleaned all his knowledge of Italy from her, or maybe he had indeed visited the country during the so-called 'lost years' when he disappeared off the radar completely for a seven-year period. Or even, she added as a hesitant conclusion, maybe the 'dark lady' had been the real writer and William Shakespeare, the actor, simply the necessary male validation in an era when women writers were considered to be the work of the devil.

The conversation continued over an excellent lunch of artichoke salad followed by beef stew and polenta and she enjoyed herself immensely. From the expression on the professor's face, he found the conversation equally agreeable. At their feet, the Labrador snored happily, his head resting on Suzie's foot. No doubt the prospect of the leftovers of beef stew was far more intellectually alluring to him than the likelihood that *Romeo and Juliet* had been written by a woman.

The only negative thing that Sunday lunchtime was watching the professor struggling with his meal. His hands were shaking badly and he even spilled some wine down his arm as he lifted his glass. Suzie could see from the expression on his face just how frustrating this must have been for him and she almost rushed to his assistance when, at one point, he dropped a forkful of stew on the floor. Before she could jump up, however, there was a sudden movement at her feet and she glanced under the table just in time to see Dogberry dispose of the evidence. From then on, the dog relinquished her feet in favour of his master's – for obvious canine reasons.

After lunch they went back into the sitting room and Paolina brought them coffee. As she sipped from the little espresso cup, Suzie's eyes strayed around the room and landed on a painting, noticing it for the first time. It was instantly recognisable. She set down her cup and pointed.

'I saw the original study for that painting the other day.' Seeing the expression on his face, she went on to explain how she had met Michael and how he had offered to cast an eye over Alex's work. As she spoke, she saw an expression of deep sadness spread across the old man's face and his voice was sombre as he replied.

'You know about his wife? What a truly awful thing to happen. And they made such a lovely couple. I'd known them for a good while through various charities with which we were both involved and then he and Grazia rented my flat in Verona for a year or so while all the building work was going on up at their house. That painting was an immensely generous gift to me from a fine man. That awful accident was so, so tragic. I'm afraid I get out so little these days, ever since I had to give up driving, and I haven't seen him since the funeral. How's he holding up?'

Suzie answered honestly. 'It'll take time. He's fit and healthy but, underneath, you can see he's still hurting.'

Mack nodded slowly. 'Are you going to see him again? Do give him my best wishes.'

'I don't know if I will see him, but if I do, I'll be sure to pass on your message.'

Suzie left the house at just after four, knowing that her bus would be coming past in ten minutes or so. Before leaving, she gave Mack a battered copy of Shakespeare's sonnets that she had found in an antiquarian bookshop in Verona and she saw his eyes light up.

'Whether he was a man or a woman, Shakespeare knew a thing or two about love. You know something, Suzie, I think I enjoy his poetry every bit as much as I do his plays. Such a brilliant grasp of human nature and the power of love.' He gave her a little smile as he quoted from *Romeo and Juliet*:

"*Love is a smoke raised with the fume of sighs;*
Being purged, a fire sparkling in lovers' eyes;
Being vex'd a sea nourish'd with lovers' tears."

'Always remember, Suzie, there's nothing more impor-tant than love.'

She hugged him warmly and her eyes were burning as she went out of the gate onto the road. He was a lovely man and she felt so sorry that somebody who believed so strongly in the power of love had managed to end up on his own. Hopefully, she told herself, this was not the fate that awaited her. She had no time for further introspection as an unmistakable long white car whispered to a halt beside her and a familiar voice addressed her.

'Suzie, how great to see you again.'

She woke from her reverie. 'James, how good to see you too. And you, Roberto.' She found she really was pleased to see them. 'How was California, James?'

'It was fine.' James looked round intently. 'Is Alex with you?'

Suzie shook her head and explained about her lunch with the professor. 'And Alex has got her father with her today, so she's stayed in Verona. But he's leaving again this evening.'

She couldn't miss the disappointment on James's face, but he hastily regained his composure. 'Would you like to come in for tea? I've just got off the plane and I'm dying for a real cuppa.'

'I can't, I'm afraid, James. My bus back to Verona will be coming in ten minutes or so and I think it's the last one of the day.'

'That's all right, Roberto or I will give you a lift back.'

'No, I couldn't possibly...'

Roberto added his support. 'I've got to go into Verona in a little while to see my brother, so I can easily give you a lift. Really.'

'Well, if you're sure.'

Suzie followed the car in through the gates of James's villa and up the drive. It was pleasantly cool here under the trees and the scent of pine was in the air. She breathed deeply. Yes, James's father certainly knew a thing or two about choosing houses.

She and James sat outside on the terrace, sheltered from the sun by a parasol, and looked out over the lake. There was very little wind today and James expressed his surprise. 'The thing about Lake Garda is that the winds are normally so dependable. In the mornings we get the *Pelèr* and in the afternoons the *Ora*. *Pelèr* blows north to south and *Ora* from south to north. It's quite unusual to have little or no wind.' He gave her a grin. 'I was quite looking forward to getting out on the water after a day on an aircraft.'

'There's always tomorrow. Besides, you probably need a rest after your journey anyway. How long are you staying?'

'Not as long as I'd like, but long enough to see Alex. I've missed her, you know.'

Suzie nodded and smiled, but inside, she was torn. Should she say something to pour cold water on his expectations or was that best left to Alex? She had just made up her mind to say nothing when James pre-empted things.

'Has she said anything about me?'

'Yes, she often talks about you.' Suzie gritted her teeth and hoped he wouldn't press her for details. Alas, she was to be disappointed.

'Suzie, do you think she likes me? I still can't seem to get inside her head. I thought everything was going so well, but I'm not so sure now. You know her well by now. What do you think?'

'She definitely likes you, James. You can be absolutely certain about that.' She saw an expression of relief on his face and hoped she wasn't making things worse. Hastily, she did a bit of clarifying. 'From what she's told me, you're just about her oldest friend. Like you, she told me you two have played together since you were toddlers.' This, she felt sure, was the truth and not likely to give him the wrong idea. She saw him nod.

'We certainly go a long way back. I used to think of her as my sort-of cousin, or even my sister.'

Suzie was quick to capitalise on his choice of words. 'That's almost exactly what she said to me.' She waited for him to comment, but he remained silent so she decided to add a hint of what was bothering Alex. 'If anything, she maybe likes you too much.'

This definitely got his full attention. 'How can you like somebody too much? Surely that's a good thing, isn't it?'

Suzie decided to bow out before things got too complicated. This was, after all, Alex's fight, not hers. 'Of course it is. You need to sit down and talk to her, I'm sure.'

Fortunately, at that moment, Roberto appeared at the French windows and held up two fingers. '*Due minuti*, OK?'

Suzie gave him a smile and a nod and turned to James, glad to have been thrown a lifeline out of their conversation about Alex. 'Thank you for the tea. I don't want to take up any more of your time. I bet you're dying for a shower and a lie-down.'

James gave a weary nod of the head and then he made her a very generous offer.

'Suzie, are you staying long in Verona? I've got to go back home later this week, but if you want to borrow any of my windsurfing kit, just call Roberto and he'll give you free run of the boatshed. Use whatever you like, whenever you like.'

Suzie beamed at him. 'I have no idea how long we'll be here, but that's really kind of you. I'll see what Alex says. We were planning on going on to Mantua and Padua, but there's an art course she's thinking of doing here in Verona, so that might change things. But, whatever happens, thanks so much, James.'

Outside, Suzie was greatly relieved to see that Roberto was driving an ordinary-looking Fiat, not the Rolls-Royce. Before getting into the passenger seat she gave James a hug and two kisses. 'Thanks again. And James, talk to Alex.'

'I will.' Then, just as Roberto started the engine, James ducked his head back down to the open window. 'By the way, I almost forgot. My cousin sends his love.' His face split into a broad grin. 'Tommy would've murdered me if I'd forgotten to tell you. I think you've made a conquest there, Suzie.'

Her cheeks were still glowing long after the villa had receded into the distance behind them.

Chapter 16

Back at the hotel, she found Alex sitting on the terrace, alone.

'Your dad gone?'

She went over and took a seat alongside Alex. There were clouds on the horizon tonight, but the air was still warm, although October would start the very next day.

'Half an hour ago.'

'And still no change of heart? He's still dead set against your doing the Academy course?'

Alex nodded. 'The man's not for changing.' She took off her sunglasses and rubbed them on the hem of her skirt to clean them. As she did so, Suzie couldn't miss the moisture in the corners of her eyes. She reached over and caught hold of Alex's arm.

'There's something else you need to know. I've just seen James.'

Alex gave a long sigh. 'So he's back. Where did you see him?'

Suzie told her about their chance meeting and the ensuing conversation. Alex gave her a grateful look.

'Thanks for doing the groundwork, but I'll have to give it to him straight tomorrow. Do you think he's going to call tonight?'

'He's just stepped off a plane and he was looking pretty bushed, but I'd be surprised if he didn't call. The first thing he asked me was where you were.'

Alex nodded slowly. 'Ah well, I knew it was coming.' She sighed softly. 'Don't get me wrong – part of me's really happy he's come back. He's my oldest friend and it'll be good to see him again. The thing is, as he *is* such a close friend, I don't want to hurt him, and I'm not sure I know how to do that.'

At that moment, Alex's phone started to ring. She picked it up, checked the caller ID and mouthed the words, *It's him.*

'Hi, James. Welcome back. How was the wedding?'

Suzie left her to it and went back into her room. As usual she checked her emails, but there was nothing hopeful on the employment front. There was, however, a text for her which cheered her up immediately.

> Hi Suzie. The forecast for tomorrow is for a good wind, force 5/6. Would you like to come windsurfing with me in the afternoon? I can lend you the kit. I've even got a wetsuit that should fit you. Michael

Suzie digested his message and the single phrase that stood out above all the others was *a wetsuit that should fit.* No prizes for guessing who had been the previous occupant of that wetsuit. One thing she knew without a shadow of a doubt was that she was not under any circumstances getting into any item of clothing that had once belonged to his dead wife. She was just reflecting upon what to do when Alex tapped on the window and came in.

'James is coming to pick me up in time for lunch tomorrow. He asked whether you'd like to come as well.'

'I don't want to get in the way, Alex. Probably best if you go by yourself, although...' A thought suddenly occurred to her. 'Although maybe I will.' She went on to show Alex the text from Michael and then to repeat James's offer of windsurfing kit. 'Why don't I come along for a bite of lunch and then go off with Michael in the afternoon, leaving you two to talk things over? How would that be?'

—

By the time James arrived to pick them up next day, the wind had also picked up. The sun was still shining, but clouds regularly blocked it out and it was clear that a change in the weather was on its way. As he drove them back to the villa, Suzie explained that she was going windsurfing with a friend that afternoon and felt she should ask if he wanted to come along, although she really wanted him to sit down and talk to Alex. His response reassured her.

'No, you go without me, Suzie. Alex and I have got a lot of catching up to do.'

Lunch was excellent and Suzie enjoyed the fact that there were just the three of them, rather than the big, noisy group from before. By the look of it, James also appreciated being able to dedicate himself to Alex. As Suzie went off to the boathouse after lunch, she exchanged glances with Alex and gave her a little wink. Hopefully the conversation to come with James would not be too hard on either of them.

She had arranged to meet Michael at the jetty at half past two and she found him already there when she emerged in her wetsuit, carrying her board. As she caught sight of him she was conscious of her heart giving a little leap that she was helpless to control.

'Suzie, hi.'

He jumped up and padded across the old timbers towards her in his bare feet. He looked as handsome and appealing as ever – and a wetsuit could be very unforgiving. He looked athletic, fit and immensely desirable. As his eyes landed on her, she felt the colour rush inexorably to her cheeks, provoking the familiar sense of annoyance with herself that only served to make her blush all the more. He stretched out his arms towards her and she only just realised at the last moment that he was reaching for the board in her arms and managed to avoid making a faux pas by throwing herself at him. She handed it to him and hurried back into the boatshed for the rig. As she came out, a strong gust caught and filled the sail, almost ripping it out of her hands, and she knew it was going to be another great day out on the water.

They barely exchanged a few words as they got ready, but what he did say was interesting and potentially cheering.

'It's great to see you again, Suzie. I've been thinking about you so much since the other night. I'm sorry I managed to spoil what started out as such a great evening.'

'You didn't spoil anything. I'm glad you felt like sharing your feelings. Like I said before, I can only begin to imagine how you must have felt and how you must still be feeling.' She gave him a little smile. 'Just remember that I'm here for you if you need me.'

He managed to smile back at her. 'Thanks, Suzie, that means a lot to me.'

Determined not to dwell any more on this sad subject, she waded into the water and glanced across at him as she checked her harness and picked up the sail, making sure to keep it feathered away from the full force of the wind.

'You lead. I'll follow.'

'Ladies first. You go ahead. I know my place.'

Suzie chuckled in response. 'Anywhere special you want to go?'

He shook his head. 'Just try to keep upwind as much as possible. With a blow like this we'll end up at the head of the lake otherwise.'

As Riva del Garda at the northernmost tip of the lake was about fifty kilometres away, she knew he was joking, but she resolved to do as instructed. With a smile at him, she lifted the sail and, as it filled, she stepped on and set off across the lake like an arrow. The board slalomed through the water as she snaked up and down the faces of the waves towards the middle of the lake. It was exhilarating, it was challenging and she couldn't have been happier. At one point a rogue wave some four or five feet high appeared before her and she deliberately steered up the face of it and flew through the air for quite a distance before landing again and carrying on. As she did so, she heard a wild scream of joy and realised with some surprise it was coming from her. Seconds later, she saw movement alongside her as Michael came past, turning his head towards her as he did so and mouthing what looked like a silent *Wow!*

They were out for about an hour and a half and by that time she was exhausted. In fact, after a spectacular fall a few hundred metres from the shore, she took the opportunity to lie in the water, arms draped across the board, for a rest. Within a minute or two, Michael arrived with a flourish and flopped backwards off his board into the water. He let the wind blow his board up to hers and she felt the warmth of his shoulder against her. Even through two layers of neoprene, it felt good.

'Wow, Suzie, you were on fire out there!'

She turned towards him, wiping the hair from her face, and beamed. 'I haven't had so much fun for ages. Last time I came out was great, but it was so extreme, it was a constant fight against the elements. Today it's tough, but it's manageable. Thanks for getting me out.'

'Thanks for coming with me. Now all I've got to do is to break the news to Beppe that I've found a new partner.'

There was a moment's silence, punctuated only by the splash of the water and the whistling of the wind through the sails, before he realised what he had said.

'Windsurfing partner, I mean.'

He looked as embarrassed as Suzie felt, but she was determined not to let emotion get the better of her.

'Well, any time you want company out here on the lake, just say the word.' She lay there for a few seconds before carrying on, taking courage from the fact that her cheeks had already been burning with the exertion before his remark so her blushes maybe hadn't shown. 'Although I don't know how much longer we're going to be in Verona.'

'I was wondering about that. The director of the Academy called me this morning with a message for Alex. They've got what he called a three-day taster course starting tomorrow if she's interested.'

'I bet she would be. The problem is that her dad's said no.'

Michael didn't really need to reply. His expression said it all. 'Well, he can't stop her doing a three-day course, surely. Tell her anyway, will you?'

'Definitely.' Suzie glanced back towards the shore. Without her glasses, it was a bit hazy, but she thought she recognised the figure watching from the shore. 'Or you can tell her yourself. That looks like her on the jetty. Shall we head back? I'm knackered.'

It took barely two or three minutes to get back to James's jetty and as she neared the shore she saw that Alex was indeed standing there, alone. That didn't look like a good sign. She sailed right up to the wooden pontoon and stepped off her board, dropping the sail into the water and reaching up to stretch her aching shoulders.

'Hi, Suzie. I was getting worried for a moment when I saw the two of you lying in the water. Everything okay?' Alex sounded normal, but Suzie knew her well enough by now to see that all was not well. She glanced over her shoulder and saw Michael still fifty yards off, approaching fast. Turning back towards Alex, she lowered her voice.

'I'm fine, thanks, just tired. But how about you? How did it go with James?'

Alex dropped her eyes. 'I bottled out.'

'You didn't tell him?'

'Sort of. I told him it felt weird because we're such old friends but then, at the end, I just said I thought I needed more time.'

'So he still thinks he's in with a chance?'

Alex nodded. 'Yes.' She looked up. 'Suzie, am I a terrible person? Shouldn't I have told him the truth and been done with it?'

Out of the corner or her eye, Suzie saw Michael sweep up to the jetty and swing the board round in a full circle on its tail before jumping lightly off into the waist-deep water. Hastily, she sought to offer reassurance to Alex.

'Of course you're not a bad person. You just wanted to let him down gently. That's a sign of real friendship.'

Pulling herself wearily onto the jetty, she went over to Michael who was fiddling with his sail in the shallows.

'Come and tell Alex about that three-day course. I think she might need a bit of cheering up.' She reached out her hands to help him up onto the jetty, but he managed it by himself and she felt a little twinge of regret.

As Michael and Alex chatted, Suzie lifted her board onto the woodwork, removed the rig and carried it back to the boathouse. By the time she returned, James had joined them, bearing a jug of fresh lemonade and four glasses. As far as Suzie could tell, he was looking his normal happy self in spite of the conversation with Alex. She introduced him to Michael and the two men sat down together. Inevitably, they started talking about windsurfing, so Suzie deliberately took a seat beside Alex and changed the subject.

'Did Michael tell you about the three-day course at the Academy?'

Alex nodded enthusiastically. 'Absolutely, and I'm going to do it. It runs from tomorrow until Thursday night and then there's a free painting day on Friday. Are you happy to stay in Verona for the rest of this week? We were going to go on to Mantua or Padua, weren't we?'

'I'm very happy to do whatever you want and I can't imagine anywhere nicer than Verona. I can always take the train down to Mantua one day if I get bored – not that I think that's going to happen. After all, it's only half an hour away.'

Alex glanced across to where the two men were still deep in conversation and lowered her voice. 'And what about you and Michael? How have you and he been getting on today?'

Suzie answered in guarded tones. 'I've had a great afternoon windsurfing with a friend. What more could a girl ask for?'

'What, indeed?'

Suzie didn't meet Alex's eye.

Chapter 17

The week passed very pleasantly, even though the weather was no longer perfect. James went back to the UK, still hopeful that things would work out between him and Alex, while she spent the days at her art course and returned to the hotel each evening positively glowing with enthusiasm. On Thursday Suzie did indeed take the train to the delightful little city of Mantua and spent the day ducking in and out of the vaulted medieval walkways, dodging the showers as she walked around the ancient *centro storico*. The setting, surrounded on three sides by the broad expanse of lakes carved by the river, could have come straight out of a Shakespeare play, and she couldn't forget that Romeo himself had been exiled here. The ducal palace and its surroundings were delightful and positively exuding history, from the cobbled streets to the trademark splayed crenellations, and Suzie would have had a wonderful day except for two things.

None of her attempts to find work had so far amounted to anything and it now seemed definite that her return to England in just over a week would mean a return to unemployment. And, if that wasn't bad enough, there was also the fact that Michael hadn't been back in touch since their afternoon on the lake on Monday. He had spent half an hour talking to James that day before coming to say goodbye to her. He looked a bit uncomfortable when she kissed him on the cheeks, but his parting words were heartening.

'I haven't had an afternoon like that for a long, long time, Suzie. That was lovely, thank you.'

Since he had freely acknowledged that the sail he had had with Beppe the previous week after the big storm had been awesome, she took this to mean that he was somehow indicating that her presence had meant something to him, not just the windsurfing conditions. She had seen him hesitate, searching for words, but then he just gave her a little smile and waded into the water with his board. As she watched him sail off to where he had left his car she had felt that same lasting sense of regret she had been feeling ever since the evening of the concert, maybe just tempered by the glimmer of hope his comment had aroused in her. Still, she told herself, as she ate a sandwich under a damp parasol in Mantua's Piazza Sordello, in just over a week there would be a thousand miles between them.

And that would be that.

That evening, she and Alex met up for dinner and the mood was sober in spite of the bottle of wine they split between them. Alex had loved every moment of the short course and was looking forward to the day of free painting tomorrow. Suzie could see how much she had enjoyed herself at the Academy and how badly it hurt that she wouldn't be able to stay on and do the full diploma course. As the meal progressed, she made another attempt to get Alex to see sense.

'That promise you made to your mum, I've been thinking about it. I'm sure she can only have meant while you were a little girl. Any mother would want her child to be happy, wouldn't she? I'm sure you'd be doing the right thing if you decided to tell your dad to stuff it and then stayed on here.'

Alex looked across the table with a rueful smile on her face. 'And what would I live on? What would I pay for the course with? Where would I live, for that matter? There's no way I could continue to stay here in this hotel, or any hotel.'

'Haven't you got any savings?' Suzie was amazed.

'There's less than a thousand pounds in my bank account. My allowance comes in every month and I spend it. It's as simple as that. That's what my father expects of me, so I do it. This holiday's all being charged to the family credit card and my father told me on Sunday that he intends to put a stop on it if ever I disobey him.'

'Bugger.' Suzie took a mouthful of Prosecco and shook her head sadly. She couldn't help letting the thought of Lord Capulet, Juliet's father, come to mind. In his own way, Lord Tedburn was being almost as radical as the man who had ruined his daughter's life, and unwittingly short-ened it, when he told her to obey him or she could *hang, beg, starve, die in the streets*. Alex's father wasn't going that far, but he was still behaving like a tyrant. She reached over and squeezed Alex's hand, doing her best to be encour-aging. 'It'll sort itself out.'

Alex didn't respond, but her expression showed how little she thought that likely to happen.

Things began to look a bit more hopeful, at least for Suzie, when she got back to her room and checked her emails. Along with a rejection by a university for a lecturing position, she found one that sounded really rather intriguing. It was from Professor Macgregor-Brown and it contained another invitation to his house – this time to afternoon tea on Saturday. In the email he included these tantalising lines:

> I would like to talk to you about a little project I've been working on for some years now. Having met you, I think this might be the perfect moment to embark upon it.

What, Suzie wondered to herself, could this mean? And why was it significant that he had met her? Did he maybe want to talk about another book about his beloved Shakespeare, or was there likely to be more to it than that? Was he even looking for her collaboration, maybe? Being linked, even in a minor way, to such an iconic name in the world of English literature would be an amazing step up for her and would, without question, increase her chances of finding a position at a UK university. Shaking off her gloom, she went to bed in a more optimistic mood.

After spending the whole of Friday wandering around Verona looking – with mixed results – for the sycamore trees mentioned in Act One, Scene One of *Romeo and Juliet*, she returned to the hotel to find Alex on her knees on the terrace, doing her best to sweep up broken pieces of fine china with her bare hands. Worryingly, she was red in the face and there were fresh tears on her cheeks. Suzie went straight across to her.

'Dropped a cup? Never mind, room service will take care of clearing up the bits.'

Still on her knees, Alex looked up and the anguish on her face was clear to see. 'Not dropped, smashed.' She wiped the back of her hand across her eyes. 'It was a stupid thing to do, but I was so furious, I threw the bloody thing across the terrace.'

Suzie crouched down and helped her pick up the last pieces of china and then they perched side by side on the slightly damp wicker sofa. The sky was overcast and although it was barely six o'clock, it was already quite dark. The sky matched Alex's mood.

'It's just so bloody unfair!' She retrieved a tissue from her jeans pocket and wiped her eyes angrily. 'I've really loved these last few days at the Academy, and Professor Milanese tells me he thinks I've got real talent. He insists I should carry on to the diploma course. I've just phoned my father to make one last plea and all that achieved was to make me break a perfectly good cup and saucer.'

Suzie laid her hand over Alex's. 'Still no?'

'Not only a firm no, but strict instructions to be on the flight back to England next Saturday or else he'll put a stop on my card *and* my allowance, and I'll be broke.' She suppressed a frustrated sob. 'It's so unfair.'

Suzie gave her a reassuring pat on the arm as she reflected on the best course of action. She had no doubt at all what she would do if she were in this position – but then she wouldn't be breaking a promise made to a dying woman or turning her back on untold wealth. Even so, she told herself, Alex was right. Her father – for whatever reason – was behaving in a heartless way and was demonstrating a total lack of consideration for his daughter's feelings, hopes and aspirations. However, she kept this firmly to herself for now. This wasn't her decision to make. It had to come from Alex. She offered a bit of gentle encouragement.

'Maybe if you try talking to him again face-to-face when we get back to England next weekend. You never know, if he sees you in this sort of state it might finally get through to him how strongly you feel.'

'The course starts the Monday after. I suppose I could miss a few days...' Alex's voice tailed off hopelessly. 'But anyway, there's no point. He won't let me do it. Like I've told you before – once he's made his mind up about something, that's that.'

Suzie was determined to do her best to shake Alex out of her depression. 'I could do with a drink. Come on. I'm buying. Let's go to one of the bars in Piazza delle Erbe.'

It took a bit of doing but, eventually, she managed to convince Alex to dry her eyes and follow her out into the twilight. By now the market stalls had miraculously disappeared and it was possible to see all the way down to the far end of the square over the heads of the crowds, whose voices echoed around the piazza. A group of Latin American musicians supplied a charming soundtrack of panpipes and drums, lights had come on all round the sides and the mood was romantic – but neither of them was feeling in a romantic mood tonight. Yesterday's rain had dried up and it was quite a warm evening so they sat under an awning and Suzie did something she had never believed she would ever do again. When the waiter appeared, she ordered two shots of grappa. Then, to be on the safe side, she also ordered two glasses of mineral water. After Alex – at Suzie's prompting – had downed her glass of the powerful spirit and was gasping for breath, Suzie resumed their conversation.

'So, apart from stopping your credit card and allowance, what else do you think your father might do if you aren't on that plane next Saturday?'

'He'd be furious, so who knows?'

'But he wouldn't go all Shakespearian on you, would he?' The thought of Lord Capulet was still at the forefront of her mind. 'He wouldn't disown you or cut you out of your inheritance or banish you or anything of that sort, surely?'

Alex did her best to smile at the thought, but Suzie could see it was a struggle – grappa or no grappa. 'I have no idea. I'm sure he wouldn't go so far as to disown me. Apart from anything else, that would be likely to cause a scandal and he's far too proud of the family reputation for that. But financially, I suppose he could do anything; maybe even cut me out of the will and leave the lot to Rafe.'

'But you and your brother are close, aren't you? He'd sort that out if it ever came to it, surely?'

Alex took a mouthful of water and nodded uncertainly. 'In theory, yes, but money does funny things to people. I wouldn't like to count on it. Besides, hopefully my father isn't going to die any time soon and, in the meantime, I'd be on the breadline.'

Suzie reflected to herself that 'the breadline' to somebody with Alex's background would probably be not having enough money for First Class and having to slum it in Business Class, but she didn't comment. Instead, she started doing some hasty mental arithmetic. She knew from her own personal experience how little it was actually possible to live on. If only Alex could find cheap accommodation and maybe even a part-time job. The image of James's villa with all its empty bedrooms came to mind and she realised that he would no doubt leap to her assistance if she asked for it. But, from what she had said, that wasn't likely to happen. Still, she risked floating the idea.

'Have you considered asking James if you could stay at his villa? There's a pretty good bus service to and from Verona. It would mean an hour's commute each way, but that's not the end of the world, is it?'

Alex looked up. 'And the quid pro quo? He's a nice guy, but it's only human nature to want something in return for a favour.' She shook her head. 'I couldn't do it, Suzie. It's too weird.'

'I still think he'll understand if you talk to him straight about the way you feel. You *are* the best of friends, after all, and have been for ages. I'm sure he'd let you stay there if you ask – with no strings.'

Alex shook her head. 'There's another reason it's a non-starter. If he offers me accommodation, it would be helping me to stay here, which is going against the express wishes of my father. I feel sure my father would then speak to James's father – and don't forget, the villa belongs to him – and then, hey presto, I'm kicked out and James is in the shit as well. It's hopeless.'

'Well, then the answer is to find somewhere dirt cheap here, even if it means getting a part-time job to pay for it.'

'A job? I hardly speak a word of Italian. What sort of job could I get? Not even washing dishes, I expect. And, remember, Italy's in all sorts of financial trouble these days. I bet it's almost impossible to find anything.'

'What about asking at the Academy? Couldn't they help with accommodation?'

189

'I asked this afternoon. They gave me a list of places, but even the cheapest of rooms would be more than I can afford and I would soon be broke.' She pulled out a tissue, wiped her eyes and blew her nose before catching Suzie's eye and shaking her head. 'It's no good. He's won.'

Suzie's heart went out to her friend and, as it did so, she realised that Alex really had morphed into a very close friend. And friends need to help friends. She had been mulling the problem over for some days now and had gradually been moving towards a decision. Now, she told herself, it was time to go with it.

'No, he hasn't won. Listen, he deposited four thousand pounds into my bank account for this month in Italy with you and I've hardly spent any of it. If we're careful, that should give us enough to put down a deposit on a little flat out in the suburbs and survive at least until Christmas. By that time, you'll know if you want to keep going at the Academy and maybe we might both be able to find jobs. More to the point, if your father sees you getting stuck in and proving you can work hard and stay out of trouble, he might change his tune. I speak reasonable Italian. I'm sure I should be able to find something in hospitality or tourism that would generate enough money to keep us going.'

Alex's eyes looked as if they were about to pop out of their sockets. 'You would do that for me? Suzie, that's crazy. What about your career? You're worth so much more than some part-time job. I couldn't possibly ask you to do something like that for me.'

'I'd be doing it for myself as well. I like Italy. I love Verona. I have nothing to go back to in the UK – at least for now – so why not stay here and see what happens?'

She held up her hand. 'And before you say it, this isn't about Michael. I know what the situation is with him and I accept that nothing's going to happen there – at least not for a long, long time. It's a pity, but that's the way it is. No, this is about trying something new and giving a friend a helping hand.'

Alex threw herself into Suzie's arms and dissolved into tears. As heads turned towards them, Suzie's cheeks inevitably started to burn, but she let Alex sob herself to a standstill all the same. When Alex finally raised her head from Suzie's shoulder, she was still crying, but a smile had formed on her face as well.

'I don't know what to say, Suzie. Nobody's ever offered to do something like this for me before, but I can't accept. It's just too much to ask of any friend.'

'You can and you must accept. And, apart from anything else, I feel I owe it to you.'

'You owe me?'

'Yes, for misjudging you. I just accepted your father's verdict on you from the start, without considering how things were from your point of view. That was a big mistake and I'm very sorry. Now that I've got to know you, I realise he's got it all wrong and if I can help to prove that to him, so much the better.' She gave Alex's damp cheek a little pat. 'Like I say, I'm happy to stay here and I know we're doing the right thing for you… and maybe for me too, who knows?' She pulled a handful of paper napkins out of the dispenser on the table and passed them across. 'Here, dry your eyes, drink up and let's go and eat.'

'Suzie, I can't thank you enough.'

'Don't bother. It's fine, but there's one stipulation. Promise me you'll work your socks off and try to become the best bloody painter in the world.'

'Better than your Michael?' Alex managed a little grin.

'He's not my Michael.'

'Says who?'

'Says Michael.'

Chapter 18

Next morning at breakfast, Alex showed Suzie the email she intended to send to her father outlining her plans and informing him that she was fully prepared for whatever retaliatory measures he might decide to adopt. The email made it clear that Alex knew she would have to do this without his money or his help, but she had decided to put her future career ahead of his wishes. She even included the line *I'm sure this is what Mother would have wanted if she had still been alive*. Suzie was also impressed that Alex insisted upon getting her to go through it line by line with her, adding and subtracting as she saw fit. There was no doubt about it. This relationship, which had started on such rocky foundations, had blossomed into real friendship and Suzie had no doubts about the wisdom of what the two of them were setting out to do. Alex needed to realise her potential, and friends need to help friends.

Alex then went on to prove that she wasn't as wet behind the ears as her father might think.

'While the credit card's still functioning, I've already paid for the full academic year online this morning so Father won't be able to stop that. And I'm not going to send him the email until Monday, so if there's anything you want, just say the word and we'll get it for you this weekend.'

Suzie grinned at her. 'I've got all I need, thanks.' In fact, now that she had taken the decision to stay on in Verona there was one thing she did intend to buy, but it was only fair for her to use her own money. This was a wetsuit. She would be happy to keep using borrowed windsurfing kit, either from James or from Michael – if he ever contacted her again, and it had been five days now – but, with winter on the way, she knew she would need a good warm suit if she wanted to be able to carry on sailing.

It then transpired that Alex had also got clothes on her mind – albeit of a very different kind.

'And I've been thinking, Suzie, I've got a load of really quite expensive designer clothes and shoes with me. I've found a website specialising in that sort of thing, so I'll get started on putting some of the stuff up for sale and that should help to pay the bills.'

Now Suzie was even more impressed. She had rarely seen Alex in anything but designer clothes and this decision to slum it couldn't have been easy. She smiled back. 'So, just like your father feared, now that you're an art student, you'll be going bohemian?'

'Don't worry.' Alex was grinning. 'I'll still keep washing regularly and changing my underwear. But the others on the taster course with me were just dressed in T-shirts and shorts or jeans, so I won't need the pricey stuff any more. Besides, I want to try to fit in.'

Suzie nodded approvingly and went on to show her the email she had received from Professor Macgregor-Brown. Alex sounded as intrigued as she was.

'I wonder what it is. I do hope it's something exciting.'

Professor Macgregor-Brown's news was definitely all of that and more. When Suzie got to the villa, sat on the sofa and finally dissuaded the happy dog from climbing onto her lap, she listened in fascination to what the old man had to say. The first thing he said was unexpected.

'I'm not sure if I ever told you, Suzie, but my wife was from Verona.'

'Your wife? I must admit I hadn't realised you were married.'

He nodded slowly. 'I met her at a conference in Verona and it was love at first sight.' He managed a little smile. 'Just like Romeo and Juliet. The marriage lasted forty-five years and they were the very best years of my life. When she died ten years ago, I thought my life had also ended. I felt lost, abandoned and alone.'

Even after all these years, there was still a catch in his voice and Suzie had to control the urge to go over and hug him.

'I'm so sorry. Do you still miss her?'

The answer was immediate. 'Every day of my life, Suzie. Every single day.' He paused for a few seconds and then she saw him take a deep breath. 'Anyway, life goes on and before long it'll be my turn next. For the past few years I've been thinking about what my legacy might be. Yes, I've written a few books, achieved a certain degree of academic success, but I want to go further.'

Suzie didn't interrupt, wondering what was coming next. After a few moments of reflection, he continued.

'Ines – that was her name – came from a very wealthy family and I inherited this villa and a fine house in Verona from her. When she passed away, I ended up with the houses and far more money in the bank than I'll ever need… although I'd happily relinquish it all just to have her back.'

He reached out with his foot and absently scratched Dogberry's backside and Suzie heard the dog grunt with pleasure. His heavy black head, as usual, was resting on her feet and she felt sure she caught a smile on the dog's face as he glanced up at her. She leant forward and scratched his ears and heard his tail thud lazily on the floor as she gently prompted the professor, who looked miles away.

'So what sort of legacy are you thinking of?'

'We never had children and I've no close family left so, rather than see it all go to some second or third cousin I've never even met, I'd like to create something worthwhile. I've been toying with the idea of establishing a bursary and a research position at Oxford – they'd jump at it, I'm sure – but there's always the risk of university politics coming into play. I'd like the scholars who come after me to be able to make their own decisions, to decide what and whom to study, without any pressure from above. So I've gradually been changing my mind, and your arrival here and our fascinating chats about Shakespeare have convinced me that an alternative is needed.' He looked across at her and nodded. 'And now I think I've come up with the solution.'

The animation on his face was wonderful to see and Suzie leant forward, listening attentively as he laid out his plans.

'Over the centuries, Italy has inspired so many English-speaking poets, writers and playwrights. And I'm not just talking about Shakespeare.' He smiled. 'Whoever he *or she* might have been. It's clear that Chaucer was definitely influenced by Boccaccio's *Decameron* and let's not forget the great romantic poets like Shelley and Byron as well as twentieth-century writers like E.M. Forster, Ernest Hemingway and Robert Graves. What I'd like to do is to establish a research centre here in Italy to help academics from all over the world who are studying the influence of Italy on anglophone literature.'

'When you say "here in Italy", are you talking about Verona?' Suzie could hear the excitement in her own voice.

'Precisely. Verona has a long and illustrious pedigree as a centre of learning. Have you been to visit the old library yet, the *Biblioteca Capitolare*? It's reputed to be the oldest library in the world and it's almost certain that such giants as Dante and Petrarch used it. Now, as it happens I'm good friends with the current director of the library and we've been talking.' He smiled again. 'He's very enthusiastic about my idea and, with his support, I think it really could become something worthwhile.'

Suzie felt her heart racing in her chest. 'And do you think I might be able to help with your project?'

He shook his head and a wave of disappointment swept over her, but only for a second or two. 'I don't want you to *help*, Suzie, I want you to run it.'

'You want me to run it…?' Her voice tailed off help-lessly and she saw his smile broaden.

'I'm far too old now for being anything but a gnarled old figurehead, while it seems to me that you're perfect for the job. Your academic track record is ideal, you speak both languages and, above all, you're the sort of person who gets on well with people, and believe me, that will be essential. You'll need all your people skills to get the local authorities on our side, and considerable tact to get the academic world in Britain and beyond to take us seriously, but I'm convinced that if anybody can do it, you can.' His expression was suddenly more serious. 'So, tell me, are you interested?'

'Am I...?' Suzie was stumped for words for a moment. Hastily collecting herself, she felt she had to make a few things clear first. 'Prof... Mack, I'm so amazingly grateful and honoured that you should even begin to consider me for something of this magnitude and I'd love to do it, but are you certain I'm the right person for the job? I'm sure you know me well enough by now to have worked out that I'm not exactly an outgoing extrovert and my threshold of embarrassment's very low. As your representative, I wouldn't want to let you down.'

'You'd never let me down, Suzie, I'm sure.' He was smiling now. 'And don't worry about the self-confidence thing. It'll come. What I intend to do is to use the house in Verona, assuming we can get planning permission from the council. It should lend itself well to transformation into the sort of facility I have in mind and as the research centre grows in size and influence we can start looking for something bigger in due course. For now, there's ample room on the ground and first floors for the centre and, if you're interested, you could have the use of the apartment on the top floor – naturally, free of charge. You'll need somewhere to live and I think you'll find it's quite comfortable. It's furnished and there are two bedrooms so it should be big enough for you and a friend if you want. You'd get a fairly modest salary at first but, hopefully, as the centre begins to grow in importance, that could increase. And as it becomes better known, I'd like to think we should be able to obtain sponsorship to help it expand and thrive. How does that sound? Does it appeal to you?'

This time Suzie couldn't resist jumping to her feet, surprising the snoozing dog as she did so, and rushing across to shake the professor's hand like crazy. If he hadn't just told her he was going to become her employer, she would have kissed him. He caught her hand in both of his.

'Can I take that as a yes, then?'

By this time Dogberry had also jumped to his feet and was standing on his hind legs, scrabbling at the two of them with his massive paws, tail wagging furiously. Suzie stroked him with her free hand before looking back at the professor.

'You most certainly can. Yes, please. And thank you so very, very much, I can't imagine anything better. When would you like me to start?'

Apart from the offer of a job, the realisation was beginning to dawn upon her that the use of the apartment immediately removed the main stumbling block for Alex's plans for the future as well. They would now have somewhere to live, and it would be free!

'Excellent. You can start as soon as you like. Shall we say a week on Monday? That way you can finish your holiday and make all the necessary arrangements first. Now, let's have some tea and a slice of Paolina's cake and we can start discussing the details. It'll mean the creation of a charitable trust, with trustees and so on. I'm afraid that over these next few months it'll be a pretty steep learning curve for you as you get to grips with the arcane mysteries of the Italian legal system and the country's crippling bureaucracy.' He released her hand and she straightened up, the smile still on her face. 'But you'll soon pick it up. And I'll be behind you all the way.'

By the time Suzie emerged from the villa with a set of keys to the professor's Verona house in her bag, the smile on her face still hadn't faded in the slightest. The more they had discussed the project, the more fascinated she had become. Slowly but surely the realisation had dawned upon her that she not only had a job, but this would be doing something perfectly suited to her background, qualifications and experience. Even in her wildest dreams she could never have imagined anything so amazing. As he had said, the pay wouldn't be massive, but with free accommodation she calculated that she would actually be better off than she had been in London. And also, a little voice whispered inside her head, this would mean that she would be able to remain close to a certain artist – whether he wanted her close or not.

As she waited for the bus, she pulled out her phone and called Alex to break the good news. Alex was delighted – for Suzie and also for what this would mean for herself.

'You mean we've got the offer of a flat and it's free?' Suzie could hear the disbelief in her voice. 'Are you sure?'

'So sure that I suggest you and I meet there in, say, an hour's time. He's given me a set of keys.'

She dictated the address, adding that the professor had told her it was bang in the heart of the *centro storico*, less than 200 metres from the Arena, and they agreed to meet there at six. After that she called her mother and told her about this amazing stroke of good fortune and all the way home on the bus she couldn't stop smiling. Her mum had sounded delighted – and relieved. Suzie knew full well that her parents had been worried for her after she had lost her job in London, and she could sense the joy at the other end of the line. They had always been so very supportive and they knew just what this meant to Suzie, even though it would keep her further from them. The professor's job offer had been a boost to the whole family and Suzie had a feeling her father might well get the sherry bottle out for a celebratory drink this evening as a result.

Alex was already waiting for her when she got to the professor's Verona house at ten to six, staring at it in silent appreciation. It was a fine old townhouse, part of a row in a narrow street deep in the heart of the old town, a stone's throw from Piazza delle Erbe, and they all looked hundreds of years old. She unlocked the three separate locks, turned the handle and pushed. After clearing a pile of junk mail from the mat, she opened the door fully and they went inside.

The first thing that struck her was how elegant it was in there, in spite of its fairly bland exterior. The ceilings were high, and swirls and curves had been painted onto the plaster, giving it the impression more of a palace, rather than just a home. There were two large rooms and a small kitchen on the ground floor. The room at the rear opened onto a lovely little garden area with a palm tree in the middle and an ancient rambling rose climbing all over the walls, pink petals littering the ground beneath it, its perfume wafting in through the French windows. Upstairs was a big bathroom and more large rooms, one of which even had a fresco of nymphs and cherubs painted on the ceiling. A locked door gave onto a staircase that led up to the apartment on the top floor.

This proved to be perfect. The kitchen was modern, the bathroom spotless, the living room huge and the two bedrooms both a good size. It was furnished with some rather fine antique pieces; not least two massive beds with tall carved wooden headboards. There were radiators mounted on the walls and no doubt these would come into their own as the months went by and winter approached. Even better, they had a fine view out over the rooftops towards the mountains and, outside, there was even a rooftop terrace, although it was piled high with clutter. Alex was positively jumping for joy.

'What a place! I was already bracing myself for only being able to afford some rat-infested slum. Instead of which we've got this super little flat. It's amazing.'

Suzie agreed entirely and she also approved of the accommodation on the lower floors which should be easily convertible into the sort of academic research centre the professor had outlined. She took a few photos to send to her parents and then, by mutual agreement, they decided to go out for a celebration dinner.

Suzie decided to take Alex to Beppe's restaurant. Whether this was just for the sake of the food or on the off chance of bumping into Michael was something upon which she refused to let her mind dwell, but Alex knew her so well by now. As they stood outside under the *Da Beppe* sign, looking at the menu in the window, Alex caught Suzie by the arm.

'So, what if your Michael's in there? Do we go and sit with him?'

'He's not my Michael...' Suzie realised that she was beginning to sound like a stuck record and gave a little snort. 'If he's here and if he invites us to his table, then of course we'll join him, but he won't be, I'm sure.' Before she got too carried away on that train of thought, she decided to redirect the focus onto Alex. 'By the way, have you told him you've enrolled on the course?'

Alex nodded. 'Yes, I sent him an email this lunchtime, but I haven't had a response. His phone's probably off.' She grinned mischievously. 'I could try calling him now and tell him we're here. Maybe invite him?'

'Leave him alone, Alex. He's probably working. Besides, I don't want to give the impression I'm hounding him.'

The restaurant was well over half full, but Michael was not among the diners. Suzie couldn't help a little twinge of disappointment, but she hid it as Beppe came over to greet them. To her surprise, he caught her shoulders in his powerful hands and kissed her on the cheeks.

'*Ciao, bella.*' He released her and shook hands with Alex. 'Another beautiful lady. It's my lucky night.'

He spoke in Italian and, although Alex's command of Italian was still little more than rudimentary, Suzie could see that she had understood him. After all, the words *bella* and *fortunato* were pretty self-evident. Alex gave him a big smile as she replied.

'*Buona sera, Beppe.*' She grinned. 'I'm afraid that's about all I can say in Italian, but I'm trying to learn.'

Beppe smiled back at her and accompanied them to the same little table where Suzie and Michael had sat the previous week. After Beppe had left them to make up their minds, Suzie pointed out the windsurfing photos on the walls. Alex nodded towards the photo of Michael with his bare chest and winked at Suzie. 'It's enough to put you off your food. What a hunk!'

Suzie had to agree, but she knew it was wiser to try not to think of him in such terms. They were, after all, just good friends. He had made that perfectly clear.

The meal was excellent. After a mixed salad starter, they both opted for Beppe's homemade lasagne and it definitely hit the spot. Alex rolled her eyes and told Suzie they would definitely have to come back. When Beppe returned to the table to remove their empty plates, Suzie was delighted to hear Alex making a real effort.

'*Lasagne molto buono, Beppe.*' To reinforce the message, Alex brought her fingers to her lips and kissed them in the Italian way. The big man beamed at her and replied in heavily accented English.

'Thank you, beautiful lady.' He then turned to Suzie and carried on in Italian. 'My wife and I really need to improve our English. Our eight-year-old speaks it better than we do. We get so many foreign customers these days, it's absolutely essential. I know, why doesn't your friend give us English lessons and we'll give her Italian lessons? That way we'll both be happy.'

Suzie relayed the suggestion to Alex, who jumped at it, and an appointment was fixed for Tuesday at five o'clock here at the restaurant. Hopefully this would also help to accelerate Alex's assimilation into the Italian way of life.

Chapter 19

Sunday was a quiet day for both of them, but the same couldn't be said for Monday. Around mid-morning on Monday, all hell broke loose. Suzie was in her room, investigating other similar research centres around the world on the Internet to get a better idea of what would be expected, when there was frantic knocking at her door. It was Alex and she had her iPad in her hand.

'Half an hour ago I sent the email to my father. I've just had his reply.' She shrugged her shoulders helplessly. 'You won't be surprised to hear he's gone through the roof.'

As she spoke, Suzie heard her phone bleep. Somehow she had a shrewd idea of who the sender of this email might be. She wasn't wrong. It was from Lord Tedburn. It was polite, but terse, and it contained instructions for her to *talk some sense into Alexandra, who will be quite unable to exist without the luxuries to which she has become accustomed.*

She held it up for Alex to read. 'Not a happy man. What does yours say?'

Alex passed her iPad over and Suzie read the email carefully. There was no doubt that he was annoyed, angry even, but she was pleased to see that he made no dire threats to throw her out of the family or anything equally draconian. He repeated his warnings about cutting off Alex's money supply and it was clear that he assumed this would mean a rapid return to the fold for a chastened daughter once the cold hard reality of poverty struck home. Suzie glanced up from the screen.

'To be honest, it's not as bad as I was fearing. Yes, he's annoyed, but we're certainly a long way away from anything too Shakespearian.'

'Wait for it. Did you see what he says at the bottom? Rafe's on his way over on Wednesday; no doubt to give me the third degree.'

Suzie did her best to sound supportive and optimistic. 'That's all right. You can explain everything to him and he'll understand, I'm sure.'

'I wish I had your confidence.'

Suzie took the bus down to Bardolino in the afternoon and spent two hours talking to the professor about their new project. When he finally indicated that he was feeling a bit tired, she stood up to go and he made a suggestion.

'You've been sitting down all afternoon, Suzie. Why don't you go for a walk?'

Suzie glanced at her watch and shook her head. 'The last bus is in fifteen minutes. I need to catch that and then I'll have a walk around Verona this evening.'

'Don't worry about that. I've been thinking about the buses. It's very awkward for you to have to spend so much time on the bus in order to come and see me. I don't really like driving any more, but my car's in the garage and it's still insured. Why don't you borrow it and use it for travelling to and fro?' Seeing the expression on her face, he continued. 'Really, I don't use it at all these days and it would make me feel better about asking you to keep coming here to see me. You can drive, can't you?'

'Well, yes, but I can't take your car...'

'It's not being used. Take it.' He smiled. 'Now that that's settled, I think I'll go and have a little snooze. Would you like to take Dogberry with you on your walk? He so rarely gets a chance to stretch his legs these days, now that I'm less mobile. He pulls a bit on the lead, but he's not too bad.'

Suzie and the dog had a lovely walk. After a bit of a tug of war to start with, she soon reached an agreement with him that he wouldn't try to pull her arms out of their sockets as long as she let him stop, sniff and mark interesting spots along the way. They had never had a dog at home, but she soon got the hang of it – even the little poo bags – and she enjoyed the company. The sky was quite overcast today and the wind had picked up again. She tried to remember the name of the afternoon wind blowing from south to north, but she had forgotten. There were a number of kite and windsurfers out on the water and she stopped for a rest on a bench and watched them while the dog sat at her side, leaning heavily against her knee and panting. It was a delightful scene with the multicoloured sails and kites standing out clearly against the dark hillsides beyond. She was totally unsurprised to realise that her eyes were searching for Michael, but it was impossible to recognise anybody at this distance.

As she returned to the professor's house, she stopped off at James's villa to say hello to Roberto and Rosa and found herself invited in for tea and homemade biscuits. Dogberry was delighted to be offered a whole biscuit all to himself, although it disappeared down his throat without him making any attempt to pause and savour the taste. Roberto repeated James's offer to use the windsurfing kit and informed her that he had had an email that morning informing him that James and some friends were coming over later in the week. Suzie's ears pricked up and she resolved to let Alex know. Maybe this would provide the opportunity for her to finish her conversation with him. Also, it suddenly occurred to her, it might mean a return visit from Tommy. How, she wondered, would she react to seeing him again?

The professor's car proved to be ideal. She had been slightly worried that it might turn out to be some massive old classic car, but in fact it was a fairly new Mini. She had learnt to drive in just such a car and so it felt really quite familiar, even though the steering wheel was on the other side. She bade farewell to Mack and the dog and drove back without incident, arriving at the hotel in the gathering dusk. A porter came out, relieved her of the keys and took the car off to the hotel's private garage so that Suzie was able to stroll into the hotel feeling quite relaxed. Needless to say, in a few days' time, once they had been forced to give up this expensive hotel, she felt sure she wouldn't find parking so easy. She remembered Michael telling them how hot the police were and how hefty the fines could be, but for now, that wasn't a problem.

When she got up to Alex's room, she found her looking concerned, but not downhearted.

'My father's sent me no fewer than five emails today and we've spent half an hour on the phone. Like he said before, he's going to put a stop on all money – including the card – as soon as Saturday comes along if I'm not on the plane home. I've tried and tried to make him understand how badly I want to do this, but I get the impression he's backed himself into a corner and he's not a man who likes admitting he's wrong. Anyway, although he's sure I'll come running home with my tail between my legs, it sounds as if he's not too terribly angry any more. In fact, his last words to me on the phone were for me to look after myself and take care.'

'Well, that's good to hear. And here's something else you need to hear – James is coming over later this week. I stopped off at the villa and Roberto told me.'

Alex nodded. 'I know. He sent me a text. He's coming over with a couple of others and we both know who's going to be with them – Rafe.'

Suzie smiled sympathetically. 'Sounds like you're going to have your work cut out this week. Still, that means you can get all the talking out of the way before your course starts next Monday.'

'Oh, and I've had a reply from Michael at last. He's been in Switzerland for a portrait commission.' She gave Suzie a grin. 'So he wasn't trying to avoid me... or you.'

'I never thought that for a second.' She avoided Alex's eye. 'Did he say anything special?'

Alex shook her head. 'Sorry, not really. Just wished me luck with the course and asked me to say hi to you.'

Hi. That was pretty much what Suzie had been expecting, but it was disappointing all the same. Still, doing her best to sound confident, she launched into a report of her afternoon, including the walk with the dog and the drive home. Alex didn't comment any more about Michael, and Suzie was glad.

–

Rafe arrived early on Wednesday evening with James and along with them was Tommy. All three greeted Suzie with kisses on the cheeks and she felt distinct warmth from

Tommy. This display of affection had the inevitable result and she felt the colour rush to her face.

They all went out for dinner together and, as it had been a sunny day with little wind, it was very comfortable to sit outside one of the restaurants opposite the imposing bulky outline of the Arena. As they ate, they chatted, mainly about uncontroversial matters like Alex's first Italian/English conversation exchange with Beppe and his wife, which had ended with red wine and lasagne. At least, Alex explained with a grin, even if her Italian prowess had a long way to go, she had apparently found an abundant source of excellent free food.

As this meal progressed, Rafe finally came to the point.

'Father's hopping mad, Al. Are you still dead set on doing this art thing?'

Alex nodded. 'Yes, Rafe, it's all been decided.'

'Even though father's said no.'

'Afraid so. I've finally found something I'm good at and I know the right thing's for me to do the course.' She looked across at her brother. 'I'm sorry Father's taken it the way he has, but I'm not a child any more. I have my own life to live.'

'You know he's going to stop your allowance?'

'He told me. But it's okay. Suzie's got a new job and a rent-free apartment. I'll start selling off my expensive clothes and I'll try and get myself a part-time job washing dishes or some such. We'll survive.' She smiled at him. 'I probably won't be having too many more expensive lunches like this for a while, but I'll manage.'

Rafe turned his attention towards Suzie. The expression on his face was hard to read – part curiosity, part respect. 'I must say it's great that you're going to be here alongside Alex. Father's very pleased, I know. So, what's the job? Does this mean you're going to be staying on in Verona indefinitely?'

Suzie gave them a brief summary of the professor's proposal and she spotted particular interest on Tommy's face. When she reached the end of her exposé, he surprised her by being the first to react.

'That sounds amazing, Suzie. You never know, I may be one of your first customers.' He then went on to tell her that he had come out of the army a year earlier and was now studying for a PhD in American Studies at Nottingham University, and the subject of his doctoral thesis was none other than Ernest Hemingway, for whom Italy had inspired such classics as *A Farewell to Arms*. Suzie looked at him with increased interest. Good looks, money and a brain added up pretty much to the complete package. And if he was still hooked on her, how did this make her feel? Doing her best to banish any such conjecture – at least for now – she summoned her most enthusiastic voice.

'Terrific, Tommy. Make sure you spread the word throughout your university. Give me your email address and I'll let you know how things progress.'

'I'll tell everybody and I guarantee I'll be here, knocking on your door, as soon as the research centre's up and running.' His eyes caught hers for a moment and she couldn't miss the eagerness in them – not necessarily for the research centre.

'I'll look forward to seeing you.' And she realised she meant it.

'So you're going to be here over the winter, Suzie?' James sounded pleased. 'I'll be coming back as often as

I can to see Alex. Hopefully we can get out on the lake for a windsurf together again. And of course there's your friend, Michael. He's hooked on windsurfing as well.'

Suzie just smiled and nodded, unsure if she would ever see Michael again – or, indeed, whether James would in fact be coming back to see Alex once she had explained the way she really felt about him.

Rafe and Alex continued to talk about her decision to stay in Verona and by the end of the meal Suzie got the impression that her brother had finally got the message that she was serious. While the others talked, Tommy devoted his attention to Suzie, asking her more about the research centre and then chatting more generally. At one point, she caught Alex's eye and saw her nod imperceptibly in his direction and wink at Suzie, who realised what she was signalling. There could be little doubt that handsome Tommy fancied her. As the thought crossed her mind, she saw Alex grin and the inevitable blushes flooded Suzie's face.

The three men were all staying at James's villa and, as they left, Suzie could see the regret in James's eyes that he had to abandon Alex in Verona. He insisted that the two of them come to the villa the next day and offered to send Roberto in the Rolls but, seeing as Suzie had a meeting with the professor in the morning, she said she would come in the Mini, drop Alex off at ten o'clock and then join them for lunch after her session with Mack.

Just as Suzie got back to her room, her phone bleeped and she was surprised and delighted to see that it was a text from Michael. So maybe he hadn't forgotten about her after all.

Hi Suzie. Good forecast for tomorrow.
Fancy a windsurf? Afternoon probably best.
Michael.

She read it through a few times. One thing was perfectly clear: there was nothing in the message that even vaguely hinted at any kind of connection between them apart from friendship. She felt a little stab of disappointment, but hastily did her best to suppress it as she replied.

Great. I'm having lunch at James's villa. Shall
we meet at his jetty at, say, 3? S

She specifically avoided inserting a little x before the S. As she dropped the phone and sat back, a thought crossed her mind. If the text had been from Tommy, would he have included a little x? The answer was almost certainly yes.

Chapter 20

Suzie and Alex drove to Bardolino on Thursday morning through light rain and, as the lake came into view, the grey clouds ringing it confirmed what she had already suspected. When Michael had talked about a good forecast, he hadn't meant it in the traditional sense. To a mad keen windsurfer, sunshine was unimportant. What counted was the wind and, by the look of it, it was going to turn out to be a good afternoon for a sail. She had brought her newly purchased wetsuit with her and looked forward to trying it out. Hopefully it would keep her warm over the next few months when the water temperature would begin to plummet as autumn turned into winter.

She left the car and Alex at the villa and made her way to the professor's house next door where she received a rapturous welcome from the big black dog and a warm, but slightly less energetic, greeting from the professor, who was looking a bit weary today. She and Mack had a good planning session over fresh coffee and Paolina's homemade biscuits – with Dogberry snoring at their feet – and the time flew by. It was almost half past twelve when she returned to James's place.

Everything appeared fairly normal at the villa and, for a moment, she wondered if Alex's nerve had deserted her at the last moment. The rain had stopped some time ago and the sky was clearing fast. James was out on the lawn, practising putting with Tommy, while Rafe was sitting down at the end of the jetty, looking out over the lake, his phone clamped to his ear. They all looked happy enough, but there was no sign of Alex at first. Then, just as Suzie was starting to get worried, the sitting room door opened and Alex appeared. There was a smile on her face – not a broad smile, but nonetheless a smile.

'Alex, hi.' Suzie glanced round to check that James and the others were still outside before lowering her voice. 'Did you set him straight, and how did he take it?'

'I told him, but it was water off a duck's back. He told me he loved me – seriously, that's the word he used – and he didn't care. I'm the only woman for him and he feels sure that sooner or later I'm going to realise that too, so he's prepared to hang about for as long as it takes.' She shook her head slowly. 'I don't know what else to do. It's like having a little dog. I'm sure I could kick him and he'd still come trotting along after me.'

'Wow! That's impressive.' Suzie shot Alex a little grin. 'I'm sure Shakespeare would have approved. That sounds like good old-fashioned infatuation. You've got to admire his commitment. You'll have him lurking around in the bushes beneath your window before long.' Her grin broadened as she made a little alteration to one of the most famous quotations from her beloved *Romeo and Juliet*.

"*But, soft! what light through yonder window breaks?*
It is the east, and Alex is the sun."

She was still grinning as a voice interrupted their conversation.

'Hi Suzie, how did it go with the grumpy old professor?'

They both turned their heads in unison to find James at the French doors with a putter in his hand. Behind him was Tommy, and a smile lit up his face as he spotted Suzie. This only served to redden her cheeks and she turned away in frustration. At the same time she found herself questioning why his smile should affect her in this way. How was she supposed to react? How did she want to react? To further confuse her, both he and James came over and kissed her on the cheeks. As Tommy stepped back again, he was still smiling and she was still blushing.

How much James might have heard of her doctored quotation was hard to tell, but he continued as if he hadn't a care in the world.

'Hi Suzie, Alex tells me you're going windsurfing this afternoon with your friend Michael. All right if Tommy and I tag along?'

'Absolutely, guys, that sounds great. And the professor's not in the least bit grumpy. I find myself thinking of him as the brainy grandfather I never had.'

James went across to Alex and stretched his arm affectionately around her shoulders. 'Pity you aren't interested in trying it, Alex. I'd love to teach you.'

She shook her head at the idea of windsurfing. 'No thanks. Neither Rafe nor I have ever had any great interest in water – unless you count lying on a beach and swimming in the lovely warm sea like we did back in Venice.'

Suzie glanced down towards the jetty where Rafe was still talking on his phone. He was turned side-on to them and she could see he wasn't smiling any more.

'That looks like a serious phone call.'

Tommy answered for them. 'In the words of the Bard, they're "star-cross'd lovers". He's having girl trouble.' He grinned. 'Or, rather, his problems aren't *with* the girl, but *because* of the girl.'

Suzie exchanged glances with Alex. This was the first time she had heard of Rafe's girlfriend. Alex added a brief comment.

'I'll tell you all about it later on, Suzie. He's just spent all morning telling me.' She smiled ruefully as she slowly shook her head. 'Definitely one for your Mr Shakespeare.'

Suzie was intrigued, but at that moment Roberto appeared and announced that lunch was served.

It came as no surprise to her to find Tommy seated alongside her, very attentive and very talkative. He kept offering her more wine but, with the prospect of wind-surfing that afternoon, she limited herself to just one glass of the very good red. After another excellent lunch, this time of mushroom risotto followed by *bistecca alla milanese* – thin slices of beef fried in breadcrumbs and accompanied by roast fennel dusted with Parmesan – they retired to the living room for coffee. By now the northerly *Pelèr* wind had changed to the *Ora* and was blowing from the south and, from what Suzie could see of the white-capped waves further out, it promised to be a really good afternoon on the water. As she sipped her coffee, she glanced across at Rafe, who had been unusually silent over lunch. From the strained expression on his face, it was clear to see that all was not well in paradise.

Just before three o'clock, she climbed into her new wetsuit and went down to the boatshed. She rigged up a medium-sized sail and took it out to the lakeside. There, chatting to James and Tommy, was a familiar figure and she felt herself smiling as she went over to him. His face broke into a wide smile in return as he saw her and she felt a charge of optimism.

'Hi, Suzie. New wetsuit?'

She went over and kissed him on the cheeks, doing her best not to dwell upon the little thrill the contact with him produced in her. 'Hi, Michael, yes, I got it the other day. It might be a bit hot for today, but I wanted something warm for the winter.'

They carried on a brief conversation together with the other two, but it was only about windsurfing. There was no opportunity for anything more personal, but Michael showed no sign of wanting to get more personal anyway, so she choked back her regret and joined in with the sailing chat. As they talked, she compared the three men. They were all good-looking in their own way and there was no question they were all fit. Michael was probably three or four years older than the other two and with his careworn face, he looked even older. In a male beauty pageant she had to admit that the points would almost certainly have gone to Tommy, but she knew deep down that Michael alone had a special something that would always draw her to him.

It turned out to be an excellent afternoon on the water. Michael and James were probably roughly the same high standard, while she and Tommy were a few degrees below them, but they all had a great time. After about an hour, as she began to tire, Suzie spotted a black shape sitting statue-like at the end of the professor's jetty and she broke away from the others and headed across to say hello. It took a moment for Dogberry to recognise this strange figure dressed in black, splashing about in the water, but as soon as he had worked it out, he launched himself bodily into the lake and doggy-paddled over to greet her. She dumped her board and rig in the water and waded to the shore with him, his tail wagging furiously all the way.

She squatted in the shallows alongside the happy dog and made a fuss of him, glad her wetsuit was protecting her from the Labrador-scented water he splashed all over her. Finally, she got up and walked out along the jetty to where she had left her board and tugged it onto the woodwork. Dogberry trotted along beside her. As she straightened up, Michael swept up in a shower of spray and joined them. As soon as the dog recognised him, he repeated his trick of diving in to say hello, after which the three of them sat down on the wooden jetty and relaxed. Dogberry and Michael were clearly old friends and Michael scratched his tummy as the Labrador rolled onto his back, legs in the air, tail wagging happily from side to side.

'I haven't seen Dogberry for three years, but he still remembers me all right.'

'Maybe he recognises your smell.' Suzie grinned at him. 'So, what's new? How've you been?'

'I've been fine. I've been in Zurich for a commission and I just got back yesterday. What about you? I've missed you, you know.'

Suzie didn't know that and it came as a very pleasant surprise.

'Well, I've missed you as well.'

She was still smiling as she went on to give him a brief outline of the professor's job offer and how this meant she would now be staying on in Verona for the foreseeable future. He sounded happy for her, if a bit pensive, but made no reference to how this might affect his life. Realistically, she thought to herself ruefully, it would probably only mean that he would have another windsurfing buddy. Then, he said something unexpected.

'He's a good-looking guy, your boyfriend.'

Inevitably, the colour rushed to her cheeks. 'My boyfriend?' Realisation dawned. 'Tommy, you mean? He's not my boyfriend. I barely know him. He's James's cousin.'

'Ah, I see. Well, he's a good-looking guy. If he's got the same sort of money as his cousin, I reckon you could do a lot worse.'

Suzie's cheeks were on fire, but she took a firm grip on herself and replied with as much decisiveness as she could muster. 'I'm not in the market for a man at the moment, thanks. I've got a fabulous new job to concentrate on. Hooking up with Tommy – or any man – would just be an unnecessary distraction.' She wasn't sure why she added the words 'or any man' and instantly regretted her choice, but by then Michael had changed the subject back to windsurfing.

Fortunately, just a few moment later, they heard a shout and saw James gesticulating from his jetty for them to come across. After making a final fuss of the dog, they collected their boards and splashed over to James's property where they were both invited in for tea. To Suzie's disappointment, she saw Michael shake his head.

'Thanks, James, but I've got to get off. I've got an appointment with the picture framer in less than an hour and I need to get changed out of my wetsuit and take a shower first.' He shook hands with the two men and kissed Suzie on the cheeks. For a moment it looked as though he was going to say something to her, but then he just stepped onto his board and sailed elegantly away, leaving her with that same sense of disappointment, now complicated by the fact that she had somehow inadvertently just told him she wasn't interested in any man. She growled to herself as she carried her board and rig into the boathouse. How stupid could she be?

–

That evening James suggested going dancing at the same nightclub he and his friends had been to before. Suzie would happily have gone back to the hotel in Verona for a quiet evening but found herself coerced into joining them – mainly by Tommy. In fact it turned out to be a lot of fun, although by the time she and Alex were dropped off at their hotel at just before two o'clock, her ears were ringing and she was feeling decidedly weary after dancing virtually without stopping. Tommy had monopolised her most of the time and on those rare occasions when he decided to step back, Rafe had stepped in. As a result, she was exhausted. One thing, however, had been hard to miss. On the occasions when the music had slowed and she had felt Tommy's arms around her, pulling her to him, it had been pretty clear that he liked her a lot. She liked him, too, but just not as much as she did her artist – but, alas, she felt sure she was on a hiding to nothing there. It was very frustrating.

However, the frustration didn't last too long. When she surfaced, later than usual, the following morning back in the hotel in Verona, she found she had a message.

Sorry we didn't have much time to chat.
How about dinner tonight? Michael.

She didn't have to think too hard. The idea had considerable appeal.

Great. Where? Beppe's? S

The answer was almost immediate.

See you there at 8. Okay? M

Suzie sent a one-word answer and then wandered out onto the balcony in her pyjamas. The French windows to Alex's room were wide open and she found her sorting through piles of clothes heaped on her bed.

'Hi Alex. Packing?' Tonight would be their final night in this luxurious hotel.

'Sort of. I'm separating out the stuff I'm going to sell from the stuff I'm going to keep.' She smiled wistfully. 'It's harder than I thought it would be.'

'No regrets, I hope?'

'Well, it's tough to say goodbye to some of these gorgeous things, but no, no real regrets. I know I've made the right decision and I'll be forever in your debt for throwing me a lifeline.'

Suzie smiled back. 'You're very welcome, but it's no big deal. The flat's big enough for two, it's free and I'd like the company.'

'Yes, but you were fully prepared to stay on here even before you got the offer of the professor's job. That means a lot.'

Suzie shrugged off her thanks. 'Like I say, you're welcome. I'm just glad you're happy. Now all that's needed is for Rafe and his girlfriend to get themselves sorted out. By the way, what's that all about?'

'It's complicated.' Alex went on to tell Suzie all about it. Apparently, this girl, Melanie, and Rafe had been seeing each other on and off for some years now and it was definitely getting very serious. There was just one problem and Suzie guessed what – or rather who – that was even before Alex told her.

'She's from an ordinary family and Father doesn't approve.'

'For crying out loud...' Suzie snorted in disbelief. 'You know, people sometimes say that Shakespeare's plays are no longer so relevant to the modern day.' She shook her head slowly. 'Your family are the living proof that that's wrong.'

Alex nodded in response. 'You aren't joking. But, like I've been telling him all day, he's got to stand up for himself, just like I've done. I've said he should take a leaf out of your book.'

'My book?'

'You're the one who got me to stand up for myself and I have absolutely no regrets – give or take an Armani dress or a pair of Jimmy Choo sandals. That's what he's got to do.'

'And do you think he will?'

'I hope so. I tell you what, Suzie. Would you talk to him this weekend? Make him see sense? James wants us both to stay over at the villa.'

Suzie hesitated. 'I'm not sure, Alex. Maybe I've interfered with your family enough already.'

'Not at all. It hasn't been interference. It's been massively helpful. Please talk to him? For me?'

Suzie nodded slowly. 'All right, if you say so, but I can't promise any miracles.' She decided to change the subject.

'By the way, seeing as this is our last night here, have you got plans?'

'Rafe and Tommy said they were going off to Padua for the day today and James has asked me out for dinner with him. To be honest, I wouldn't be surprised if he's told the other two to disappear so he can be alone with me. He wanted me to go to the villa for an intimate dinner, just the two of us, but I said I'd prefer somewhere neutral and he didn't put up much of a fight. Do you want to come along? That would suit me fine. Safety in numbers and all that…'

Suzie shook her head and told her about Michael's invitation. Alex was predictably upbeat.

'Great news. The more time you get to spend with him the better. Sooner or later he's going to have to begin thinking about starting over and you need to be by his side when that moment arrives.'

Suzie didn't reply. The question was when – or indeed if – he ever would be ready?

–

Suzie turned up at Beppe's restaurant just after eight feeling unexpectedly nervous. She had dithered all afternoon before deciding not to dress up too much for Michael. If he preferred them to be just friends, it was probably best to keep the swanky new dress and the high heels for another occasion. Predictably, Alex had objected, insisting that she should go out of her way to beguile him, but beguiling had never been Suzie's way and she wasn't about to start now. Instead, she went with jeans and trainers – not least as it had started to pour with rain by the time the evening approached. She did, however, select her favourite soft grey V-neck jumper. Rob had bought it for her a couple of years ago in a pricey boutique in Lanzarote and she had always liked it.

As she pushed the door open, she felt it taken out of her grip as Beppe did the honours.

'Good evening, madam. Welcome to my restaurant. How are you tonight?' His English pronunciation could have done with a bit of spit and polish, but she was impressed at the result of his first English lesson at the hands of Alex.

'Good evening, sir. I'm fine, thank you. How are you?'

A smile spread across his face as he returned to Italian. 'That's about as far as it goes for now, but I'm getting there.' He relieved her of her dripping umbrella, kissed her on the cheeks and pointed across the room to a table in the corner. 'He's been here for fifteen minutes, nervously looking at his watch.' He winked mischievously. 'Maybe he was afraid you'd stand him up.'

Suzie went across to Michael's side and tapped him on the shoulder. '*Ciao, bello. Come stai?*'

His head jerked up and there was no mistaking the pleasure on his face as he saw her.

'And *ciao bella* to you too. You're looking amazing as usual.'

He jumped to his feet, stretched out his arms and pulled her gently towards him, depositing a light kiss on each cheek. As she felt the touch of his lips, the usual frisson of pleasure went through her and, of course, her cheeks coloured. Doing her best to look unruffled, she took a seat opposite him.

'This was a very good idea. It's my final night in the lap of luxury before moving into the flat and I wanted to celebrate.'

'And Alex?'

Suzie went on to tell him that Alex and James had gone off in the Rolls-Royce to some Michelin-starred restaurant on the lakeside and she saw him smile.

'Moving into an attic and becoming a penniless art student's going to be quite a shock to the system for her, isn't it?'

'She'll be fine. Really… I mean it.' Suzie told him about Alex's plans to sell her designer wardrobe to generate funds and he nodded approvingly.

'Good for her. So tell me about you, Suzie. I'm delighted you've managed to land yourself what sounds like the perfect job. You must be very pleased.'

After ordering their meal, she gave him more details of the proposed research centre and he listened intently. The conversation then broadened as they ate and she found herself telling him about her previous job at the charity, her parents and, finally, Rob and his job in Canada.

'And was it sad for you to see him go?' He took a mouthful of wine and sat back. 'Had you been together long?'

'Almost three years. And no, it wasn't really tragic, but it was tough all the same. You know, you get used to being with someone, having them there and then, suddenly, they aren't there any more.' As she spoke, she instantly registered the impact of her words on him and she could have kicked herself. Rather lamely, she added a muttered addendum. 'I'm sorry. You know all about that, of course.'

He didn't respond immediately and she, too, took a big mouthful of wine. Tonight they were eating trout and had opted for a carafe of local white wine, and it was very good. She ate the final pieces of fish slowly before setting her knife and fork down, deliberately giving him time. Finally, he replied in a low voice.

'I certainly do.'

That was all he said and she was relieved. She had feared she might have tipped him into depression. To be on the safe side, she hastily changed the subject to windsurfing and the conversation became more animated once again. From windsurfing she got him talking about his child-hood in the Cotswolds and his career, and he became more cheerful as he recounted some of the experiences he had had at art college. Suzie was glad Alex's father wasn't listening in. Many of the stories, while hilarious, would have confirmed Lord Tedburn's worst fears about art school being a den of iniquity. By the end of the meal she had learnt quite a bit about Michael and she had definitely got the impression that he had loosened up and appeared to be genuinely happy in her company. She left the restaurant feeling more optimistic about the future.

However, as they were walking back to her hotel after-wards, that all changed.

The rain hadn't abated at all and they both shared her umbrella. Michael held it while she gripped his arm with her hand, enjoying the feel of his bicep beneath his coat, her shoulder rubbing up against his, as they made their way through the near-deserted streets. The only sound was the drumming of the rain on the umbrella and the splashing of their feet through the puddles. In spite of the weather, here in these historic streets it was a pleasant and potentially romantic experience – if there had been any romance to be had from him. As usual, she sensed nothing on his part. But then, as they came out into the wide open expanse of Piazza delle Erbe, he slowed and turned towards her.

'Come and shelter here under this awning for a moment, would you? There's something I've got to tell you.'

He disengaged his arm from her grip and set the umbrella down on a damp tabletop. This outdoor part of the restaurant, which would normally have still been busy on a warm autumn night, was completely deserted tonight and the square itself unusually empty. She could see the reflection of the orange street lights on the flagstones and in his eyes and she had a sudden premonition that the news she was going to receive was not going to be good.

It wasn't.

'It's like this, Suzie… I'm leaving.' She could tell that he was struggling to find the right words.

'Leaving? What, Verona?'

'Italy. I've decided to go back to the UK, for good. My mother still lives in the Cotswolds, so I'll stay with her until I find somewhere suitable with space for my studio. And then I'll try to make a fresh start.'

Suzie felt crushed. She had more or less come to terms with the fact that he wasn't ready for a new relationship just yet, but she had imagined that she would continue to see him on a regular basis, even if it was only on a sailboard. She was suddenly very conscious of the silence around them, only broken by the incessant drumming of the rain on the canvas over their heads and the drips all around them. She didn't know what to say, how to respond. The most she could manage was an inarticulate 'Oh…'

Finally, after a long silence, he continued.

'I love the house at Bardolino, but everywhere I look, I see her… Grazia, my wife. It's like you were saying earlier, you get used to having them there and then, suddenly, they're gone and it hurts.' The light caught his eyes again and this time she could see the tears in them. 'It hurts an awful lot. It's no good. I have to go.'

'And when are you planning on leaving? Presumably the house'll take time to sell.' As she said it, she reflected that this would probably mean a good few months before their separation. She was wrong.

'I'm not going to sell it for now. I've given it to a holiday rental firm and they'll manage it for me.'

'So you're leaving… when?'

'Straight away. This weekend, I think. Best to make a clean break.' He hesitated. 'I wanted to tell you myself. I know you'll understand. And I want you to know that I'll miss you, Suzie. I'll miss you a lot.'

Suddenly Suzie's dream job in Verona was looking far less appealing. Under normal circumstances she would have been returning to the UK herself tomorrow and that would, at least, have meant that the distance between her and Michael would have been greatly reduced. For one crazy moment she found herself toying with the idea of contacting the professor and telling him she couldn't, after all, accept the job offer, but then immediately rejected it. She had made a commitment and she knew she owed it to the old man – if not to her career – to stick to it. Besides, she told herself, being in the same country as Michael wouldn't change the inescapable fact that as far as he was concerned they were nothing but friends, however much she knew she would love to take things to the next level. No, she told herself firmly, better here and employed than back home, unemployed and getting nowhere as far as romance with him was concerned. She took a deep breath and did her best to sound positive.

'Of course I understand, Michael. You have to do what feels right for you. I'm glad you aren't selling the house – at least for now. Maybe, with time, you'll feel able to come back and pick up where you left off.' She caught hold of both his hands in hers. 'And I'll miss you tremendously as well, but I do understand.'

They stood there for a few seconds and time seemed to stop. Even the sound of the rain faded away in her head and all she could feel was the warmth of his hands and a developing sense of loss. All her instincts were screaming at her to lean in for a kiss, but she didn't.

And neither did he.

Chapter 21

Suzie spent Saturday at James's villa with Alex and the others. Just to compound her woes, there wasn't a breath of wind. She hadn't slept well and the way she was feeling after Michael's bombshell, she knew what she really needed was a crazy blast across the lake to let off steam. As it was, later that morning, she and Tommy went paddleboarding while James and Alex sat and talked, and Rafe remained glued to his phone. Last night's rain had cleared, the sun had come out and the water was like a millpond. It was very pleasant to make their way gently along, parallel to the shore, avoiding the noisy ducks who were remarkably unafraid of these two humans as they floated past. It was fun to peek into the gardens of the villas lucky enough to be right on the waterfront and to watch all the people walking, running or cycling along the lakeside path when it returned to the water's edge.

After half an hour or so, they stopped at a little cafe with tables outside by the water's edge and ordered coffee, which proved to be remarkably good, considering the premises were little more than a wooden shack. Suzie sat back and relaxed as she chatted to Tommy about his studies and her plans for the research centre. Then the conversation suddenly turned to more personal matters.

'James tells me you've fallen in love with Michael, the artist.'

Suzie spluttered into her cappuccino and, inevitably, felt the colour rush to her cheeks. She paused to mop her mouth with a napkin before replying.

'I haven't fallen in love with anybody.' She took a deep breath. 'We may be living in the most romantic city in Italy, but I'm not following Juliet's example.'

He grinned. 'That's good to hear. That didn't work out too well for them, did it?'

Suzie nodded and did her best to keep the conversation on *Romeo and Juliet*, rather than herself, but Tommy was persistent and soon brought the conversation back to the subject of her and Michael. 'So there's no big romance?'

Suzie sighed. 'Nothing's going to happen between me and Michael. Besides, he's just told me he's going back to England.'

'What? Permanently?'

'Apparently.' Her tone was deflated and he couldn't have missed it.

'And you've got to stay here?' He didn't wait for Suzie's nod. 'Wow, that's tough. Are you going to be okay?'

'I'll be fine, thanks. I've got the research centre to concentrate on.' Deciding to turn defence into attack, she spun the question back at him. 'So what about you? Are you married or engaged or whatever?'

He smiled. 'Whatever, I suppose. I joined the army straight from university and it's hard to combine the life of a junior officer with anything too serious on the personal front. Now, since I've left the army, I'm a bit like you. I'm concentrating on my studies. Yes, there've been a couple of girls, but nothing serious.' Now it was his turn to look embarrassed. 'Until I saw you, that is.'

'Until you saw me?' Suzie's cheeks had gradually been returning to their normal colour, but this comment changed all that.

'Do you believe in love at first sight, Suzie? You know, like Romeo when he first glimpsed Juliet?'

Suzie took refuge in the little ginger biscuit that had come with her coffee, taking her time over unwrapping it and slowly nibbling it crumb by crumb. She could hardly believe her ears. When the biscuit had finally disappeared, she did her best to give him a sensible answer.

'I'm sure it exists – at least on an initial infatuation level. But whether it leads to anything lasting, who knows? As for you, Tommy, thank you. I'm really pleased you liked the look of me and I like you, too, but I'm not in the market for a man at the moment.'

'Because of your artist?'

'I don't know. Really, I don't.' She could feel her cheeks still burning, but she felt surer of herself now. 'It's a funny thing, this love business. For Shakespeare it was all pretty cut and dried. Boy meets girl and falls in love. Girl falls in love with boy, they overcome a few obstacles and they all live happily ever after.'

'Or, in the case of Romeo and Juliet, it all ends in tears.'

'Quite, but there's no dilly-dallying along the way. It's either love or hate, and that's that. In one act of *Othello*, he loves Desdemona; in the next, he's killed her. Real life's not like that – at least not my life. My artist friend – and that's what we are, just good friends – definitely attracted me from the start. But circumstances conspired to make it impossible for any sort of romantic relationship to develop between the two of us. It's nobody's fault, but it just never really got off the ground.' She marshalled a little smile. 'And Shakespeare wouldn't have liked it at all. Not enough drama.'

'But you're still hung up on him.'

Suzie was beginning to feel more relaxed now and it was easy to answer honestly. 'I like him a lot, Tommy, but there's no way it's going to lead to a happy ending.'

'I hope it does, for your sake. But if things don't work out and you feel like having another bash at romance, you will remember me, won't you?'

'Of course I'll remember you, Tommy.'

–

After another of Rosa's sumptuous lunches, ending with homemade panna cotta, Suzie went down to the pool and lay down on one of the sunbeds, feeling quite weary after a couple of glasses of wine with the meal, her morning's exercise and a lack of sleep the night before. Although the boys had swum in the pool the previous day, they had complained that the water temperature had dropped quite a bit, so she felt no desire to go in. Instead, she lay back in the autumn sunshine and let her eyes close. However, before she could doze off, she heard a voice.

'Hi, Suzie, mind if I join you?'

She looked up, expecting to see Tommy. Instead, it was Rafe, looking unusually sheepish.

'Of course. The sun's still got some warmth in it.'

He sat down on a sunbed alongside her and a longish pause ensued before he spoke up.

'Um… Suzie… my sister's sent me down here to ask you for some advice.'

She glanced at him and saw that, for once, she wasn't the one looking embarrassed. Remembering the promise she had made to Alex, she pulled herself a bit more upright, resting on her elbows.

'If I can help in any way, I'll be only too happy to do so, but I'm no agony aunt, I'm afraid.'

This brought a little smile to his lips. 'Thanks, Suzie... I imagine Alex told you all about it.'

'Not much, really. She just mentioned that you were having a bit of trouble. Why don't you talk me through it?'

Slowly at first, he related the whole sad story. As he talked, it became ever clearer that he liked this girl, Melanie, a lot. She lived in Exeter, about half an hour away from the manor, and she was a pharmacist at the hospital. Rafe and Melanie had been going out for three years now and they got on very well together. The problem was that she wasn't of noble birth. He had spoken to his father about asking her to marry him and Lord Tedburn had poured cold water on the idea.

'Why, exactly?' Suzie asked the question, although she felt pretty sure she already knew the answer.

'The line.' Seeing Suzie's expression, he elaborated. 'The Tedburns have been at the manor since 1616. The title always goes to the senior male heir and that's me. As such, Father feels I should marry somebody from a similar social level.' He looked across at her morosely. 'Pretty much what he's told Alex to do with James.'

'And has he anybody in mind?'

'He's paraded a number of suitable candidates before me over the years. His current pick is a distant cousin of Prince Charles' who lives in Cornwall.'

'And she doesn't do anything for you?'

'She's a nice girl, but she isn't Melanie. It's quite simple, really. It's Melanie I want. I know it. Melanie knows it, but Father won't have it.'

Suzie lay back down again and let her eyes range across the big puffy white clouds far above. It was almost unthinkable that this could still be happening in the twenty-first century. She felt sure that Shakespeare would have recognised Rafe's dilemma only too well. She had no doubt at all how she would have reacted if she had been in his shoes and she decided to say the same thing to him as she had said to Alex.

'Are you sure you really want my advice?'

'Yes, please. I can see how much happier Alex is now, and that's down to you. She says so and I know she's right. So, yes, please tell me what you think.'

So Suzie did. 'You need to do what's right for you, Rafe, not what's right for your father. It's pretty clear to me that, although he's inherited some archaic ideas about parenting, deep down he loves you and Alex a lot. He will want you to be happy, even if it doesn't square with his old-fashioned ways. If I were you, I'd tell him your mind's made up and that's that.'

'And when he goes ballistic?'

'Let him go ballistic. What's the worst he could do, after all? He can hardly chuck you out of the family. That would effectively scupper all his desires to see the Tedburn line continued. Tell him you want to marry the girl you love. Remind him that even the future King of England has just married a commoner and times have changed. Make it clear to him that you're going to do it with or without his blessing.'

There was silence for a moment before he replied. 'That's exactly what Alex has been telling me.' He hesitated again. 'It's just that I've never refused to obey one of his orders before. It just doesn't feel right.'

'It's up to you to decide, Rafe. All I can say is that if I were in your shoes, I wouldn't hesitate. It's your life and your happiness.'

She and Alex spent the night at the villa. She was quite relieved that nobody suggested another trip to the nightclub and, instead, the three men did a barbecue down by the lakeside. Suzie offered to help, but was handed a glass of champagne and told to relax, so she did just that. She sat down on a bench at the water's edge and sipped her wine, dividing her attention between the boats on the lake and events closer to home. Rafe was still looking worried, and she hoped her few words this afternoon might help him. Alex appeared happy and Suzie was glad to hear her laughing a lot. As for the other two men, the expressions on their faces were so similar at times that Suzie felt like smiling, but she genuinely felt sorry for both of them – especially as she was partly to blame.

It was a very unusual experience for her to find herself, for once, with a handsome man quite evidently pining for her. And alongside Tommy, James was evidently equally smitten by Alex and, as the evening progressed, she noticed numerous longing looks on the faces of both men. She sat back and tried to analyse the way this made her feel.

She liked Tommy, and the fact that he shared many of her interests was endearing. There was no doubt they were getting on well together. So why, she asked herself, had she turned him down and told him she wasn't interested?

Of course, the short answer was Michael. However, after last night's bombshell that he was leaving, it was pretty obvious Michael was no longer anything more than a boat that had passed in the night – a very desirable, if damaged, boat, but one that was now heading in the other direction. So, she wondered, where did this leave her and Tommy? If he carried out his promise to come to the research centre in the new year, and if he still felt the same way about her, what would she do? She had never had a man admit to having been struck by love at first sight for her before. Her impression of him had been positive – give or take a few beers too many – but love? He was handsome, intelligent and, of course, ridiculously wealthy, so could she see herself developing feelings for him? She spent the evening sipping champagne and wondering.

Chapter 22

The next weeks as October led into November were bittersweet for Suzie. She often thought of Michael, but heard little from him apart from an occasional email informing her of his progress in looking for a suitable house with space for a studio back in the UK. She read and reread the few messages that arrived from him with as much care as if she were studying a hitherto unseen masterpiece by her beloved Shakespeare, but failed to identify anything in his words that hinted at anything more than just friendship. In reply she sent him updates on the progress of the research centre, but didn't allow herself anything more intimate than a single little *x* before her name at the bottom of the page.

On the other hand, she regularly received messages, emails and calls from Tommy. He kept her informed about the progress of his studies and often asked her advice. He was obviously enjoying being back at university after seven taxing years in the army, although she got the impression he missed the excitement. He told her all about himself and, gradually, she opened up to him about her background, aspirations and hopes for the future. It was quite clear that he still hoped that there would be a place for him in that future and, although she felt flattered, she knew she couldn't commit – at least, not yet. She came to enjoy, and even look forward to, her talks with him and there was no doubt that he was beginning to occupy a place in her head, but still not in her heart. That remained stubbornly filled with the memory of a heartbroken artist, however hard she tried to tell herself he was a lost cause.

The research centre itself gradually began to take shape and occupied more and more of her time, which was in many ways a blessing, filling her thoughts and stopping her from dwelling too much on what might have been. She loved almost all of the process – although her introduction to Italian bureaucracy, as the professor had warned, was less enjoyable and at times immensely frustrating. She busied herself with everything from arranging the installation of new toilets and choosing a state-of-the-art computer system to setting up a bank account – something that involved even more bureaucracy. She wrote papers, designed a new website and spent an inordinate amount of time sending out messages to academic centres all over the world to publicise the forthcoming launch of the centre, scheduled for early in the new year – as long as the necessary planning permission was granted.

She saw Professor Macgregor-Brown almost on a daily basis and was greatly relieved to hear him volunteer to liaise with the lawyers in setting up the new charitable trust. In one meeting devoted to this tortuous subject in late November, at which she was also present, she was surprised to hear a familiar name mentioned.

'*Professore*, have you drawn up a list of possible trustees?'

Avvocato Verdi, the lawyer, was a tall, immaculately-dressed gentleman in his sixties who emanated an air of trustworthiness and infallibility. He also emanated enough powerful aftershave to anaesthetise an elephant and Suzie inevitably returned from these meetings, leapt into the shower and changed clothes completely. Today she had taken a seat at the far end of the highly-polished mahogany table in the hope of avoiding the worst of it, but the damp autumn weather had suddenly turned decidedly wintry and the windows were sealed shut. Seated between her and the lawyer, Mack appeared impervious to the tsunami of cologne wafting down the table as he read out a list of names of local – and as it turned out, not so local – dignitaries as trustees. The final name on his list was, 'Michael Turner, the famous portrait painter.'

Even now, nearly six weeks after her last sight of him that wet October night, Michael's name was enough to give Suzie a little tremor as she found herself wondering if this might bring him back to Verona – even just for a day. The lawyer took the list from Mack and they moved on to other matters, but Suzie was still thinking about Michael as she walked back home after the meeting, huddled into her winter coat, her breath forming clouds in the air in front of her. The tops of the hills behind the town were now white with snow and, in the high Alps beyond, she knew that the ski resorts were already preparing for the start of the season. So engrossed in her thoughts was she, she almost bumped into Alex as she emerged into Piazza Bra.

'Hi, Suzie. A penny for your thoughts.' Alex, now wearing jeans, trainers, and a cosy jacket purchased from the Saturday market down at the stadium, was looking happy – as she had been for the past weeks since embarking upon her course at the Academy. 'You looked miles away.'

'Hi, Al. Just thinking.'

'Business or pleasure?'

Suzie looked up and smiled. 'A bit of both, I suppose.' And she told Alex about Michael's name on the list of possible trustees.

'Brilliant. That's bound to bring him back to Verona.'

Suzie nodded. 'Maybe so, but it isn't likely to bring about a change of heart.'

Alex wasn't going to be discouraged. 'Don't you believe it. He's been back in the UK for weeks and weeks now, and that's a long time if you're missing someone. You wait and see. I bet he comes back, cap in hand, and tells you he can't live without you.'

'Some hopes…' Not for the first time Suzie gave herself a mental kick up the backside and changed the subject. 'By the way, still no word from Rafe about him sitting down and talking to your father about Melanie?'

Alex shook her head in annoyance. 'He's going to chicken out, I know it. Every time I speak to him I have a go at him, but old habits die hard. He's so used to doing everything Father says, he's going to need a real push.'

Suzie nodded. 'Well, I tried my hardest when we spoke back in October. Here's hoping. Anyway, how're things with you? Are you going out this evening?'

'Yes, but not socially. I'm working tonight and tomorrow.'

Alex's English/Italian conversation sessions with Beppe and his wife had led to employment for her in the restaurant kitchen on busy nights, doing everything and anything from mopping the floor or washing the dishes to dicing carrots, peeling potatoes and filling salt cellars. To Suzie's delight, she had taken to it like a duck to water and Beppe and his wife expressed complete satisfaction with her. As this was effectively the first 'real' job Alex had ever had, this was a very good sign and Suzie was delighted for her. The extra income wasn't massive, but coupled with the steady stream of money coming into her PayPal account as her designer clothes were snapped up by fashion-conscious Italian women looking for a bargain, Alex had been able to make ends meet so far without asking Suzie for a sub. Suzie was proud of her and she could see that Alex was equally proud of herself. The big unknown, of course, remained what her father thought of her.

'Isn't James supposed to be coming back this weekend, Alex?'

'Not this weekend, but next, along with Rafe. You and I are invited to the villa for the weekend if we want.'

'If *you* want, Al. You decide. I'm always up for some free food and the chance to go windsurfing, but you're the one who's trying to keep James at arm's length.'

'Like you say, it'll be free food, so of course I'm up for it.' She grinned. 'I haven't eaten meat for a few weeks now, so a nice juicy steak would be perfect. I'll text him and say yes for both of us. He can send the car to pick us up.'

Now that they were no longer living in the hotel with its private parking, Suzie had returned the Mini to the professor, as parking spaces in the city centre were in very short supply. On the occasions when she visited him at the lake, she took the bus and found it quite easy. She nodded and smiled. Getting into the Rolls would be a little blast of nostalgia for Alex after all, although she had settled into life as a 'normal' student remarkably well.

Back at the flat, Suzie was just checking her emails when her phone rang. It was her mother, and suddenly everything changed.

'Suzanne, darling, I'm afraid your father's in hospital.'

Suzie's blood turned cold. 'Why? What's happened?'

'He's had what they're calling a "heart event". He was feeling very unwell overnight and I had to call 999 this morning. He's in the RD&E and he's having an operation this evening or first thing tomorrow morning.'

Suzie knew the Royal Devon and Exeter Hospital well. As a teenager she had broken her arm falling off a horse and had ended up there. 'What sort of operation?'

'They tell me it's nothing too major, although it sounds a bit scary. They insert a camera into an artery in his groin and follow it up to the heart to see what's wrong and then they fix it.' Her mother's voice trembled a bit and Suzie knew what she had to do.

'They can do wonderful things for heart disease these days, Mum. Try not to worry. Listen, I'll get a flight to Bristol tomorrow and come down on the bus to Exeter. I'll come straight to the hospital and I should be there by late afternoon.'

Her mother put up token resistance but finally accepted the offer gratefully. As soon as Suzie put down the phone, she dashed next door and explained to Alex what had happened. Alex was quick to offer reassurance in her turn.

'Father had that a couple of years ago. It's called an angioplasty and it's really quite routine these days. When the camera comes to a blocked bit of artery it slips in a little sleeve to reopen it. Father had two and he was fine again within a day or two.'

Suzie hoped she was right. She phoned the professor who told her to take all the time she needed and then she booked a seat on the flight from Venice leaving early the following afternoon.

–

As she was sitting at Marco Polo airport next day, waiting for her flight to be called, she had a pleasant surprise. Her phone beeped and she saw she had a message from Alex.

> Rafe will meet you at Bristol airport and give
> you a lift to the hospital. Try not to worry.
> Good luck. XX

Suzie texted back, trying to object, but Alex replied that the offer had come from Rafe himself and that he was adamant he wanted to help. Suzie was touched. She was also mightily impressed when she walked down to the pick-up area of Bristol airport a few hours later to find Rafe waiting for her in a luxurious sports car with the Aston Martin badge on the bonnet. She hugged him and thanked him warmly, but Rafe waved away her thanks.

'I had to take Melanie up to Bristol for a few days and I was planning on heading back to Devon today or tomorrow anyway. The airport's en route, so please don't worry.'

As they drove down to Devon, they chatted and Suzie was glad to talk about something other than her father's state of health. The subject turned to Alex, and Suzie was pleased to be able to report how well things were going for her.

'She's as happy as a sandboy. She keeps getting top marks and she's just had a couple of paintings accepted for a regional art contest. The way she's going, she'll be the next David Hockney.'

'Father's still amazed that she's managing to adjust to life without all the frills.'

'You can tell him that Alex bought herself a new bra at the market for five euros the other day and she says it fits just fine. And what's more – she did the whole transaction in Italian. She's made the transition to art student remarkably painlessly and she's just so happy doing what she's doing.'

'She owes a lot to you, Suzie.'

'Not at all. She's very determined. She'd have managed it without me, I'm sure.' She glanced across at him. 'But the best thing is how much more self-confident she's becoming. Irrespective of how well her art career goes, this is doing her so much good and her father needs to know that.'

'That's really good to hear. I'll be sure to tell him what you've said.'

'And do tell him that she hasn't gone all bohemian. She's a sensible girl and she's working hard.'

Rafe dropped Suzie at the hospital at just after five-thirty and she hurried up to see her father. She found him awake, with her mother sitting at his bedside. She rushed over and kissed them both before settling down on the edge of the bed, her father's hand in hers.

'Have you had the operation, Dad? You look so well.' For somebody who had just been under the knife he was looking remarkably sprightly. He smiled up at her and she felt his hand squeeze hers.

'Yes, all done, and good as new – or so they tell me.'

'The surgeon's been round and he says the operation was a complete success.' The joy on her mother's face was a delight and Suzie felt a great sensation of relief sweep over her. For a moment she felt her eyes stinging with emotion, but she wiped the tears away.

'So you'll be coming out soon?'

'Tomorrow or the next day, I believe.'

It seemed incredible and Suzie gave him a big kiss on the cheek. 'I'm so, so glad.'

'Now tell us about you, Suzanne. How've you been?' Her mother's face was pale and drawn, but the smile on her lips reassured Suzie that she, too, was recovering from the shock of events.

At seven o'clock they left the hospital and Suzie drove her mother home in the car. Neither of them was feeling particularly hungry so they had tea and toast and Suzie spent much of the evening telling her mother all about Verona. In the course of the conversation she mentioned Michael as a windsurfing friend, but her mother must have managed to pick up something in her voice.

'And you like this man?'

Suzie answered honestly. 'I like him a lot, Mum, but nothing's going to happen there.' Under cross-examination, she revealed what had happened to Michael's wife and saw her mother wince and shake her head in sympathy.

'Poor, poor man. How awful.' After a pause she looked up. 'But give him time. Time's a great healer, you know.'

Their conversation was interrupted by Suzie's phone. It was Rafe, asking for news about her father. She gave him an upbeat report on his health and then was not totally unsurprised to hear what he had to say next.

'That's excellent news. I'll tell Father. By the way, Suzie, he asks if you might have a moment tomorrow morning to see him. I could come and pick you up if you like.'

Suzie assured him she could drive up to the manor in her parents' car and agreed to be there at ten o'clock, wondering what sort of mood he would be in.

When she arrived in Lord Tedburn's study, she found him far less intimidating than the first time. He actually got up from his desk, came across, shook her hand, and then kissed her on the cheeks – which, needless to say, immediately started glowing as a result.

'How kind of you to come, my dear. Can I offer you anything? Coffee? Tea? Sherry?'

Suzie thanked him but shook her head and sat down in one of the armchairs while Lord Tedburn took a seat opposite her and asked about her father. He looked delighted to hear the good news and asked her to pass on his best wishes. Then, formalities completed, he changed the subject.

'Suzie… you don't mind if I call you Suzie, do you?' Suzie shook her head, quite amazed at the distinct thaw in his demeanour. 'Suzie, I wanted to see you to offer you my heartfelt thanks for staying on in Verona to be with Alexandra.'

'Not at all. I've managed to find myself a fabulous job with free accommodation, so no thanks are necessary. The flat's easily big enough for two.' At his insistence, she went on to tell him more about the new research centre and he expressed considerable interest.

'I'm very pleased for you, Suzie. That sounds like an exciting new challenge. I wish you and the research centre well. But Alexandra made it clear that you decided to stay on with her even before knowing about the new job. I won't forget what you've done for us.'

Suzie was particularly pleased to hear him use the pronoun 'us'. Clearly, there was no question in his head of any lasting Shakespearian-type rift between father and daughter. Hopefully, the same would happen as and when Rafe took the bull by the horns and told him his intentions as far as Melanie was concerned. She hadn't dared ask him in the car the previous day, but she felt pretty sure he still hadn't found the courage to speak up.

Lord Tedburn went on to ask her for news of Alex, and Suzie replied honestly that all was going well, mentioning the fact that she was working part-time and selling her expensive clothes to make ends meet. He appeared impressed, particularly when Suzie showed him photos of the two of her paintings that had been selected for the prestigious regional art exhibition scheduled to take place in mid-December in the magnificent Castelvecchio in Verona. By the end of their chat, she distinctly got the impression that he was both relieved and maybe even unexpectedly proud of his daughter. Suzie felt sure this boded well for a rapprochement before too long. As he bade her farewell, he took an envelope from the top drawer of his desk and pressed it into her hands.

'Here, I'd like you to have this. It's not right that you should be paying for my daughter's lodgings.'

Suzie glanced inside, saw a sheaf of green one hundred euro notes and made a quick decision. Handing the envelope back to him, she refused as politely as possible.

'Thank you, Lord Tedburn, but there's no need for this. Alex and I are friends and I'm happy to help her. If I'd needed to be paid, Alex would have found the money somehow, I know. She wants to be self-sufficient and she's succeeding. So, thank you very much, but this isn't about money.'

She gave him a smile and left the study, knowing she had done the right thing. There was no disputing that the extra money would have been useful, but accepting it would have run contrary to Alex's expressed desire to stand on her own two feet, without any help from her father. Hopefully the message would not be lost on him.

Chapter 23

Suzie's father walked unaided out of hospital next morning and she flew back to Italy the day after, relieved and satisfied that he was on the road to full recovery. Although she had planned to take the bus to the airport, this was rendered unnecessary by Rafe who insisted on giving her another lift as he was on his way to pick Melanie up again. As they headed north, Suzie gave it a little while and then asked him what he had decided as far as his future with her was concerned. His answer confirmed what she and Alex had already imagined.

'I've been putting it off and putting it off, but I *am* going to speak to Father about it. In fact, I'm planning on having it out with him this week. I just want to talk it through with Melanie one more time first.' He managed a grim smile. 'So wish me luck.'

'Good luck, but I'm sure he'll want you to be happy.' Without giving him a chance to disagree, she hastily changed the subject to Tommy and was rewarded by a little smile from Rafe.

'He sends his love and asked me to tell you that his offer still stands.'

Suzie smiled in return. 'Do, please give him my love and tell him thanks, but my answer remains the same. And also you can tell him the research centre should be open for business by mid-February if he or any of his colleagues are interested. I'll let him know when I've got a definite date.'

'He's really cheesed off that he can't come over with James and me at the weekend to see you. He said to tell you it's the fault of one of his mates from the army who's getting married, and Tommy's his best man.' He glanced across at Suzie and winked. 'I know he'd rather be with you.'

It came as no surprise to either of them when Suzie's cheeks lit up like traffic lights.

At Bristol airport she kissed Rafe warmly on the cheek and repeated her good wishes for the forthcoming confrontation with his father. She had her fingers crossed as she left him. She didn't envy him the experience.

Back at the flat in Verona that evening, she shared a pizza and a bottle of supermarket red with Alex and related everything that had happened in Devon. In particular, Alex listened spellbound as Suzie recounted her meeting with Lord Tedburn and applauded her decision to refuse his offer of money to pay the rent. Suzie could see from the expression on Alex's face that she was greatly relieved to know that her father was no longer breathing fire and fury, and maybe even beginning to realise that she really could stand on her own two feet and work hard. Alex then asked if Rafe had said anything about talking to his father and Suzie told her what he had said in the car.

'He's worried your father's going to go all Shakespearian on him, so he's been putting it off until this week. He told me a while back that there's always been a Tedburn at the manor ever since 1616. By the way, do you realise that's the year Shakespeare died? That's quite some tradition to uphold.'

'Tradition's all well and good, but without happiness it means nothing.' Alex was in no doubt. 'This week, you say? I just hope he doesn't lose his nerve. I'd hate it if he ended up having to marry somebody he doesn't love.'

'Like you and James? Or are you coming round to thinking that James might be the one for you after all, maybe?' He had been over for a quick visit that weekend while Suzie had been in the UK.

Alex shook her head, but Suzie got the impression it was with a bit less certainty than before. 'I do like him a lot, Suzie. It's just the whole sex thing…'

'Have you tried again?'

'I've barely kissed him.'

'But you have?'

'Well, yes.'

'And how was it? They say you can tell a lot from just a simple kiss.'

'Well, to be honest, it was rather nice.'

Suzie gave her a wink. 'Well, that's a good start, isn't it? And he's coming over again this weekend, isn't he? You can't say he isn't making an effort. That'll give you time for some more practice.'

After dinner, she logged onto her work computer and was surprised to see an email from Michael. It was addressed to the professor and copied to her, and it was a formal reply to the request for him to act as one of the trustees of the new charity. To her delight, he accepted with pleasure and indicated that he would be happy to come over to Verona for the opening, whenever that would be. She shot off a reply, thanking him and adding as an aside how happy she would be to see him again. As it was a work email, she avoided putting a little *x* before her name.

Next day she took the bus to the lake and met the professor, assuring him that all was now well again with her father. He expressed delight at her news, and the Labrador appeared to share his sentiments as he made a concerted effort to climb onto Suzie's lap while Mack was out of the room. Suzie dissuaded him gently and Dogberry was once more laid out on the floor when his master returned, but with one eye open, studiously watching every move that Suzie made in the hope that she should decide to get up and take him for a walk.

Although it had been getting ever colder day by day since mid-November, and there was frost in the air this afternoon, she and Dogberry had a lovely walk. It was a dry day and the air was clear. Walking along the lakeside, she could see the considerable quantities of fresh snow cloaking the mountaintops and for the first time it occurred to her that she might be able to go skiing or snowboarding this winter. She had had a couple of skiing holidays with Rob in the past and had enjoyed herself immensely. This reminded her of the skis she had spotted amid all the other junk underneath Michael's studio. However, once she had started thinking about him, she found it hard to stop. By this time she and the dog were almost level with the narrow lane leading up to his house and so, on impulse, she set off up the hill, soon identifying a path that led them away from the road and through the vines.

She was boiling by the time they reached his house and the dog was panting like a steam train. She stopped by the gate and looked into the courtyard. A flashy-looking Mercedes with Swiss plates was parked there and it was pretty clear that the rental agency had been doing their job well and had wasted no time. She glanced across at the studio, but it was all locked up. Presumably Michael had decided not to include it in the rental agreement. She hoped any local burglars wouldn't get wind of this as there were no doubt some valuable paintings in there. She stood there for a few minutes, looking across the courtyard to the vineyards – the bare vines now surrounded by a copper-coloured mass of fallen leaves at their feet – and down as far as the lake, her mind remembering how much she had enjoyed that one day she had spent here. Finally, with a shrug, she turned and set off back down the hill again, sadly reflecting that this might well be the very last time she would ever come here.

Back at the lakeside she stopped for a rest and sat down on a bench. Now that most of the leaves had fallen, the view out over the water to the mountains beyond was uninterrupted and she savoured the scene, although she couldn't rid herself of the familiar sense of regret for what might have been. A moment or two later, she felt a big heavy canine head land on her thigh and she looked down into soulful brown eyes.

'Ciao, Dogberry. Enjoy the walk?'

His head didn't move and his eyes remained fixed on hers.

'I wish he was here, dog.' She let her hand rest on his big hairy head and stroked him softly. 'I really do.'

–

James arrived early on Saturday morning to collect them both and bring them back to the villa for the weekend. When he saw Alex, his eyes lit up and he kissed her warmly on the lips and, as far as Suzie could see, Alex managed to respond. There didn't appear to be any risk of a repetition of her nausea from before. Whether this signified any significant development in their relationship remained to be seen.

It was a very cold day and the sides of the roads were white with frost, but the heavy car was sure-footed. Suzie glanced up at the cupola on top of the sanctuary of Nostra Signora di Lourdes on the hill to their right and saw that it already had a light covering of snow. It was the end of November and winter was very definitely not far away down here, and no doubt was already in full swing in the high mountains. She was quite relieved to hear James say that there was no wind at the lake and so he had no intention of going windsurfing that day. The very prospect made her shiver.

When they got to the villa, Rafe was waiting with a surprise for them both. Alongside him was a very pretty dark-haired girl with a smile on her face. Alex went over and hugged both of them, after which Rafe greeted Suzie and introduced his companion.

'Suzie, this is Melanie, my fiancée.'

Both Alex and Suzie did a double take as they heard this, and Suzie saw James smiling as the secret was revealed.

'You're going to be married?' Alex got there first. 'That's tremendous. I'm so, so happy for you guys.' And she hugged them both warmly. Suzie waited until she had released them before adding her congratulations.

'I'm delighted for you both. How exciting! Have you named the day?'

Melanie shook her head. 'That all rather depends...'

Suzie and Alex exchanged glances. No prizes for guessing the identity of the potential stumbling block.

'So you've spoken to Father?' Alex was hanging onto her brother's arm, looking up anxiously at him. 'How did he take it?'

Rafe sighed. 'How do you think? I'm the worst son in the history of the world, I'm irresponsible − by the way, he informed me that's always been your prerogative up till now, but I've just replaced you in his bad books − and he can't believe our heritage means so little to me.' He gave a wry grin. 'But I gave him the one argument he couldn't possibly refute.' He glanced across at Melanie before continuing. 'You see, Mel and I are expecting a baby.'

'A baby?' Alex looked surprised, but delighted. 'That's wonderful. When's it due?'

'The end of May.' Melanie clutched Rafe's hand and gave him an affectionate look. 'Rafe took me up to see my parents in Bristol last weekend and I saw a specialist on Monday. She's confirmed I'm three months into the pregnancy and all's well.'

'And your father, Rafe? How did he take the news? Was he even more furious when you told him?' Suzie had a feeling she might know the answer, but she was wrong.

'No, surprisingly, he wasn't. He didn't say very much, but it certainly took the wind out of his sails. When I left his study, he was speechless, but not in a bad way, if you know what I mean.'

'So do you think he's happy for the wedding to go ahead?'

Rafe smiled and shrugged. 'I wouldn't go so far as to use the word "happy", but resigned maybe. He gave up trying to talk me out of it, so when we go back on Monday, we'll sit down with him and talk it through. It'll be all right, I'm sure. He just needed to let off steam.'

'Well done, Rafe.' Alex looked justly proud of her big brother. 'You did it.'

'I think it was the toughest thing I've ever had to do. He was really livid at first. Thank goodness he calmed down again. For a moment there I thought he was going to explode.'

Suzie nodded quietly to herself. There was no doubt about it; Shakespeare would have had a field day with Lord Tedburn.

They had a very good morning together. Although Suzie was the odd one out in the middle of the two couples, Rafe and Melanie chatted with her while James monopolised Alex. Suzie learnt more about Melanie and her work at the hospital and gave her a brief résumé of the progress of the research centre and was able to confirm that they now had all their papers in order and planned to open for business sometime in February. Just before lunch, she popped next door to say hello to the professor and his lovely dog and to pass on news of the arrival of the final permit from the town hall and he was delighted. He asked her to lunch the next day and she said yes without hesitation. James, she felt sure, wouldn't mind.

Back at the villa, Rosa had produced a slap-up roast with all the trimmings and Suzie made a point of going through to the kitchen to congratulate her. They drank champagne first and then moved on to some excellent Nebbiolo from the Piedmont region. If she had let herself go, Suzie could have drunk herself into a stupor, but she decided to keep a clear head. The mood around the table, now that Rafe had finally summoned up the courage to speak to his father, was buoyant. Suzie herself was very pleased at the way the research centre was proceeding and she was maybe even beginning to find herself thinking about Michael a bit less.

That afternoon the two couples disappeared in different directions so Suzie popped next door and collected Dogberry to take him for a walk. She headed down the lake this time, away from Bardolino, walking past the little cafe where she and Tommy had come on their paddleboards back in early October. Unsurprisingly on a cold late autumn day like today, it was all locked up and there were few people out and about, compared to two months earlier. The view with the snow on the hills was, if anything, even more stunning, and she sat down on a bench and breathed it in. The sky was a cloudless pale blue and the air clear and still. Without the wind, the surface of the lake was like a mirror, with the image of the mountains on the other side inverted in it, every detail perfectly reproduced. She could pick out the occasional house and farm scattered on the hillsides opposite quite easily and she was just wondering what the view would be like from up there when her phone started ringing. She pulled it out of her pocket and saw it was Tommy's mobile.

'Tommy, hi. You'll never guess where I am.'

'Well, you can't be windsurfing if you're speaking to me on the phone. I'd guess Verona somewhere.'

'I'm down by the side of Lake Garda, at that little cafe we came to on our paddleboards, and I'm with Dogberry, my four-legged friend.'

'So how come you aren't windsurfing?'

'Simple; no wind.'

'So, apart from a lack of wind, how's life?'

They chatted for five or six minutes. She told him more about the research centre and he repeated his determination to be there as soon as it opened.

'We're still on target to be up and running by February. I look forward to seeing you then.'

'You'll see me before… that's if you'd like to see me.'

'Of course I'd like to see you. When's that going to be?'

'Next weekend. I'm coming over for the Ice Race on Saturday, a week today. James is going to do it, too. Has he told you about it?'

'So far we've only been talking about Rafe and Melanie. So, there's a race next weekend, is there? Great. Although Ice Race is a forbidding-sounding name.'

'It'll be fine, I'm sure. Apparently the first weekend of December every year the Ice Race takes place at Malcesine, up near the top end of the lake. James has done it before, but this'll be a first for me. Why don't you come up and join us? Maybe take part?'

Suzie's eyes focused on the dog's breath still pumping clouds into the near-freezing air. Of course she had her nice new wetsuit that should be warm enough, and she should be able to afford to invest in some boots, gloves and a hood. Maybe she would join in.

'If I can get hold of all the winter gear in time I'll seriously think about taking part. But, either way, of course I'll come up to see the race.'

'Terrific. We're all staying in the same hotel. James'll let you have the details. And Suzie, I'm really looking forward to seeing you again.'

After he had rung off, she sat back and did her best to analyse her feelings.

She had enjoyed the sound of his voice and she had meant it when she had told him she was looking forward to seeing him again. The sad fact of the matter, however, was that the voice she would have preferred to hear was that of her heartbroken artist and he hadn't spoken to her now for weeks and weeks. Was it maybe time to forget him and move on?

Chapter 24

Malcesine had a very different feel to it, compared to the south of the lake. Up here, the mountains plunged steeply down to the water and, starting only a few hundred metres above the town, everything was already covered with a blanket of snow. Although little more than half an hour up the lake from Bardolino, Malcesine was quite plainly in the high mountains. As Suzie drove into town late on Friday afternoon, she could see people carrying skis and snowboards returning from the cable car station that linked the little town with the snowy slopes above. Dusk was falling, it was bitterly cold and everybody she saw was wearing thick anoraks, hats and gloves. Earlier on, when she had collected the car from the professor's house, she had had to scrape thick ice off the windscreen and she was having serious second thoughts about the wisdom of venturing out onto the lake the next day in potentially sub-zero conditions.

It was almost completely dark by the time she managed to squeeze the car into the crowded hotel car park and checked in. She left the board and rig she had borrowed from James's collection securely strapped to the roof of the Mini. When they had spoken about the Ice Race last Sunday after Tommy's call, James had spent half an hour talking her through the triangular course that ran right across the lake to the chic resort of Limone and back again, warning her about possible wind shifts and tricky currents. Suzie was very grateful for the help, particularly as this had taken him away from Alex's side for just about the first time that weekend. She had been unable to judge from Alex's expression whether this was a blessed relief or a disappointment, but when they left the villa, Alex had spent considerably longer in James's arms saying goodbye than previously and had admitted back at the flat that she and he were getting on really rather well.

Inside the hotel, the first person Suzie saw was the bulky figure of Beppe. As he caught sight of her, he came striding across and embraced her.

'Ciao, Suzie. I hear you're going to take part in tomorrow's race. Is that true?'

Suzie kissed him on the cheeks. 'Ciao, Beppe. I think so, but I'll make a final decision tomorrow. It depends what the weather conditions are like. I don't fancy wind-surfing in a blizzard.'

'It's a good forecast. A good, strong wind from the north all morning and from the south in the afternoon – just like it should be here. It might be a little chilly, though.'

'A little chilly? It's freezing out there!'

'Ah, yes, but you'll soon warm up. I do this race every year and I lose two or three kilos each time just because I sweat so much.'

Suzie wondered whether to believe him, but made no comment. Instead, she turned the conversation onto another subject.

'Have you heard from Michael recently? I haven't had any news from him for quite a while now.'

She saw Beppe nod. 'He called me earlier this week. He's over in Italy this weekend and he said he's going to try to get up here to see the race. He won't be taking part as he's got stuff going on and he won't be able to get here in time.' His friendly face broke into a broad grin. 'That's good news for those of us who'd like a chance of winning. He's won so many times, it's getting boring.'

Suzie was torn – on the one hand she was glad Michael was coming, but she was a bit miffed that he hadn't thought to tell her. Doing her best to hide her feelings, she smiled back at Beppe.

'So there's hope for the rest of us.'

She lugged her bag up to her room and dumped it there along with her jacket. The room was small and far less luxurious that any of the hotels where she had stayed with Alex, but it would do fine. She had asked for a single room and this was indisputably that. From the size of the bed, there wouldn't be room for more than one person here – and not a very big one either. As the thought crossed her mind, she did her best to banish the image of Michael and herself squashed together in a lovers' embrace on the narrow bed. That wasn't going to happen and it would be better if she didn't have any more ideas like that. She went into the little en-suite shower room, washed her hands and splashed some water on her face. Contact with the cold water reminded her of the following day's race and she wondered, yet again, whether she really would be brave – or stupid – enough to take part. She was just drying her face when she heard a knock on the door.

It was Tommy, with a big smile on his face.

She smiled back at him and kissed him on the cheeks. 'Hi, Tommy, it's so good to see you again.'

'And you, Suzie. You're looking great. No glasses tonight?'

She shook her head. 'Alex has been bullying me into wearing my contacts more so I've been trying, even though I still feel more comfortable with glasses. When did you get here?'

'We've just arrived. Coming down for a drink?'

Downstairs he led her into the large bar and they were immediately swallowed up in a noisy mass of humanity. She clung to his arm as they squeezed through the crowd towards the bar, but before they got there James appeared with a bottle of Prosecco and a handful of glasses hanging down from his fingers. He kissed Suzie on the cheeks and dispensed the Prosecco.

'Drink as much as you can. The more I can get you and Tommy to drink, the more unfit you'll be tomorrow.'

Suzie found herself smiling back at him. 'Does this mean you're scared I'll beat you?' She knew this was a forlorn hope.

He grinned back. 'Terrified, but I'm counting on it being too cold for a little girl like you tomorrow. Hopefully you'll leave the serious stuff to us men and watch from the sidelines.'

'I've never been much good at watching from the sidelines. You might do well to look over your shoulder when you're out on the water tomorrow, James.'

He gave her a wink. 'At least if I'm looking over my shoulder, it'll mean you're behind me.'

Tommy joined in. 'And I'll be way behind her. Suzie'll be back here sipping champagne while I'm still only halfway back across the lake. You wait and see.' He held out his glass of Prosecco and clinked it against theirs. 'May the best man, or woman, win.'

It turned out to be a fun night. Tommy stuck to her side like a limpet and she was pleased to see him drinking sparingly. Whether this was because of the following day's race or so as to show her how well-behaved he could be, she couldn't tell, but she found him very pleasant, intelligent, attentive and handsome company. From the looks she intercepted from some of the other women there that night, she was pretty obviously not the only one to like what she saw. As the evening progressed, she couldn't help thinking that she could do a lot worse.

She finally headed for bed around eleven. The party downstairs was still in full swing for the hangers-on, but the serious competitors were clearly making sure they got a good night's rest. The course the following day would be almost ten kilometres and, with a strong wind, the waves and the near-Arctic temperatures, it would no doubt prove to be gruelling. She walked up the stairs to her floor with Tommy and James and bade them good night without any preamble. For now, she told herself, all her attention had to be focused on tomorrow's race. After the race, there would be time to think of other things – like men.

–

Next morning when she woke, the first thing she did was to look out of the window towards the lake. It was a cloudless day, so no chance of a blizzard, but it looked bitterly cold out there and she found herself seriously doubting the sanity of anybody willing to venture out into these freezing conditions on a sailboard. However, after a hot shower, she emerged from her room determined to give it a go, if only to show James that she wasn't just a weak little woman. In the dining room she found James and Tommy sitting at a table with a couple of other racers, so she marched over and told them.

'I've made up my mind. I'm going to do the race.'

James looked at her with respect. 'Good for you, Suzie. Make sure you wrap up warm.'

'Excellent, Suzie. I'm sure you'll enjoy it. We all will.' Tommy was smiling. She sat down beside him as James poured her a cup of black coffee. She normally had tea at breakfast, but she didn't object. She felt sure she would need all the adrenalin pumping through her veins she could get if she was going to survive the Ice Race.

Unusually for a windsurfing race, the Ice Race began with a Le Mans-type start from the pebbly beach. As she lined up along with about fifty other lunatics, board and sail in her hands, she looked round, doing her best to stop her teeth from chattering in spite of her thick suit, boots, tight-fitting neoprene hood and gloves she was wearing. All morning she had been keeping her eyes peeled for a sight of Michael, but without success. Beppe had said he was hoping to be here. Maybe she would have to accept that he wasn't going to make it after all.

As the countdown to the bell started, she checked that her number was well attached. She had ended up with number fifty and she hoped this wouldn't be her finishing position. Behind the beach, quite a large crowd had gathered, all wrapped up in thick winter clothes, and they shouted out the numbers in chorus as the start approached:

'*Cinque… quattro… tre… due… uno… Via!*'

As the bell started ringing furiously, Suzie ran forward with the others and splashed into the water, throwing her board in ahead of her. Even through her wetsuit and boots, the icy shock was palpable. The wind close to the shore, protected by the headland, was little more than a light breeze and she found herself having to pump the sail violently to get the board moving. To her left, she saw a big man fall off and another competitor ahead of her follow suit as the wind failed. She just managed to take avoiding action and squeeze past him. Fortunately, within a very few minutes, she emerged from the shelter of the promontory into the full force of the wind and she felt the sail almost ripped from her hands as a powerful gust caught and filled it. She just managed to hook into her harness and hurl her full weight backwards to compensate and avoid being thrown off. Ahead of her, two competitors were not so lucky and she heard both of them yell as they fell into the icy water.

She set off across the lake as fast as she could, following maybe a dozen others, and she recognised the sails of Beppe and James, neck and neck with a handful of others in the lead. She risked a brief glance over her shoulder and saw the rest of the field behind her already well strung out, with several figures still struggling in the water. By this time she was beginning to enjoy herself. The excitement of the start and the vigorous pumping of the sail had warmed her up far more than she could have imagined and she wondered whether Beppe had actually been telling the truth when he had talked about sweating off a couple of kilos. Certainly, she was far from cold now. As they made their way diagonally across the lake towards the far side, she overhauled three other boards and was doing well by the time they reached the first buoy and gybed round, before running downwind to the second turn.

It was when she was on the final leg, within sight of the finish, her arms aching and her shoulders almost set solid, that disaster struck. One minute she was sailing along, close-hauled, skimming across the waves in third place, the next there was a muffled thud as her board struck something beneath the surface and stopped dead. She was thrown violently forward as the impact flung the board into the air and tore her feet from the foot straps. Her forehead made contact with something solid and everything went black.

Chapter 25

'Suzie, Suzie, can you hear me?'

At first she couldn't work out what was happening. Somebody was shaking her and somebody else was pouring buckets of icy water all over her. She opened her mouth to speak, swallowed more water and started to choke. She felt the strong arms grip her more tightly as his voice came again.

'Suzie, can you hear me?'

It was surprisingly difficult to get her eyes to open, but she finally managed to get them partially open and, as she did so, it all came back to her. She was bobbing up and down in the midst of a chaotic jumble of waves, her weight supported partly by a sailboard and partly by a figure in a hooded wetsuit. As her eyes started to focus, she saw that the figure was Tommy and he was grinning from ear to ear.

'Thank God, Suzie, you're alive.'

She did a lot of coughing and had to make a couple of attempts before she was able to speak. When the words finally came out, it sounded as if somebody else were doing the talking. 'Was I dead?'

He was still grinning stupidly. 'No, of course you weren't. You were just knocked out for a few minutes.'

Suzie did her best to smile back at him, but another wave smashed into them and she choked once more, but his arms supported her. Then, mercifully, she began to hear another noise above the all-pervading hiss of the wind and the splashing of the water. It was unmistakably a powerful motor and, seconds later, an inflatable appeared alongside them. Hands reached down and dragged her out of the water into the boat, but her brain was working slowly and she didn't react. She was vaguely aware of voices and felt arms holding her as somebody wrapped a thin sheet of gold foil around her shoulders. Then the engine roared into life once more and the boat set off for the shore at high speed, bouncing though the waves. Whoever was holding her did a good job, as she remained solidly in place all the way to the beach.

Less than five minutes later, she found herself lying on a narrow bed inside a white-painted room. For the first time, she managed to open her eyes fully and blinked in the light. Her head began to clear and her eyes regained focus. Only now did she realise that she could taste blood. She raised a hand to her face and felt it come away wet. Holding it up in front of her, she squinted at it and saw the fingertips covered in bright red blood.

'Don't worry, it's just a little cut.'

She turned her head towards the voice and saw an unfamiliar face. It was a youngish man in a white coat and he was talking to her in Italian. Behind him was unmistakably a female paramedic in uniform. As the doctor saw her eyes focus on him, he smiled. 'It's all right, I'm the doctor. My name's Dario. You knocked yourself out, but you're going to be fine.'

'What happened…?' Her voice still sounded strained, but at least it now sounded like it belonged to her again. 'I was in the race and then, suddenly, I was in the water.'

'Good, good, you can remember that. They told me your board hit a tree trunk that was submerged just below the surface. You're going to have a black eye for a few days, but you'll be fine. Now, do you think you can try to wriggle out of your wetsuit so I can check you over? Carla here will give you a hand. One of your friends has gone back to your hotel to get you some dry clothes.'

After a struggle, Suzie managed to get out of the wetsuit and was wrapped in a towel and thick blankets to help warm her up again. The doctor gave her a full check-up and had just finished sticking little strips of tape across the cut over her right eye when there was a tap on the door. For the first time Suzie realised she was inside what looked like a caravan, not a building, as the door opened and a head appeared up the steps, accompanied by a blast of arctic air. It was Tommy and he was still smiling.

'Hi, Suzie. I hope you didn't mind me going through your stuff. The manager let me into your room. By the way, he sends his best wishes for a speedy recovery.'

Suzie smiled back. 'Hi, Tommy. Thanks for helping out. I thought I was going to have to walk out of here in just a blanket.'

He dropped the clothes on the bunk alongside her, stepped back and hesitated. 'Now I'd better leave you to it. I'm really glad you're all right, Suzie.'

'Don't go, Tommy. Wait a moment, there's something I've got to ask you. I'm afraid it's all a bit of a blur, but did you just save my life?'

This time he definitely blushed. 'Not really. I just grabbed hold of you, pulled your head out of the water and held you up until you came round again.'

'That sounds like saving my life to me.' She turned towards the doctor for confirmation and only then realised that she and Tommy had been speaking English. The doctor, however, nodded and replied in very good English with just a hint of an Italian accent.

'That very definitely sounds like life-saving to me, too. I reckon you owe this gentleman your thanks.'

Suzie gave him a broad smile and held up her arms to Tommy. 'You heard the doctor, Tommy. Please would you come over here?'

Hesitantly, he made his way across to the bunk and, at her insistence, leant down towards her. She stretched her arms around his neck and pulled him to her until she could kiss him, hard, on the lips. She felt him press tightly against her for some moments before a cold draught struck her again as the door of the caravan was pulled open. A man in a heavy jacket appeared, his eyes wide, trained on the scene before him.

'Suzie, are you all right?'

She released her hold on Tommy as the blood rushed to her cheeks.

'Michael, you're here!'

'I'm sorry I was late. I've only just got here. I was just in time to see your accident. How bad was it? Tell me, are you all right?'

She could see him staring at Tommy, who was now on his feet, staring back at him. The atmosphere was suddenly tense.

'What happened is that I hit a tree trunk and Tommy saved my life. I've just been thanking him.'

To her surprise, and no doubt Tommy's initial consternation, Michael took three steps across to him and enveloped him in a bear hug.

'Tommy, you're a hero. Very, very well done.'

Then, instead of transferring his attention to her, Suzie saw him turn back to the door. As his hand caught hold of the handle, he looked back over his shoulder for a few moments. She could see him doing his best to choose the right thing to say. He didn't look angry or jealous, just bewildered, and her heart went out to him. In the end, all he managed to get out was, 'I'm so glad you're all right, Suzie. Get well soon.'

And he was gone.

Suzie lay back against the pillow and wiped her eyes. To her surprise, she discovered that she now had tears pouring down her cheeks. She did her best to wipe them away as she looked back up at Tommy.

'Sorry for the tears. I suppose it's just delayed shock or something.' She glanced across at Doctor Dario, who smiled and nodded. Returning her attention to Tommy, she avoided any mention of Michael's whirlwind visit. Instead, she renewed her thanks. 'Thank you with all my heart for saving my life, Tommy. It sounds such a pathetic thing to say in response to something so major. I don't know how to thank you enough. I'm sorry if I cost you the race. Were you going to win?'

He shook his head, the concerned expression on his face changing to a smile. 'You must be joking! Beppe the chef won pretty easily, with James in second place. You were doing really well, though. It looked as though you were catching them when you hit that tree trunk and I was a good long way behind you. The main thing is that you're all right.'

The doctor told her to take it easy for the rest of the day and to avoid alcohol or driving for twenty-four hours, and she followed his advice. Tommy positioned himself firmly at her side as they sat down to a snack in the empty dining room, but she found she had little appetite. Although she had the reassuring feel of his hand in hers or even his arm around her shoulders for much of the time, her thoughts were of another man. She kept her eyes peeled for any sight of him, but to no avail. Seeing her kissing Tommy had no doubt confirmed to Michael that she and Tommy were now an item, but the sight of him had proved to her – if she had needed proof – that her heart still belonged to him. The fact that he had then left without even a kiss to the cheek was something she couldn't fathom and she found herself sniffling a bit over her half-sandwich. Hopefully, Tommy would put it down to delayed shock.

A bit later on, he escorted her to her room and saw to it that she that she lay down to rest as instructed by the doctor. His attitude was caring and considerate. Before letting him leave her, she held out her arms towards him once again.

'Thanks for everything, Tommy.'

He caught hold of her and kissed her lightly on the lips, just once and very briefly, but then he straightened up and stepped back.

'You're a lovely girl, Suzie. I wish you felt the same way about me that I feel about you.'

She was too tired to dissimulate. 'Is it that obvious?'

He gave her a gentle smile. 'I just hope your friend Michael realises what a lucky man he is. You deserve to be happy.'

She looked up and smiled back at him. 'And you're a lovely man, Tommy. A really lovely man.'

—

She fell asleep almost immediately and snoozed for the rest of the afternoon, not surfacing until well after dark. She found Tommy downstairs in the bar, looking concerned. As he spotted her at the door, there was no mistaking the relief on his face. He came across to guide her through the crowd and she was surprised to find that she appeared to be the object of many people's attention as she received numerous greetings, hugs, pats on the back and good wishes. As they reached the table, she saw Beppe sitting alongside James, both smiling up at her and, standing behind them, an unfamiliar face. Beppe leapt to his feet, embraced her and then made the introductions.

'Suzie, so great to see you up and about again. This is Alessandro. He's one of the organisers of the race. He's been waiting to talk to you.'

'Suzie, I'm delighted to see you're not too badly knocked about after your accident.' Alessandro held out his hand towards her. 'How do you feel?'

Suzie shook his hand as she replied. 'A lot better, thanks. A bit of a headache, but I've just taken some paracetamol, so I should be okay soon.'

'Very good, very good. Anyway, Suzie, on behalf of the organising committee, I have something for you. You've been awarded the *Medaglia della Combattività*. That's an award we give to the competitor who, in the opinion of the panel of judges, has demonstrated the greatest courage. This year, unusually, we have awarded this honour to two of you – yourself and Tommy, this brave guy who leapt off his board and rescued you. You're both heroes. Congratulations to you and best wishes for a speedy recovery.'

There were cheers and applause on all sides as he handed over a little box containing a silver medal to each of them and Beppe immediately insisted that Suzie pin it onto her top. Needless to say, her cheeks were glowing by this time. She thanked him warmly, hugged Tommy once more and sat down.

She managed to eat a little at dinner and was definitely feeling much better by the time the disco laid on by the organisers started, although she would have felt better if there had been some sign of Michael. The throbbing coming out of the loudspeakers went straight to her sensitive head and she decided it wouldn't be the best of ideas to try dancing – even if she felt like it – so although it was barely nine o'clock, she bade everybody good night and decided to return to her room. Ever attentive, Tommy was at her side, a supporting hand on her arm, as she climbed back up the stairs. When they got to the door of her room, she turned the handle and hesitated.

'Thanks again for everything, Tommy, starting with saving my life. I'm sorry I've monopolised your time.'

'Not at all. You're very welcome. Now make sure you get a good night's sleep.'

Before she could answer, he turned away and disappeared along the corridor.

Next morning she got up late, feeling much more normal, although her reflection in the mirror was scary, and she found Beppe sitting in the breakfast room.

'Hi, Suzie. How're you feeling? You look pretty battered.'

'A lot better, thanks. Almost normal, I would say, apart from a bit of a headache and a big bump on my forehead.' She sat down opposite him and summoned a smile. 'Did you get a chance to talk to Michael yesterday?' She glanced round the room. 'He went straight off after seeing me, right?'

He nodded. 'Yes, pretty much. He told me he had a lot of stuff he needed to get his head round.'

'Like seeing me kissing Tommy.'

'He didn't mention that.' Beppe must have seen the doubt on her face as he was quick to reassure her. 'No, really, he didn't. So does that mean you and Tommy are serious about each other?'

'He's a lovely guy and he saved my life and that's something I'll never forget. But no, we aren't a couple. He would like us to be a couple, but I'm afraid there's somebody else I can't get out of my mind.'

'Michael?'

'Michael. Although the more time passes, the more impossible it all seems.'

'You like him a lot, don't you?' Beppe's voice was unusually soft. Without waiting for an answer, he carried on. 'These past three years have been terrible for him, Suzie. He and Grazia were very, very much in love. Losing her was like losing part of himself. I can only begin to imagine what he's been through. But I can see that he really likes you, too. A lot. He just needs time.'

Suzie managed a little smile. 'That's what my mum said.' She caught the waitress's eye and ordered a pot of tea. 'I feel so very sorry for him. Like you say, it must have been awful. I just wish he'd let me help him.'

'Do you know why he was over here in Italy this weekend?'

'Not just to watch the race?'

He shook his head. 'He flew over on Friday. You see, it was the third anniversary of Grazia's accident and he met up with her family for a memorial service in their local church in Brescia. After staying there overnight, he came across here yesterday afternoon. He told me it had been an emotional time and that's why he was late getting here. He gets on very well with Grazia's parents and he stayed on to comfort them.' His tone was deadpan. 'It was this time three years ago, just before the race, that the call came through to him from the highway patrol. You can imagine all the memories that must have been flooding through his brain. He told me to say he was sorry he had to go off, but he needed to get his head straight. That's what he said – he wanted to get his head straight.'

'I just hope he can.'

When the time came to leave and go back down the lake to see the professor as agreed, Suzie saw that her kit, rescued from the lake by some kind people, was already strapped on the roof of Tommy's hire car along with his own gear and James's. He asked her if she was sure she felt well enough to drive. Otherwise, he said one of them would be happy to drive the Mini back to the professor's house in Bardolino and then drop her back in Verona. She told him she felt fine and gave them both a warm hug and a kiss before they left.

'Once again, Tommy, thank you from the bottom of my heart for saving my life and for being such an understanding friend.'

He kissed her chastely on the cheeks. 'I'll always be your friend, Suzie.'

As she was getting into her car, she heard her name being called. It was Beppe. As she turned towards him, he caught her in a bear hug, and when he released her he gave her a meaningful wink.

'Next time you come to the restaurant, your dinner's on me.'

'That's very kind, Beppe, but what for?'

'I'm not sure how much you remember, but you were coming up fast on James and me when you hit that log. For all I know, you might have overtaken either or both of us. As it was, we both carried on to the finish, blissfully unaware of all the drama unfolding behind us. Your friend Tommy saved you, I won the race, you're all right and he's a hero. If that's not worth a free meal, I don't know what is.'

Suzie gave him a big kiss on the cheek and, as he turned away, she surreptitiously pulled out a tissue. Puzzlingly, although her lips were smiling, the tears were once again pouring down her cheeks.

She drove down to Bardolino very slowly and carefully, just in case, but her head was feeling pretty normal again by now. When she got there, the professor was initially appalled at the state of her bruised and battered face, but she was quick to assure him that it was just cosmetic, and that she would be as right as rain soon. The dog greeted her warmly and positioned himself strategically between her and the cake, adopting his 'they never feed me' expression that Suzie knew of old and ignored. The hopeful thump of his heavy tail on the floor carried on all the way through their tea and cake. The professor, however, was thinking of things other than cake.

'I've been wondering. Now that we have all the papers in order, I wonder if you think it might be possible to bring forward the opening of the research centre.' This had been planned for mid-February. 'I was wondering whether we could maybe even make it sometime in January. I'm sorry to give you extra work, but I'd like to speed everything up if we can and it would be wonderful to open the doors of the research centre a bit earlier than planned.' He glanced across at her and grinned. 'I'm not getting any younger, after all. Do you think that might be feasible?'

Suzie had already been thinking along similar lines. 'I'll make sure it is.' She gave him a confident smile. 'We'll get there. I'll do a bit of chasing and I promise we'll be ready before the end of January, even if I have to paint the walls myself.' It occurred to her that one advantage of this change of plan would be to give her a valid reason for contacting Michael and, hopefully, of seeing him again sooner than she had hoped.

A little later on she took the bus back to Verona, and returned to the flat. As she walked in, Alex took one look at her and almost had a fit.

'Good God, Suzie, you look like you've just head-butted a brick wall. What the hell happened?'

Suzie gave her an encouraging smile and told her all about it. As she did so, she checked herself out in the mirror on the kitchen wall and had to admit that she was a pretty scary sight. Apart from the cut above her eyebrow and a black eye – or, rather, a bloodshot eye surrounded by blue and purple bruising – she also had a big lump in the middle of her forehead, along with scratches on her left cheek. Still, she told herself, it could have been worse. Much worse.

'Tommy saved my life.'

Alex grinned at her. 'Of course he did. And was that the cathartic moment that made you realise you love him? Have you spent every minute since then wrapped in each other's arms?'

Suzie managed to smile back. 'Afraid not. You see, somebody else showed up just as I was kissing Tommy.'

'Michael?'

Suzie nodded and recounted the events of the previous day, including Michael's surprise arrival and sudden departure. After that, she poured herself a glass of mineral water and went on to tell Alex the reason Beppe had given for his sudden disappearance, and she read sympathy in her friend's eyes.

'I suppose his head must have been swirling with memories. Little wonder he bailed out. Anyway, I've got my conversation exchange with Beppe on Wednesday. I'll see if I can wheedle any more information out of him.'

'You do that, but the thing is, Michael didn't even kiss me. He didn't even shake my hand. He just left.'

'Remember what Beppe said, and what your mum said, and what I've been saying. Give him time.'

Suzie sat down at the kitchen table opposite her. 'I know, but it's just so bloody frustrating. Somehow I don't think it's meant to be. The stars just haven't aligned for us, I'm afraid.' She stifled a sigh. 'Anyway, what about you? Everything ready?'

The reason Alex had stayed on in Verona on Friday afternoon had been to collect her two paintings from the framers. On Saturday afternoon she had then taken them to the Castelvecchio in readiness for the exhibition opening, scheduled for next Friday night.

'Yes, I've handed them in. I worked that evening and then last night I went to a party.'

'Oh, yes? Any good?'

Alex shook her head. 'It's the funniest thing. There was booze, the whole place reeked of marijuana, there was loud music and boys, but I felt like a fish out of water.' She snorted. 'It sounds crazy but, at the ripe old age of almost twenty-six, I felt old, really old.'

Suzie laughed. 'Think how an old woman like me would have felt. Did you manage to have a good time all the same?'

'Yes, I suppose I did. I danced a bit and had a few beers, but my heart wasn't in it. Even when this totally gorgeous guy I'd never seen before offered to take me back to his place for the best time of my life I was just, sort of… no, can't be bothered.'

Suzie found herself giggling. 'I think that's a thing called maturity. Well, your father would have been pleased, and I'm proud of you.'

'Talking of my father, I almost forget. Hot off the press: he's coming here next Friday night for the opening of the exhibition, although he's flying back again straight away the next morning. I've booked him into our old hotel for the night.'

'Wow, that's great.' The more Suzie thought about it, it really was good news. 'And how did he sound?'

283

'To be honest, he sounded good. He and Rafe have done a lot of talking and the wedding's set for the beginning of February. And of course you'll be getting an invitation, by the way. Rafe called me last night and told me it had all gone remarkably well. Now that Father's got to know Melanie a bit better, he seems to have calmed down, and he sounded pleased that she and Rafe are happy together, even if she hasn't got a title.'

'Brilliant! So do you think this means he might let you off the hook as far as James is concerned? Surely he can hardly let his son marry a commoner and then insist that his daughter goes through with an unhappy marriage for the sake of the family tree.'

Alex looked more than a little embarrassed. 'To tell the truth, Suzie, I think I may be changing my way of thinking about James. I've met quite a few men since I started doing the course and there was that guy at the party last night, but there's no getting away from it – I haven't met anybody I like anything like as much as I do James.'

'I told you he was the man for you.' Suzie was delighted at what she was hearing.

'The other thing is now that I'm proving to my father – and myself – that I can be independent, it occurs to me that it doesn't matter if I end up with James. I'm my own person now and I'll hook up with whoever I want. If it happens to be somebody Father approves of, then so be it, but the decision will have come from me.'

'Terrific news. So what happens now? Isn't there still the problem of you and him being like brother and sister?'

There was no doubt about it. For once, Suzie wasn't the one with the bright red cheeks. Alex's face was positively glowing.

'Um, that might not be so much of a problem after all. Somehow, bit by bit, I'm coming round to realising I actually quite fancy him. You see, I've been dreaming about him.'

'Oh, yes… and…?'

'Well, let's just say they haven't been the sort of dreams a sister would have about a brother.'

Suzie reached across, took hold of both her hands, and gave them a squeeze. 'That's the best news I've heard all week. You and James look good together and there's absolutely no doubt that he's potty about you. So, when are you going to see him next? Christmas?'

'At the weekend. He's coming back over for the exhibition as well.'

'And you're going to tell him about your dreams?' Suzie grinned at her. 'Or maybe let the dreams become reality?'

Alex was still red in the face and looking unusually embarrassed, so Suzie relented and let her off the hook, secretly delighted things appeared to be working out. And not just for Alex with James. It also looked very much as though things were finally coming good between Alex and her father, and Rafe and Melanie had now reconciled with him as well. The Tedburn family finally appeared to have managed to set its house in order. Suzie felt really happy for all of them, but she wouldn't have been human if she hadn't felt a little bit envious. She and Michael were hopefully still friends, but that was as far as it went.

Chapter 26

The week passed quickly. True to the promise she had made to the professor, Suzie contacted the plumbers on Monday morning and did her persuasive best to get a commitment that they would install the new toilets as soon as possible. Fortunately, the boss of the company had known Professor Macgregor-Brown for years and as a result on Wednesday a van arrived and work started. Suzie immediately went out and bought doughnuts for the two plumbers and made sure she was always on hand to make drinks for them whenever they wanted from then on, determined to keep them there at all costs.

Interestingly, while British tradesmen normally tended to function best on liberal quantities of tea, she discovered that Italians preferred coffee, and one of the men in particular managed to consume a never-ending succession of powerful espresso shots each day. Suzie felt sure that she would have been awake for a week if she were to do the same, but it didn't appear to hamper him in his work and maybe it actually helped. Whatever it took, she was determined to keep the plumbers on site and working.

She had received a text message from Michael on Monday morning, apologising but not explaining his sudden departure. She sent him a photograph of her face so he could see how the bruising was developing and he replied immediately telling her she was already looking a lot better, but saying little more. After that, radio silence resumed and she felt disappointment descend upon her once again.

As soon as the plumbers moved up to the first floor, Suzie set about clearing the big rooms downstairs completely. She slaved away, polishing the floors and cleaning everything from top to bottom before borrowing the car and scouring the furniture factories in the area around Verona – of which there were surprisingly many – until she found somewhere that could supply and deliver a fine-looking conference table, desks and several dozen chairs before the end of the year. The new computer system was scheduled for installation during the first week of January and the boxes of books that kept arriving began to fill the bookshelves. Gradually, it was all taking shape. And the harder she worked, the less time she had to think of Michael and what might have been.

–

James and Lord Tedburn arrived together late on Friday afternoon and by this time Alex had got herself into a real state. Torn between wearing something suitably formal for the opening of the exhibition – not to mention something conservative for her father's benefit – and something alluring for James, she had begun to panic now that she had disposed of all her designer dresses. Suzie even offered her the posh dress Alex had bought for her, but Alex thanked her and chose a skirt and the best top she could find in her seriously depleted wardrobe. The fact that it had a fairly revealing neckline would no doubt please her boyfriend, although it might not create quite the right effect for her father.

Nevertheless, when the two men arrived at the flat, Alex was looking really good, and Suzie sensed no disapproval on her father's part and a lot of attraction on James'. As for herself, she decided to wear the smart dress and put her hair up, but no amount of makeup would cover her bruises, so she didn't bother. Hopefully there wouldn't be any small children at the opening party to be terrified by her appearance.

The four of them sat down together in the comfortable living room – which Suzie and Alex had scrupulously tidied and cleaned in advance – and gradually they all relaxed. Alex positioned herself beside her father and, before long, was chatting to him quite freely. For his part, he also looked and sounded far more relaxed than Suzie had expected. She distinctly got the impression that he approved of their new lodgings, even though they were a far cry from the five-star luxury of the hotel where he was staying. Then, at six, after a bottle of very good champagne brought by James, they set off and walked through the quiet streets to the Castelvecchio.

Every time Suzie saw this magnificent medieval castle which also housed a museum, she never failed to be impressed. Tonight, with the façade floodlit and an unexpectedly large number of people milling about, all decked out in their finery, it looked even more impressive. It gave her an idea of what it must have been like back in the days of the man who had ordered its construction. Cangrande della Scala, the most famous ruler of Verona, had been known both for his military achievements and for his interest in the arts, especially his patronage of Italy's greatest poet, Dante Alighieri. Not that this had prevented him from meeting an untimely death by poisoning. The Middle Ages had been a dangerous time here in Verona.

Inside the castle tonight, however, the atmosphere was far from poisonous. This was the first opening night of a major art exhibition that Suzie or Alex had ever visited and, as Alex commented in hushed, awestruck tones, it was a hell of a lot more impressive than the annual opening of the local art club exhibition in their Devon village.

The exhibition turned out to be a triumph for Alex. Best of all, both of her paintings had little red stickers on the labels when they got there, signifying that they had already been sold. She whispered gleefully in Suzie's ear that the money she would get from the sales would be more than enough to pay for return tickets to England for both of them at Christmas, as well as a few presents. And then, just as it looked as though things couldn't get any better, one of her paintings was singled out by the judges as being of special artistic merit. Suzie could see that Alex was on cloud nine and she was delighted for her. She was also really pleased to see Lord Tedburn looking and sounding happy and proud of his daughter.

Suzie wandered around the exhibition with a glass of Prosecco, pleased to see that very few of the works on display appealed to her as much as Alex's. She met several familiar faces and stopped to say hello. Little by little she was beginning to get into Veronese society and she already felt a growing sense of identity with the inhabitants of this gorgeous historic city. It was while she was standing in front of the larger of Alex's paintings – a marvellously atmospheric woodland scene where tree trunks and boughs entwined in a serpentine way – that she was joined by none other than Lord Tedburn himself, and there was a broad smile on his face.

'Hello, Suzie. I love my daughter's work, don't you? All these years I'd never realised how good she could be.'

'I think the course she's doing at the Academy has been very useful for her. And, of course, she got a lot of great advice back at the beginning from a good friend of ours.'

'Is that the portrait painter she's been telling me about?'

'Michael Turner, that's right.'

'I must go and thank him.'

Suzie was puzzled. 'You know where he lives?'

Lord Tedburn shook his head. 'Not at all, but I understand he's just arrived here tonight. Alexandra told me she'd seen him talking to the judges.'

If there had been any more than a dribble of Prosecco left in her glass, Suzie might well have thrown it in her own face this time as she literally jumped at the news.

'He's here? Michael's here?' She turned and cast her eyes around the room.

'Yes, I believe so.'

She was already thinking of the most polite way of asking to be excused before running off to see Michael when Lord Tedburn changed the subject and she had to stand there, desperately fidgeting to be off, but doing her best to listen politely.

'I'm fascinated by this new research centre you're setting up. Tell me, have you got enough money for everything?'

'We're doing fine at present, although all the renovation work and buying new equipment and resources has stretched things a bit. The plan is to wait until it's up and running and then start looking for sponsorship.' She gave him a grin. 'I was thinking about maybe approaching some of the big grappa companies.' She cast another fruitless glance around the room.

'I was wondering if I might be able to save you the trouble. Maybe I might be allowed to help?' Suddenly Suzie's attention returned to Lord Tedburn. Seeing the expression on her face, he elaborated. 'As I think I told you, I have a deep love of English literature and Shakespeare in particular. I would be honoured if you felt like accepting me as a sponsor of this new endeavour.'

'You want to be our sponsor?' Was she hearing what she thought she was hearing?

'Yes, I would love to contribute towards this remarkable new venture. Do you think Professor Macgregor-Brown might be prepared to consider my offer? I would ask for nothing in return.' He smiled. 'I'm not asking for the place to be renamed in my honour or anything. I just think it would be a worthwhile use of the funds at my disposal. And according to my accountants, it could work out to be beneficial to me from a tax point of view anyway. Do you think you could use the extra financial support?'

'Lord Tedburn, that's incredibly generous of you.' Suzie was genuinely stunned at his generosity – tax deductible or not. 'I don't know what to say. Could I talk it over with the professor and get back to you? Thank you so much for the amazing offer.' She let her eyes flit around the room once more and prepared to launch into her apology at having to leave him, but Lord Tedburn hadn't finished.

'Not at all. Please talk it over and let me know what you think. And, Suzie, there's something else. Now, please don't get upset, but I'd like to give you a present.' Suzie started to protest, but he carried on. 'Let me finish, please. I can't begin to tell you how impressed I am at the way my daughter has grown up and blossomed, and so much of it's thanks to you. I know you didn't do it for money, but I'd be grateful if you would accept a gift from me just to say thank you. And, besides, it is Christmas, after all.'

At that moment a waitress came round with a magnum of Prosecco and paused to replenish their glasses. As the girl moved on again, Lord Tedburn demonstrated that he had been doing his homework.

'I've spoken to Rafe about this idea and he tells me he thinks you might like a new sailboard and rig. Apparently James has been lending you his equipment, but it would be good for you to have your own kit, wouldn't it? Please humour me. It would mean a lot to me to be able to demonstrate how grateful I am to you.'

Suzie put up token resistance, but ended up accepting his generous offer. As he had said, it would be good to have her own kit. In spite of her anxiety to get away, she forced herself to be patient and they continued to talk for a few minutes before he told her something that almost took her breath away.

'You may have been wondering why I've proved to be such an inflexible – some might say interfering – father.' She saw his eyes were no longer fixed upon her or the painting. They were staring out of the window into the beautiful courtyard of the castle. It was still freezing cold outside and there were even little dry snowflakes in the air, whirling and dancing in the floodlights. 'It's all because of a promise I made to my dear, departed wife. A matter of days before her death, she asked me to promise to keep a close eye on both children and see that they did well and made successes of their lives. Of course I promised I would – I would have done so anyway – but it's only over the past few weeks that I've come to realise that my concern for their well-being has led me to be far too prescriptive. Both Rafe and Alexandra are adults now and, as such, it's only fair they should make their own decisions.' He turned back towards Suzie with a gentle smile on his face. 'And as I've told them both, the decisions they've been making recently strike me as eminently sensible. I'm proud of them.'

Suzie was genuinely amazed. So Lord Tedburn had also been tied by a promise made to a dying woman. Without wanting to, Alex's mother had almost brought about the opposite of what she had sought to achieve. Instead of the happiness of her children, relations had soured until a break-up of the family had loomed large. Not for the first time, she found herself reflecting on how much Shake-speare would have loved the Tedburns. Thankfully, in their case, tragedy had been averted and things had finally worked themselves out. She smiled back at him.

'And you're right to be proud. Rafe's a good man and his future wife strikes me as ideal for him. And, as for Alex, I just know she's going to have a brilliant future, and it'll be all the better now that she's got the full support of her father.' She held up her glass and clinked it against his. 'And now, Lord Tedburn, if you don't mind, I must go and look for Michael, the portrait painter.'

Michael was standing in front of the second of Alex's paintings, arm in arm with her, clearly congratulating her. As he caught sight of Suzie, a smile spread across his face and a corresponding hot flush crossed hers. It was really, really good to see him again. Alex looked round and grinned.

'Surprise, surprise. You didn't know he was coming, did you?' She was looking positively mischievous. 'I did. In fact, I was the one who insisted he absolutely had to come to my first ever exhibition.' Suzie was still just standing there, gawping. 'I only found out he was definitely coming this afternoon and I should have told you, but I wanted to surprise you, and the expression on your face is priceless.' She took a big mouthful of Prosecco and disengaged herself from Michael's arm. 'And now I'll leave you two and go and talk to my father.'

As she walked off, Michael stepped towards Suzie and stopped, a foot or so from her, a nervous smile on his lips. She could see him studying her battered face intently. The blue of the bruises had started to disintegrate into multicoloured patches, the colours now less intense. The scar above her eye had closed up and she no longer needed the strips of tape. She still felt she looked like a zombie, but definitely better than before. She saw him nod to himself a few times before speaking.

'You look breathtaking, Suzie.' There was emotion in his voice. 'The bruises are much, much better. And that dress is perfect. Yes, you look amazing.'

'You look very good, too, Michael.' He was wearing a very smart midnight-blue dinner jacket with a crisp white shirt and bowtie. He looked every inch the sophisticated man she had first seen in Venice. She remembered her initial impression of him as being way out of her league and, as the thought crossed her mind, she suddenly felt less secure. 'How wonderful to see you. I had no idea you were coming.'

'It was a last-minute decision. I knew I had to see you.' The nervous look was still in his eyes and she wondered what was coming next.

Initially, it was a hug. He moved the remaining few inches towards her and, hesitantly, opened his arms and caught hold of her. He stared down into her eyes for a moment before pulling her towards him and hugging her so tightly, her feet almost came off the floor and she felt a warm glow spread throughout her whole body. If he had released his grip on her, she would probably have collapsed in a heap on the floor – a very happy heap, but still a heap. He didn't kiss her, but he didn't need to. Somehow she could sense a major change in him and her heart began to beat more rapidly.

'We need to talk. I think there are benches in the museum. Shall we go and sit down?'

She nodded and followed him out of the exhibition area into the main part of the museum. A few people were wandering around the exhibits, but it was very quiet and very private. He led her to a wooden bench set among a collection of suits of armour, where they sat down side by side and he took her hand in his. Here, after a long period of silence, he slowly started to speak.

'I got to Malcesine last Saturday just after the Ice Race started and I watched your progress from the shore. When I saw you disappear into the water and not emerge, for a moment I thought you were dead. All I could see from the beach was the upturned board and the half-submerged sail and, of course, I was powerless to help. It was then that the realisation started to dawn on me. I thought I'd lost you, too, just like I lost Grazia, and it broke my heart. Life is for living and time's too precious to waste.' He was staring down at her fingers, entwined with his. 'And then, in that First Aid post, with you shivering under a blanket, your arms round Tommy's neck, suddenly my head started spinning. It was as if a lightning bolt went right through me. From then on, I was in a daze.'

Suzie could hardly believe her ears. She was finally hearing what she had been waiting so long to hear.

'But, tell me, why did you run off? There's nothing between me and Tommy.' She produced a little smile. 'Apart from the fact that he saved my life, of course.'

He hung his head. 'I know. Beppe told me. And, for that matter, so did Alex. I'm sorry I chickened out and ran off without talking to you, but I had so much going through my mind, I knew I wasn't going to be coherent.' She saw him take a deep breath. 'Back in October, when I told you I was leaving Italy and returning to the UK, I said it was because of memories of my wife, but that wasn't really the whole truth. You see, what made me make that decision was a conversation I had with my brother-in-law, Grazia's brother. He and she were very close and the accident hit him hard... probably as hard as it hit me. Anyway, I had dinner with him back in early October and I told him I'd met this girl – that's you – and I liked her a lot. He almost had a fit and he told me in no uncertain terms that I owed it to Grazia to get as far away from you as possible.' He looked up, straight at her. 'So I took his advice. I know now that it wasn't good advice.'

She gave his hand a squeeze, but he didn't seem to notice. His eyes dropped once more as he continued.

'October and November have been miserable months for me, constantly thinking of you but feeling I owed it to Grazia to stay clear of you, not even to contact you, although I longed to hear your voice. And then, when I came back last weekend and realised I'd almost lost you, I knew I had to do something. I sat down with Beppe and asked for his advice. He told me to talk to Giovanni – that's my brother-in-law – and get him to see sense, and then to talk to you and see if you'll have me. I flew back to England and I spent a miserable few days trying to get my head straight.' He looked up from the floor. 'And then last night the mists finally cleared. I got yet another text from Alex – she's a persistent little devil, isn't she? – and I realised I needed to see you to explain, but first, I needed to go to Brescia.'

Suzie tightened her grip on his hand, but didn't interrupt. She noticed for the first time a light mark on his ring finger. His wedding ring was no longer there.

'I got the early morning flight to Bergamo today and went straight to my in-laws' house in Brescia. I called Giovanni and he came round and we sat down together. I told them everything, from first setting eyes on you to thinking that you'd drowned, and her parents understood. I've always got on well with them and in many ways, especially since the accident, they're almost like real parents to me. They understood and, bit by bit, they managed to convince Giovanni.' He stared straight into her eyes. Suzie could see the hurt still lurking there but there were no tears. His tone became firmer as he continued. 'What they told me is that life goes on, Suzie. I know that now. One chapter of my life is over and a new one has started. One doesn't diminish the other. I suppose, deep down, I've known it since I saw you in Venice, but the thing is, I've finally got my head – and my heart – straight. The mists have cleared and I know I want to be with you… if you'll have me.'

She had absolutely no hesitation. 'Of course I'll have you, Michael, but only when you feel the time is right. I'll wait for you. For as long as it takes.' She could feel her eyes stinging, but she steadfastly refused to let tears run.

Funnily enough, she found that she wasn't blushing. In spite of the emotions swirling inside her, she suddenly felt reassured and an inner calm descended upon her. She saw an expression of relief on his face and noticed for the first time that the dark rings under his eyes were far less pronounced now. He looked a new man and a much happier man. As their eyes met, he managed a little smile.

'The time is right now, Suzie. Of that, I'm sure.' He hesitated and glanced around. 'Do you think there's a no kissing rule in this museum?'

Suzie leant towards him, feeling her normal reticence start to ebb away as she realised a whole new chapter was opening in her life as well. 'Rules are made to be broken.'

Chapter 27

The grand opening of the Macgregor-Brown Research Centre on the twenty-third of January went really well. Both of the large rooms downstairs were packed with people and Suzie even had to open the French windows to allow some overspill into the garden, in spite of the frosty night. The professor gave a little speech in English and immaculate Italian, followed by the head of the famous *Biblioteca Capitolare*. After these two august gentlemen had spoken, Suzie had to give her own welcome to the crowd. She had been dreading this, but Michael had schooled her well, making her recite the bits in English as well as the bits in Italian until they were engraved in her memory. He had taken his job so seriously that he had even made her recite parts of it while lying in bed with her, although the touch of his hands on her naked body had not made the task any easier – definitely a lot more pleasant, but not easier.

The speech was very well received and she felt she had managed to get it right, surprising herself by getting through it all without blushing, and she caught his eye as she reached the end. He was beaming and she beamed back. Mind you, she thought to herself, she had had a permanent smile on her face for weeks now.

Alongside him in the front row, she saw another smiling face. Alex, too, had been looking very happy ever since moving into the villa with James a few weeks back. James had managed to organise his business affairs so as to allow him to take a six-month semi-sabbatical and he and Alex had set up home together at the villa by the lake. While Alex went up to Verona every day to do her course, sporting her new engagement ring on her finger, he worked from home, honed his windsurfing skills and practised his Italian with Roberto and Rosa.

Between Alex and Michael was another happy face. Sitting at their feet was Dogberry, with a canine smile on his face as his nostrils had already picked up the alluring aroma of the canapés being readied for the guests. Knowing him so well by now, Suzie had no doubt he had already worked out that in a crush like this, it was almost inevitable that succulent mouthfuls would end up on the floor. In true Labrador tradition, he would be only too pleased to provide an efficient waste-disposal service.

Once the speeches had finished, the guests were invited to inspect the other floors, the resources at the disposal of academics and all the other facilities available. Suzie and Alex had both moved out of the top-floor flat in early January and this had now been transformed into a relaxing area with tea- and coffee-making facilities, periodicals and a large television screen. With the aid of Lord Tedburn's generous cash injection, there were now more easy chairs and sofas up there and the scruffy old terrace from where you could see across to the Scaliger castle had been cleared, restored and rendered serviceable once again.

Lord Tedburn himself was waiting for Suzie as she stepped down from the little dais they had erected for the speeches. He, too, was beaming.

'Excellent speech, Suzie. Thank you for mentioning my contribution, but like I told you, there was no need. I'm just happy to see Professor Macgregor-Brown's dream come to fruition.'

Suzie grabbed two glasses of Prosecco from a passing tray and handed one to him. 'Well, I meant it. With your support, the centre's future is secure.' She clinked her glass against his and they toasted each other. 'And that means mine as well.'

He took a sip of wine and nodded approvingly. 'Excellent wine. By the way, I bring apologies for absence from Rafe and Melanie. She's been suffering from morning sickness and he didn't want to leave her, but they wish you well with this enterprise. And of course, you've moved, haven't you? How are you finding your new home? Alexandra tells me it's got an exceptional view.'

Suzie nodded, doing her best to swallow her fizzy mouthful cautiously before risking a reply. As of three weeks ago, she and Michael were officially cohabiting and she couldn't have been happier. He had told her of his plans in her bed the morning after Alex's triumphant exhibition back before Christmas.

'I've been thinking.' At the sound of his voice, she had turned towards him and rested her bruised cheek against his bare chest, letting her hand run gently over his skin. 'My decision to move back to the UK was a big mistake. There's so much I miss over here in Verona. I left a lot of friends behind and coming back to see the Ice Race reminded me of them all. But of course, the main person

I knew I'd miss would be you – and I'm not going to let that happen. I've made up my mind. I don't want to be separated from you any longer.'

That had sounded perfect to her and, as a result, she now found herself living in the Old Stables with him, and both he and she had settled in just fine. Any lingering memories didn't appear to trouble him any longer. Cat had mysteriously reappeared the very first day and had plonked himself down in proprietorial fashion on her lap and she had felt completely at home from the off.

She gave Lord Tedburn a smile. 'I love the place. It's a real home in a gorgeous position and it even comes complete with its own cat. And I've got a dog only five minutes away if I ever feel like going for a walk. The lake's just down the hill and the ski slopes are little more than an hour away. What more could I ask for? You must come out and see us sometime. Please give Mel and Rafe my love. Tell them I'm looking forward to seeing them at the wedding.'

'Hi, Suzie, lovely to see you.'

She turned at the sound of the voice and smiled as she saw who it was. When she and Michael had finally got together, his had been one of the first numbers she had called.

'Hi, Tommy, it's great to see you, too. I'm so glad you could come.' She hugged him warmly and kissed him on the cheeks, before repeating the process with the pretty girl on his arm. 'Hi, I'm Suzie.' After introducing Lord Tedburn, she returned her attention to Tommy's new girlfriend. 'In case you didn't know it, this is a wonderful man you've got here. Has he told you he saved my life?

Without Tommy, I wouldn't be here now. Hang onto him. He's worth it.'

The girl smiled back and Tommy looked embarrassed. 'This is Debbie. We're both doing postgraduate research at Nottingham. I'm doing English, she's doing History.' His eyes caught Suzie's for a moment. 'Thanks for telling me your big news. I'm so happy for you that you managed to get your man in the end.' He looked and sounded sincere and she gave him a big smile in return.

'Thanks, Tommy. It took time, but he was worth it. I'm delighted to see you both here tonight. I wish you all the very best and I look forward to seeing you using the study facilities here as soon as you like.'

Suzie left them after a few minutes and mingled with the other guests. She soon bumped into Beppe carrying a tray of bite-sized canapés which smelt fantastic. Unsurprisingly, a black shadow at his feet was following his every step.

'Suzie, you've got to try these. They're slices of deep-fried polenta, topped with roast beef, horseradish and porcini. It's a variation on an English recipe I got from Alex. The porcini and polenta were my additions.'

Suzie did as bidden and licked her lips. They were divine. He smiled indulgently at her.

'Take another one. You need to keep your strength up.' He added a lurid wink for effect, but she knew him of old by now and his innuendo didn't even manage to bring a flush to her cheeks. Instead, she grinned.

'For the windsurfing, you mean? Don't forget the big race coming up on Valentine's Day. I need to make sure I'm strong enough to beat you this time.'

'Ah, the Love Race. You know something, somehow I think you've already won that one.' He was smiling now. 'And you've managed to mend a badly broken heart in the process.' Suddenly serious, he carried on in a low voice. 'He's my best friend, Suzie, and I'll always be grateful to you for bringing him back from the edge.'

Feeling a sudden flood of emotion threatening to engulf her, Suzie helped herself to another of the canapés and bent down to feed it to the dog, taking advantage of the momentary respite to wipe the back of her hand across her eyes before straightening up again. She reached up and kissed Beppe on the cheek.

'Thanks, Beppe. You're a sweetie.' She was just turning away when she heard his voice again.

'Hey, you can't just feed the dog my food and not have some more yourself, you know. Here, take another one of these.'

She gave him a grin, took another piece of polenta and headed off into the crowd. By the time she got up to the top floor, she had consumed half a dozen different canapés and was on her second glass of wine, and she was feeling relieved and happy. Everyone she spoke to sounded complimentary and she felt encouraged that her efforts had not been in vain. Her new life here in Verona looked as if it was now assured. The doors to the terrace were open and she stepped outside into the crisp winter air. It had snowed the previous night and there was still snow on the roofs of the town, although she had swept the terrace clean this afternoon. All around her, lights twinkled, and somewhere in the distance a bell was pealing. It was a delightful scene and she breathed deeply, relishing the peace and quiet.

'Room for two on the terrace?'

She turned towards him and smiled. 'Definitely room for you anywhere, Michael.'

'I thought your speech went very well. *Complimenti.*' He caught her in his arms and pulled her to him.

'I had a good teacher.' She snuggled up against him and kissed his neck softly. As she did so, she heard him whisper in her ear.

'Want to know something?'

'Mmm.' She didn't really mind what he said. It just felt so perfect to be here with him like this.

'You know they call Verona the city of love?'

She nodded against his shoulder.

'Well, it's true. You see, I'm not sure if I've told you this before, but I love you, Suzie.'

She turned towards him, slipped her hands around the back of his neck and grinned at him from close range. 'That's only the third time today you've told me.'

He grinned back. 'But who's counting?'

'Well, just for the record, I love you too.'

'Well, that's all right then.'

'All right? It's bloody marvellous.'

And she kissed him.

> *Doubt thou the stars are fire,*
> *Doubt the sun doth move,*
> *Doubt truth to be a liar*
> *but never doubt thy love.*

William Shakespeare

Acknowledgements

With warmest thanks to my editor Emily Bedford, Michael Bhaskar and all the lovely people at my wonderful publishers, Canelo.